STEVI MITTMAN

What Goes with BLOOD RED, Anyway?

WHAT GOES WITH BLOOD RED, ANYWAY?

isbn-13:9780373881048

isbn-10: 0373881045

This edition published by arrangement with Harlequin Books S.A.

TheNextNovel.com

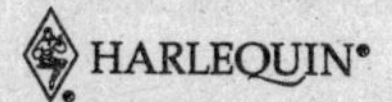

PRINTED IN U.S.A.

Praise for the writing of bestselling author Stevi Mittman

"A vibrant, funny story that wraps around your heart—Mittman makes you laugh, makes you think, makes you feel...and always makes you smile."

—*USA TODAY* bestselling and RWA Hall of Fame author Jennifer Greene on *Who Makes Up These Rules, Anyway?*

"Don't miss this book—it has all the heart that her historicals held, as well as Stevi's wonderful and wacky sense of humor."

—*USA TODAY* bestselling author Elizabeth Boyle on *Who Makes Up These Rules, Anyway?*

"*Who Makes Up These Rules, Anyway?* is filled with humor. Teddi jokes even while her life is falling apart, and there's a great surprise ending. A keeper."

—*Romantic Times BOOKclub* Top Pick! 4-1/2 stars

"If any writer is going to sit on the throne so recently vacated by the wonderful LaVyrle Spencer, it just may be Stephanie Mittman. With *A Kiss To Dream On,* she proves that she can spin a story of real people dealing with genuine problems as love—not fantasy love, but true love—grows between them."

—*barnesandnoble.com*

"One of those special books that will make your heart smile...Sit back, kick off your shoes and enjoy."

—*New York Times* bestselling author Debbie Macomber on *A Taste of Honey*

Stevi Mittman

Stevi Mittman is having the time of her life. She'd had a ball writing eight romance novels under her given name, Stephanie, and winning numerous awards and accolades, when she suddenly found herself going off in another direction—contemporary women's fiction. From there it was a hop, skip and a jump to funny mysteries set in suburbia. Think *Desperate Housewives* meets Jessica Fletcher.

Now she likes telling people she's left historical romance to write hysterical mysteries, which she writes under her nickname, Stevi. *What Goes with Blood Red, Anyway?* is her second book for Harlequin NEXT in her LIFE ON LONG ISLAND CAN BE MURDER series featuring Teddi Bayer, the reluctant suburban sleuth who has plenty of trouble of her own.

In addition to the books, Stevi is blogging on her Web site (www.stevimittman.com) while Teddi blogs on her own interior design site (www.TipsFromTeddi.com). It's an ideal situation for Stevi, whose own home on Long Island was featured in *Distinction* magazine after she decorated it herself. She even plans to feature some of her own room treatments on Teddi's site.

Stevi lives in a dream house in Ithaca, New York, with her wonderful husband and two incredibly affectionate cats, who will no doubt show up in pictures on the Web site.

From the Author

Dear Reader,

For those of you who can't get enough of Teddi Bayer, who want to know what she's doing between books, what that ex-husband of hers is screwing up now, who's on her radar screen and who's off, and for more of Teddi's decorating tips, there's a place you can go—www.TipsFromTeddi.com. It's loaded with Teddi's favorite decorating ideas, as well as links to Web sites that help you measure for wallpaper, painting tips and provide answers to your decorating quandaries.

And then there's Teddi's journal, in which she records dates, thoughts, her New Year's resolutions and her suspicions about various neighbors and friends.

For more murder, mayhem and matching drapes, be sure to check out www.TipsFromTeddi.com!

Teddi's had a great time creating it, and can't wait for you to drop by.

Stevi Mittman

This book is dedicated to all the incredible women in my life, especially Miriam Brody, Cathy Penner and Janet Rose, who are always there for me; and to Tara Gavin, my editor, and Irene Goodman, my agent, both of whom are the best pom-pom-less cheerleaders I know. And, of course, to the one incredible man in my life, Alan, with thanks…

CHAPTER 1

Design Tip of the Day

> The most neglected area of any house tends to be the ceiling. Look up. Now imagine what antique mirror tiles on your library ceiling could do (*click here*). Imagine baby-pink and apple-green circus stripes that extend down 12 inches onto the walls of your baby's room (*click here*). Imagine ornate white molding against a deep blue ceiling in your dining room (*click here*). Imagine a field of flowers over your bed (*click here*) achieved simply by stapling sheets to the ceiling and running ribbon over the seams. Look up again—what do *you* see?
> —From TipsfromTeddi.com

Elise Meyers's eyes are staring at the ceiling I've designed for her new kitchen. It's a Marrakech-bazaar tromp l'oeil sort of thing. She's lying on the newly tiled but not-yet-sealed terra-cotta floor in a getup that men in dark theaters wearing wrinkled raincoats can only dream about, and I can't really tell how she feels about the work I've put my heart and soul into.

"So, what do you think?" I ask, fingers crossed, breath held, staring up at the ceiling myself. She doesn't acknowledge me, doesn't even blink. I suppose she just doesn't understand how important this is to me, that this new business I've started isn't just a job. It's security, self-respect, sanity. "You hate it. I can change it. Just tell me what you don't like. Is it the colors? The red is a little soft with the mustardy gold. Maybe it could be deeper—"

She just keeps staring at the ceiling, ignoring me. I mean really, how can I fix things if my clients don't tell me what's wrong? I'm not a mind reader.

"Elise?"

I stamp my foot, trying, I suppose, to snap her out of her reverie, or stupor, or whatever it is. Only she still doesn't blink.

And then I notice the trickle of blood.

"I should have known," I mumble, more to myself than to Detective Harold Nelson of the Nassau County Police Department, who is taking down my statement. He is keeping one eye on me and the other on his partner, who is donning rubber gloves and kneeling over the body of the very scantily clad Elise. "Maggie May was waiting by the open door, and I thought, 'I'll probably find Elise dead....'"

"Maggie May?"

I gesture with my head toward a pathetic little ball of

white fluff whimpering on her little red monogrammed L.L.Bean bed in the dining room. The detective appears to melt. I'd have pegged him for a mastiff man, which just shows how much I know about men.

"Right," he says. "So you thought she'd be dead because…?"

I hesitate. There's a uniformed policeman investigating the new vegetable sink that was supposed to be installed today—a hammered copper bowl that just sits on the center-island counter with a faucet poised over it. The idea was for it to make you actually want to eat an avocado or something equally healthy. Not that it matters now. And I don't see the bar faucet, which I'd had to special order, but I don't suppose that matters now, either.

And there's something else different, but for the life of me I can't think what.

The detective is waiting to hear why I should have known. Because things were going too well. Because it was a gorgeous September morning and the sun was shining. And, most important, because Elise was loving how the kitchen I was redecorating for her was turning out. So, I ask you—how could I *not* have known that something dreadful was going to happen? Still, even if I had sensed disaster looming, I'd have thought *leak*, *crack*, *incorrect measurement*—not *murder*.

"Well, because I'm a worrier," I explain to the patient Detective Nelson, whose eyes keep straying over to Elise. She really did have a great figure for someone in her forties.

Better than mine will be when I get there, which is sooner than I want to think about. I concentrate on the detective and let him concentrate on Elise's body. "And this just proves that if you don't worry about a particular thing, that's the one that's bound to happen. Then you can spend the rest of your life worrying about what you're not worrying about."

Well, I've got his full attention now. He's staring at me like it's my marbles on the floor and not the bunch of pills I stepped on. He seems to be framing his next question carefully so as to prevent another babblefest, but it's futile. When I'm upset I can't help saying stupid things. As if to prove it, I shake my head and out comes a pronouncement that my mother has been right all these years and my ex-husband, once again, was wrong.

"How's that?" he asks, apparently fascinated by the pull-out warming drawer in the center island, despite the fact that Elise is lying face up on the unsealed tile floor with pills and change scattered around her.

"See?" I say, pointing to the broom just inches from her hand. "A little housework *can* kill you."

The police photographer looks up at me. He is taking pictures of every angle of the kitchen and of Elise. And of the dark red stain that is seeping into the floor.

And, except for Elise, it's all very familiar, the red stains in the kitchen, the police, the questions…

"You seem pretty cavalier about all this," the detective says.

"If you'd had this dream a few hundred times, you'd be

cavalier, too," I tell him. Ever since the thing last year with my soon-to-be-ex-husband, Rio, when he tried to drive me crazy and I sort of shot him, the police have been regular fixtures in my dreams. Rather than think about that black time in my life, I choose to imagine myself as Cinderella trying to scrub out those stains.

When Cinderella *before she meets the prince* is a step up, you know you're in trouble.

"This is no dream, lady," he says.

I take great comfort in the fact that he knows the script. "The detective always says that. And as soon as he does, I wake up."

Only nothing happens.

I ask the detective to pinch me, which sometimes works in my *the-police-are-coming-to-get-me-again* dreams. It occurs to me that this guy doesn't look a whit like Jerry Orbach, who is the usual detective in my dreams, nor, for that matter, like David Caruso, who is my dream detective. At any rate, he's watching the fingerprinting guy and he ignores me.

So I pinch myself.

It hurts. And I'm still in Elise's up-to-the-minute, high-tech-appliance-with-old-world-charm kitchen. And Elise is still dead.

"This isn't a dream."

I say it slowly, feeling as though I'm somehow under water and every movement is that much harder, every word that much more distorted. The photographer, now snapping close-ups of the blood patterns on the terra-cotta floor, is coming closer and closer to me. Gently, with a glance for permission from the detective, he pulls on the cuff of my white jeans, lifts my leg and takes a picture of the bottom of one of my brand-new driving moccasins.

I kick the shoe off and it goes flying toward a young female officer leaning over Elise. I shut my eyes tightly and hear an ear-piercing scream. I figure I've hit her with the shoe, but she isn't the one screaming.

Things around me double and turn yellow like those old color photographs from the early '50s. Blackness hovers. Someone pushes my head between my knees and rubs circles on the back of my white Banana Republic V-neck T—soft, slow, seductive circles. I tilt my head slightly and peer up to find someone who looks too good to be real. I figure his looks must be enhanced by either the angle or my weakened state.

"Keep your head down," he says, crouching beside me, murmuring about how I'm going to be all right. "And close your eyes."

To be perfectly honest, what the good-looking detective is doing to my back with his talented fingers is not helping me get my bearings. If anything, things seem even less real and almost...dare I think it with Elise lying dead? Delicious.

"So, here we all are in a kitchen again, Mrs. Gallo," Detective Nelson announces, bringing me back to reality and making sure I know he was there the last time.

"It's Bayer now," I tell him. It's a little awkward, me with one name, the kids with another, but it's not as if their teachers don't know the situation. Heck, anyone who picked up a copy of *Newsday* or turned on a TV learned the whole story last summer. His jaded look says he thinks I've already hooked up with a new jerk to replacc the old one. "Teddi Bayer. I've gone back to my maiden name."

Detective Number Two nods, but Nelson says, "A rose by any other name."

Whatever that's supposed to mean.

Detective Cliché adds something on the order of, "outta the frying pan, into the fire." I assume he is referring to the gazillion times the cops have had to come and take my mother, June Bayer, to South Winds Psychiatric Center, her home away from home.

I just shrug, and then there is this awkward silence, which I break by saying aloud what I'm wondering—who would want to kill Elise Meyers?

"I just can't imagine how anyone could murder someone as nice as Elise Meyers." Isn't it amazing how much nicer you think people are after they're gone? Elise could be a real pain in the butt, but lying there on 12-by-12 tiles that she wasn't so sure about but decided to trust me on...well, she looks almost angelic. That is, if you don't count the hot-pink satin and black-lace getup she's got on.

Nelson asks what makes me think it was murder while

he casually places his card on the table by my arm. "Looks to me like the dog knocks the pills and stuff off the counter, she hears him, comes down and slips cleaning up the mess. Bang. Dead."

I roll my eyes the way my twelve-year-old daughter does when she wants to ask how I can be so old and still so stupid but wouldn't dare say it in so many words.

Detective Nelson catches the look and says something obnoxious, like *Why don't you give us your version, Sherlock?* at which point Detective Number Two pulls out his card and places it on top of Nelson's, as if he's trumping it. *Detective Andrew Scoones*. And his isn't wrinkled, either. His card, I mean.

"Well," I say, brushing some wayward bangs out of my eyes so that I can see better. Maybe so I look better, too. "First off, Maggie May is a bichon frise and couldn't reach the counter with a ladder. So tell me how she could have knocked anything off a work island three feet above her head. Second, the dog was out front when I got here, but only the backyard has an invisible fence, and it doesn't look like Elise was taking her out for a walk, does it?"

Thinking about the details is easier than thinking about Elise lying dead on the floor.

"Since the tiles aren't sealed yet, they aren't slippery. And, on top of all that, the faucet is missing." I'm on a roll now, imagining myself in a movie or on TV, and I continue. "In addition, since the alarm wasn't going off when I got here, she must have disarmed it, which means she either knew the killer or didn't care about his opinion, since her…uh…*cellulite* was showing."

Everyone is staring at me. They are either incredibly impressed with my deductions or they figure I've gone nuts. Considering I've been down the latter road before and I'd recognize the signs (they always want you to sit down and stay calm, no matter what the situation is), I'm betting it's the former.

"Just call me Mrs. Monk," I say smugly. Of course, I miss the most important detail—the television character, Mrs. Monk, is dead, as Nelson quickly points out.

"So your theory is that someone broke into her house and killed her for her faucet?" Nelson asks. He pretends to be taking down what I say in a little notebook, but I don't think he really is. "You get that, Drew?" he asks his partner, who actually is taking what appear to be copious notes.

"I'm saying that I left the faucet on the counter yesterday when I delivered the bar stools and that it's not there now."

The detectives exchange a look as though I've picked up on something they already know but I'm not supposed to.

I don't bother mentioning my feeling that something else is not quite right in the kitchen because they are already acting like I've got a screw loose and because it seems as though something is more right than wrong.

I mean, if you don't count Elise.

Detective Scoones puts on a new pair of rubber gloves

and picks some of the pills off the floor to look at them. He lifts one off the little teddy Elise has on.

"Looks like she interrupted a robbery," he says.

"Only, her ring's still on," I say, embarrassed that I checked while I waited for the police to show up, and pointedly not looking at Elise now because I don't want to see them looking at a dead woman's finger even though I did.

Detective Nelson suggests that maybe they just couldn't get the ring off Elise's finger.

I think about how she waved that diamond around like it was a medal, and I swear I can hear her voice in my head echoing Charlton Heston's sentiments— "From my cold, dead hands." Only I guess she wouldn't let go even then.

Things aren't adding up, but Detective Harold Nelson isn't interested in my theories. And, truth be told, I'm not interested in Detective Nelson, so I direct my observations to Andrew Scoones, aka The Handsome Detective.

I tell him that, in addition to the ring, she's got a Bvlgari watch worth about ten thousand dollars. They start to cover Elise's body with a sheet and stop to look for the watch, which I already know isn't there.

"You should check upstairs in her nightstand," I say. Elise had been very specific about needing a small drawer beside her bed for "everyday" jewelry. If I had a ten thousand dollar watch, it a) wouldn't be "everyday" jewelry, and b)would be kept in a safe. But then, I had a husband who would have stolen it and given it to one of his girlfriends and then accused me of losing it, like he did with the little diamond anniversary necklace he gave me. "She kept her watch in the top drawer on the left side of the bed."

"You just happen to know which side of the bed she slept on?" Nelson asks, one eyebrow raised like this tidbit of information actually proves his theory that I'm the killer and I've just hoisted myself by my own petard. A little slow on the uptake, it finally occurs to me that they know damn well that this is a murder. They are simply toying with me to see what they can get.

"There anything else you want us to check out on this murder theory?" he asks, as though the fact that I'm an interior designer means I couldn't possibly have anything valuable to offer beyond what color to paint a focal wall.

They suggest I leave the house for a breath of fresh air and Detective Scoones, *Drew*, instructs an officer to accompany me. When I ask if I can go home, he tells me he'd like me to stick around.

Meanwhile, Detective Nelson tells one of the uniformed cops to check upstairs. When the cop reminds him they already have, Nelson tells him to check again, *thoroughly*. The thought that the murderer might still be there hadn't occurred to me, and that—combined with the blood on my shoe—leaves me weak-kneed all over again.

Or maybe it's the idea that the good-looking Detective Drew wants me to hang around. Funny how your brain (or is it just mine?) can operate on two levels at the same time. Like when your great-aunt in NYC dies and for just a split second you wonder if her rent-controlled apartment can pass to you. I mean, you're sad and all, but there's this little section of your brain, this piece that sentiment and emotion doesn't touch....

Never mind. I'm sure it's just me.

As an officer escorts me toward the door, limping because I am down to one of my good Todd's driving moccasins that I'll probably never find on sale again, it occurs to me that maybe the reason I can't leave is because I'm a suspect. "They can't possibly think *I* could have killed Elise, right?" I ask as he opens the front door for me. He looks me over. My working wardrobe consists of only black, white and beige, so that I never clash with swatches I'm showing a customer. Today I am wearing white jeans from T.J.Maxx's clearance rack with some designer's name on the back pocket. They're a size ten, but they run small, and I look pretty good. I mean, for me.

"I wouldn't think so," the patrolman says. "No blood. If you hit that woman, you'd be pretty spattered in blood."

I stiffen, holding my arms away from my clothing. Suddenly I don't know what to do with my hands. My body seems alien to me—a piece of evidence. Even though they don't have Elise's blood on them, I will have to throw out the clothing I have on because every time I even glimpse them in my closet I will remember that I was wearing them when I found Elise.

Outside, four police cars are parked at odd angles to the curb, and neighbors are beginning to cluster at the ends of driveways. Two women in jogging suits round the corner and stop in their tracks to stare at me. They converse with each other in hushed tones and then take off in the other direction. It is eerily quiet and I think about how different this neighborhood is from my own.

I am in a foreign country, or maybe on another planet.

In my world the residents would be all over the police, demanding to know what happened. There would be a lot of yelling, and every sentence would have either "Syosset" or "this community" in it, driving home what the police already know—that we don't tolerate bad things happening in our neighborhood. Someone, probably Joan Favata, would be marshaling her daughters to take all the littler kids around the corner to Mrs. Kroll's place where they could play on the new swing set, and someone else would be pushing money at the older ones to stroll down to Carvel for soft ice cream so that no one would see something awful come out of the house, like a body bag.

Here in The Estates, there appear to be no children. There isn't a single basketball hoop in anyone's driveway, no bikes litter the road. There isn't a single Sesame Street Plastic Playhouse or so much as a doll stroller blocking the sidewalks. A lone woman in a midcalf skirt and man-tailored blouse with a Ralph Lauren–ad dog leaves a nouveau Victorian with a wraparound porch that's a shade too small for the wicker furniture on it. She throws a fisherman's knit sweater over her shoulders as she casually saunters by the patrol car. Striking a pose, she stops to talk to one of the patrolmen while signaling her dog to stay off Elise's perfectly manicured lawn and sit beside her. The cop pats the dog and appears noncommittal as the woman gestures toward first Elise's house and then her own.

Across the street a man has the hood of his Mercedes up, pretending to look at the motor. He waits for the woman to leave Elise's driveway and meets her in the street, where they both rub their arms to ward off the fall chill and glare suspiciously at the cop and at me.

The gardeners across the street start putting their tools in their trucks, but they are asked to stay put until they are released by the police. They begin to argue—they have other leaves to blow, this is no business of theirs, and the neighbors begin to demand to know what's going on. The policeman guarding me, if that is what he is doing, goes into the street to calm everyone down, but his presence seems to do the opposite.

And then, with the exception of a gasp or two, all sound stops abruptly when a car marked Medical Examiner pulls up to the curb.

I reach into my handbag and fish around for my cell to call Bobbie Lyons, my business partner/neighbor/best friend. When I turn on the phone there are several messages waiting for me. The officer returns to me, probably to tell me I'm only allowed one call, and I show him that two of the messages are from Elise.

"Do you think it's okay for me to hear them?" I ask, thinking that I don't really want to hear Elise's voice from the other world and realizing that maybe in her moment of need she was calling me for help.

The officer, I suppose thinking the same thing, tells me to wait and ducks inside the house.

The crowd, which had turned into one of those living tableaus, comes to life and closes in. Before I can answer any of their questions, a strong arm yanks me back into the house.

"Whatcha got?" Drew asks me. His partner is nearby, examining some of the sports memorabilia that I've creatively placed in the hallway I expanded to accommodate it. A sort of Hall of Fame, if you will, which allowed me to move the stuff out of the living room to please Elise and still keep it in plain sight to please her husband. I hand Drew my phone and tell him which keys to press. He gives me a look that says he didn't make detective being stupid, and I back away from the phone.

I am still close enough to hear Elise's excited voice as she tells me how much she loves the new look. Do I think she should reconsider my suggestion that we do the back wall in deep Chinese Red? She's thinking that the new, mustard-color upholstered bar stools would look great against the red, just as I told her they would. *Look*, we hear her say (my head is now inches from The Handsome Detective's and I notice he smells good, too).

I press the button that lets us see the picture Elise has sent. I touch the screen lovingly. *Yes, Elise, the wall would have looked perfect in a vintage claret wallpaper with a small golden-mustard accent design.* And the bar stools, as I can see in the picture, actually looked better where I placed them than where they are now.

Drew says they'll need to confiscate the phone and bring it down to the lab to examine the picture for any possible clues—which I totally understand. I mean, Bobbie's sister Diane is a rookie cop and she's always reporting that they confiscated this or that.

On the other hand—and I don't want to seem petty here—this is my *phone*, my link to the outside world, my security blanket. I tell him we can just send the photo to the precinct via e-mail. Nelson says he's already got Elise's phone and sees that the picture is saved in there. Just as I ask if I can have my phone back, there is a commotion outside and Jack Meyers, Elise's hot-shot sports agent husband, pushes his way in.

All my nasty thoughts about how he doesn't know "jack" about decorating evaporate as his face goes gray and he tries to grasp what the police are telling him.

He keeps asking what they mean by *dead*, as if there are different types or degrees. Probably like he thinks there are different degrees of fidelity or marriage. "Hit on the head," he repeats over and over again. "A blow to the head."

"It appears that way," Nelson tells him. "We won't know for sure until we see the autopsy report."

If there's a color grayer than gray, Jack turns it. I force myself to forget what I know about him and guide him to the "Martin Crane" chair in the living room, the one he refused to let me recover, never mind replace, and I help him sit. I open the antique armoire I've had retrofitted to accommodate a bar and pour him a straight Scotch.

After a healthy belt, he collects himself and tells us all how he wasn't home last night because he was out fishing on his boat with a client and they got caught in rough seas and had to spend the night in Connecticut. Now, Jack's a very successful agent and I know he hooks his share of big fish, but I'm willing to bet he doesn't do it with a rod and a reel from his boat. Considering that most of his clients are women athletes, I'll concede a rod, but not a reel.

At any rate, all of us know it's a fish tale, but wouldn't you know that Nelson takes down all his details, which are sketchy at best. He's so awed by Jack's circle that he just nods when Jack, with a nervous glance at me, assures him he'll have the office call with the client's number later.

As Drew is walking me out, I hear Jack tell Nelson he won't consent to an autopsy. He says it's against his religion. I have the utmost respect for religion and religious traditions, but how religious could he be with no mezuzah on the door frame? I kind of tap the doorjam where the little prayer holder ought to be, but, not being Jewish, Drew probably misses my subtle hint. I don't believe that Jack doesn't want that autopsy on religious grounds. I think he's hiding something, or wants to, and I'm suspicious.

Oh, hell, let's face it. I'm suspicious of every husband, and Jack's no prize. Still, that doesn't make him a murderer, does it?

Alone in my car I carefully back out, listening to my own breathing, and I realize that Elise will never breathe again. In my chest I feel my heart lub-dubbing. My blood is pounding relentlessly in my veins. A headache has settled into my left temple and my ankle itches where my jeans tease it. It seems I am taking inventory of everything that makes me alive.

Halfway down the street I realize I can't see through my tears and I pull over. The thing that bothers me most about Elise's murder—beyond the obvious—is that it happened in her own home. I don't know about you, but if I ever get murdered I want it to be in some dark alley that I should have known better than to go into in the first place. Home is where you are supposed to be safe. And I wouldn't want to get murdered there.

I wipe my cheeks with my bare arm but the tears continue to stream down my face. I think about calling Bobbie, but I don't know what I expect her to do. I don't want to talk. I just want to crawl under the covers and cry.

If only I hadn't used up all my Go Back To Bed Free cards last year….

CHAPTER 2

Design Tip of the Day

> Fabric is the self-decorator's best friend. Done right, a couple of coordinating fabrics can pull a whole house together. Just by covering a pillow in the living room, a bench in the hall and a couple of kitchen bar stools in one fabric and making a dining room tablecloth, a photo mat and a second pillow in the living room in a companion fabric, you can move items from room to room and have them look as though they always belonged there.
> —From TipsfromTeddi.com

I can't help crying. I may be woman, I may be strong, but at the moment I'm not roaring. I'm just grateful that no one can see me. I cry until I hiccup, and I hiccup all the way down Jericho Turnpike, where I hang a right into the parking lot of Precious Things because I don't want to go home. Who wants alone when they can have hot coffee and a sympathetic ear?

"Did he call you?" Helene, who owns the shop where just

yesterday I picked up Elise's custom-covered bar stools, asks before I've got one foot in the door. "I told him to call you last night. If he didn't, he's in big trouble."

He is her brother, newly single, just squeaking past the Dr. Joy one-year rule. According to Helene, he is my soul mate. In fact, he did call and he does sound nice. And if I was the least bit interested in ever allowing a man into my life again, I would consider him.

"Elise Meyers was murdered this morning," I say just as the phone rings. Helene tilts her head slightly, as if she is having trouble processing what I've said, and chirps a greeting into the phone. While she talks, she keeps one eye on me, rearranges some ebony candlesticks on the counter, and weaves a stray strand of her highlighted brown hair into her French knot at the same time. Her makeup is flawless and her short nails sport a perfect deep red manicure. In the last week I have popped two acrylics, which makes my left hand look like it's missing the ends of two fingers, and the last time my makeup looked as good as hers, I was leaving the Bobbi Brown counter at Bloomingdale's.

She points at the receiver, gives me a knowing glance and then says into the phone, "Well, Audrey, I could certainly sell it to you direct, but it will cost you the same thing as paying for it through your decorator. I can't very well undercut her and expect her to keep doing business with me, now can I?"

Audrey Applebaum. Just yesterday she told me she changed her mind about redecorating.

"I'm not saying I charge people who come in off the street *more*, Audrey. I'm saying I charge decorators *less*. It's how business is done. You redecorate one house every few years. They redecorate several houses every month...."

Helene rolls her eyes at me while she points to some new glass-and-wrought-iron stacking tables she thinks I might like.

Only I'm more interested in her telephone call than her telephone tables. I grab the phone out of her hand and shout into it. "Don't you feel any obligation to your decorator? Don't you think you ought to pay for her advice, her expertise? You think she can pay for her kids' braces with your thanks?"

I want to slam it down, but portables don't give you that satisfaction, so I just hit Off and throw it toward Helene, who barely catches it. For a minute Helene doesn't say anything.

And then she begins to laugh, saying between the bursts how she can't believe I did that.

I can't, either. I don't know what the connection is to Elise's murder, except that it pushed me over the edge. When I don't laugh, too, Helene studies me.

"Teddi, what's wrong?" she asks, leading me toward the only piece of furniture in the shop not covered with swatch books or cords of trim. It's a red plush chair in the shape of a spiked heel and it has a big Sale sign on it, marking it clearly as a mistake in judgment.

I sit on the instep.

"I told you," I say flatly. "Elise Meyers is dead."

"Oh my God!" she says, covering her mouth. There's a silent beat. Another. Then, "Which one's Elise Meyers?"

I remind her that Elise is the customer who couldn't wait for Gina, Helene's assistant, to arrange for the delivery of her furniture. Elise is the woman who had to have everything yesterday, always, all the time. I don't mean to make her sound difficult. She was, but still, that doesn't mean she deserved to be murdered.

"Murdered?" Helene whispers, as if not saying it aloud gives it some dignity. I think of Elise in that hot-pink satin job and dignity goes out the window.

I start at the beginning because, except for the police, I really haven't told anyone, not even Bobbie. I tell Helene how I'd just hung up with Bobbie—whom she knows almost as well as she knows me—turned off my cell phone and got out of the car, when I noticed the dog on the lawn. At this point in my story, Gina, the twentysomething young woman who works for Helene, comes out from the back of the store with some swatches of fabric for Elise that have just come in. Helene tells her about Elise and she says how awful it is. They want to know everything, not so much because either of them care but because there's something about being the first to know, to know before it's on the six o'clock news, that appeals to people. I tell them everything I know and then Gina asks if I'm going to the funeral.

"How can she not?" Helene says as if Gina has asked if Helene wants to sell the high-heel chair.

You should be warned that *How Can You Not?* is the national anthem of Long Island. It explains the Perrier-filled water glasses at the bar mitzvahs, the catered first birthday parties, the BMWs for seventeen-year-olds, and the four-carat diamonds given to wives who have found out their husbands are cheating. There are a lot of large diamonds on Long Island.

Don't let me give you the wrong impression. *How Can You Not?* also applies to allowing your neighbors to run a one-hundred-foot extension cord from their refrigerator to the outlet in your house because a storm has knocked the power out on their side of the street. It means letting some kid move into your house for the last three months of his senior year because his parents have found the perfect house in another state and you can't imagine the poor kid transferring with only months to go. It means inviting a couple you hate to your daughter's bat mitzvah because they're friends with a couple you love. The rules are complicated, but they're a comfort, too. Like in Tevye's shtetl, everyone knows what's expected of them.

Okay, not everyone.

It is my firm belief that somewhere there is a *Secret Handbook of Long Island Rules* and that certain women are given copies. My mother has one. Actually, she may be its original author. Bobbie has one. These women have been sworn to secrecy and refuse to admit it exists, but there just isn't any way they could know all the rules without it.

I'm still waiting for mine to arrive in the mail.

Men don't seem to know the rules, or maybe they don't care. They surely don't have to live by them. Which brings us to Gina's question.

"So where was Mr. Meyers when Elise was bludgeoned to death?"

It seems wrong to tell Gina about the sham of a marriage that Elise and her husband had. First off, who am I to judge how blind Elise was or wasn't? I mean, Rio, my ex, pulled the wool down over my eyes so far that I didn't know what *I* was doing, never mind what he was up to! Second, Elise was one of those Long Islanders who would have been appalled if I aired her dirty laundry in front of anyone beneath what she perceived as her social station. I don't really know how she'd feel about my sharing it with those above or within her circle, but since I'm from the Plainview side of Syosset, and not from Woodbury, I don't really swim in her social pool.

And while I don't subscribe to it, I do understand the hierarchy because I was born in the Five Towns, that area on the South Shore of Long Island where the nouveau riche have *riched* their limit, and clawing your way to the top of the social ladder while appearing not to care (or even notice) is not simply an art form, but a requisite survival skill.

As luck would have it, I married out of it. Just ask my mother. It's hard to know which she and my father view as more of a disgrace—my marrying out of the faith or out of the neighborhood.

Besides, Elise is dead. And everyone knows that you don't speak ill of the dead.

At least not until after they're buried.

"Jack Meyers claims to have an alibi," I tell her, but still, my money is on him. When I admit that the police seemed to suspect me for a minute, Helene stops me and flips the Back in Ten Minutes sign on the door, then locks it. She and Gina lead me back to their offices in the rear of the store and Helene puts on a pot of fresh coffee.

Gina doesn't really have an office, but a corner of the storeroom seems to belong to her. She works there at a computer surrounded by a bunch of Snoopy paraphernalia and some family photos. There's the requisite picture of two little tow-headed girls on an outdated Christmas card with "Season's Greetings from our house to yours!" Pinned to the same bulletin board, held in place by a fuzzy little yarn ball with goggly eyes, flat feet and a tag that says Have A Great Day! are two Charlie Brown and Lucy comics cut from the newspaper. A Snoopy tack holds a comic from the Internet about computers. Another holds a picture of a guy in a camouflage outfit somewhere in the desert.

"Is that your husband?" I ask, because it's better than talking about finding Elise bleeding on her floor, or about Elise's husband screwing some client while his wife bled to death. Or concussed to death, or whatever it was that killed her.

Anyway, Gina's in love. I remember the feeling well.

Okay, vaguely. I remember *thinking* I was in love. For twelve years.

"Not yet," she says, and she waves a darling little chip of a diamond under my nose. I think of Elise and her rock and what a terrible marriage she had and wonder if the size of the diamond is inversely proportional to the happiness of the marriage. Of course, it's not, but for the moment, for Gina's sake, I wish it were. "We're getting married the day he gets back."

The picture looks like he's in some desert so I ask if he's in the Army or the Marines. People from the Five Towns (that would be Lawrence, Hewlett, Woodmere, Cedarhurst and Inwood), where I was raised, don't join the service. Neither do people where I live now, in Syosset, so one uniform tends to look the same as another to me. It's the boys and girls from Wyandanch, from Roosevelt, from Freeport, who mow the lawns and clean the gutters of those who live in the Five Towns, who don't have trust funds to pay for college or even a used car, who sign up and serve.

But Gina says that Danny is in construction and that he goes all around the world building things like dams and bridges. "He was in Iraq for a while, and Saudi Arabia and now he's in Qatar."

And Helene adds that Gina was late this morning because she had to go to the post office to get off a letter to *Bob the Builder*. Then she offers me Valium for my nerves, Percocet for the throbbing pain in my head and the number of her masseuse, who, she assures me, can make the world go away. I'd be happy if the phone would just stop ringing.

Helene answers it, placates the person on the other end, explains that the shipment was held up in customs (shrugging at me as she wonders if the customer will buy that excuse or if she'll have to come up with another) and finally hangs up.

"Sorry," she says, "but you of all people know how my customers are."

I know all too well, and, if there was another way for me to give my children all the material things I want for them and that they need without sacrificing my self-respect (assuming that Rio even could or would pay child support if I allowed him to, which is a big assumption, a *huge* assumption), I'd be in some other line of work. Maybe I'd still be painting custom designs on furniture or, if money were irrelevant, giving art lessons to old ladies who wear funky hats and feed squirrels in little pocket parks in Forest Hills. Unfortunately, my father knew what he was talking about when he said that money doesn't grow on trees, and I have three kids, a mortgage, a toilet that drips, a freezer that won't freeze and a pledge to myself to finish repaying my parents for my final semester at Parsons (where I finally got a degree in interior design last spring after quitting to marry Rio thirteen years ago).

The point here being that Helene's customers are my customers. Bobbie and I call them Type S women, as in spoiled, self-indulgent and self-consumed. All those commercials you see on TV where people lounge by private pools while wild jaguars race by? The ads in the *New York Times* for thousand-dollar designer purses? They aren't talking to you and me. They are talking to the *S*'s, for whom Long Island is apparently a breeding ground. Here they thrive in our strategically located gated communities, which they only leave in their GPS-navigated Lexuses (with the individual DVD players in the backseat) to cut off normal Toyota-driving people like me as they head for the South Shore in pursuit of Princess In Training T-shirts for their offspring. Off they go, weighing less than their jewelry and dressed in the latest hot designer fashions as they foray out into the real world armed with attitude and determined not to be taken advantage of, not to be overlooked and, most certainly, not to be ignored.

For some people, worse than being seen as a bitch on Long Island is not being seen at all. This, I don't have to tell you, makes it hard on the rest of us, who spend our lives worrying we'll be mistaken for one of *them*.

Helene begins to mother me, pushing the hair out of my eyes, handing me a tissue. "Come, sprinkle some cold water on that pretty face," she says, taking my father's cast-off BlackBerry out of my hands and leaving it on the chair I've vacated. She leads me farther back in the shop and parts a velvet curtain for me. "Don't tell a soul I have a bathroom in here," she says dramatically. "They'll be coming in here in droves to use it if the word gets out."

She is not joking. Small shops save their bathrooms for people spending over five hundred dollars. You think I'm kidding? Ask if you can use their restroom and they'll tell you to go next door to Carvel or down the block to Burger King. Now put several costly items on the counter and tell them you'll be back for them after you find a restroom and they'll act as though the carpenters just finished installing the fixtures in theirs. *Please, be their guest.*

The bathroom, no bigger than a broom closet, is outfitted for her big spenders, with a hand-painted porcelain pedestal sink that matches the wallpaper and the paper hand towels. There are no toothpaste smears on the basin, no strands of hair clinging to the neat little brush that sits on the glass shelf below the mirror. Beside the toilet there is no book turned over to hold the reader's place, no ratty magazine with free samples of moisturizer ripped out. There are no chocolate-smeared towels piled on the floor, no pots of flavored lip gloss left open on the tank behind the toilet.

This is the kind of guest bath my mother expects to find in my house, despite three children living there and me working full time. It's just one of the gazillion ways I disappoint her. Thank God she can't see what I'm seeing in the mirror—a very ugly, bedraggled version of me staring blankly back. I have dark eyes anyway, only now, below them, my mascara and all that liner I carefully put on and then smudged to perfection has formed dry river beds that resemble a map of the Finger Lakes. Very attractive—perhaps in a few weeks, for Halloween. My nose, ordinarily an acceptable size and color for my face thanks to the nose job my mother insisted I have at sixteen, now rivals Ronald McDonald's in size and hue. My very dark hair, which usually has a sort of just-got-out-of-bed come hitherness, looks like I washed it last for New Year's Eve. And my white T-shirt looks like it needs to be laundered just to become a rag.

As I try to wash up without messing up Helene's *House Beautiful* powder room, the cell phone in my purse begins to play The Looney Tunes theme, which signifies my mother is calling. (Hey, some call it sick. I call it survival.) While dear June doesn't know her theme song, she does, of course, know I have caller ID, and rather than argue about whether I chose to take her call or not, I flip the phone open.

"On the television," she says without any preamble. "I have to find out that my daughter escaped from the jaws of death by moments on the television? You discover a dead body and you think...what? That because we have problems of our own, *real* problems, you and the children aren't still the most important thing in our lives? Roz Adelman called and I had to pretend I'd already heard it from you.... And your father! Your father is beside himself with worry."

"There's nothing to worry about," I say, and I ask her how she knows about Elise and the fact that I was there.

"You're on the news. The phone hasn't stopped ringing. Your father is forgoing the back nine and we're coming over as soon as he gets home so you shouldn't be alone."

I tell her that they don't have to do that.

"What kind of parents would we be if we didn't come?" she asks. "Besides, he's losing anyway. You want me to bring you some Xanax?"

I'm thinking that the only way I'll need Xanax is if she comes over, but I don't tell her as much because she's insisting that the kids and I shouldn't be alone in the house.

She and my father will pack a bag.

And I will shoot myself.

My call-waiting clicks. I tell her to hold on, but she is on a roll about the food she will have my father stop to pick up along the way and she ignores me. Since she'll keep talking without me, I hit the button and cautiously say, "Hello?"

Detective Scoones identifies himself and asks how I'm doing. He leaves the *g* off *doing*, and it comes out sort of intimate.

"I was thinking that possibly I could come over tonight to discuss a few details regarding the case," he says.

I can't think of a thing to say. For some inexplicable reason I'm seeing David Caruso's naked butt.

"I'd hate to drag you down to the precinct to—"

"Am I a suspect?" I stop fussing with my hair, trying to fix the unfixable in the damn bathroom at Precious Things, where no one, least of all Drew Scoones, can see me.

"Nothing like that," he says. Is that the same as *no*? "I'm just curious about Mr. Meyers and I thought that you, working with the two of them, and knowing Mrs. Meyers pretty well..."

I ask about Jack's alibi and Detective Scoones says they are checking into it. Helene knocks on the bathroom door and asks if I am all right.

"So about seven, Ms. Bayer?" he says. It seems that only the time is in question. "I'll come by your place."

And then he clicks off and I hear my mother's voice.

"I said, 'Does Jesse like chocolate or regular rugelach?'"

"Oh, he likes them both," I lie, planning to eat the ones with the raisins while Jesse, ten, and Alyssa, six, gobble the chocolate ones. (Dana, the stick, will no doubt makes noises about how she'll be fat for her bat mitzvah while scarfing down the rainbow cookies my father always brings for her. At twelve, she is old enough to watch the other two, and I could tell my mother not to come, not to bother. But rugelach sounds like exactly what I need at the moment. And I do, after all, have a date with the police. So in the end, as always with my parents, I fold and tell her that sure, they can come over to look after the kids. And yes, I add, they can pick up some pastrami and knishes as long as they are stopping at Ben's Deli.

I exit the bathroom to find Gina staring at me like I'm an ax murderer, clearly on the road to the electric chair.

She hands me my BlackBerry. "Your reminder went off," she says apologetically.

Today is a day I'm not likely to forget.

As if none of this has happened, Helene returns to the subject of her brother, Howard, and reminds me that he is a food critic for *Newsday*. "You'd never starve," she says with a wink as I gather up my belongings. I smile and wave, opening the door without comment. "The divorce was his wife's fault," she shouts after me. "His *ex*-wife!"

Yeah, yeah, my wave says. I bet that's what Rio tells every woman he meets.

My phone rings again as I am getting into the car, and of course, it's Bobbie. The neighborhood grapevine has already begun to produce fruit. Or is it whine? She apologizes to me fifty times for refusing to come to Elise's with me this morning. When her sister, Diane called Bobbie from the precinct to tell her what happened, she couldn't believe it. And then, after we dispense with all the *oh my Gods!* that we both need to get our of our system, we start hypothesizing about who could have killed Elise Meyers.

I didn't mention it to the police, but between you and me Elise Meyers was a little off her rocker—not that I'm one to talk, which is probably why I didn't say anything to them. Still, she was. Here's an example: once when Rio called me on my cell at her house to yell at me for refusing to sign our joint tax return before my lawyer looked at it, she told me I should keep a list of every obnoxious thing he ever did. She said it could be very therapeutic. Then she told me that she kept lists, tons of them. She had brightly colored, leather-bound Kate Spade journals of every injustice ever done to her, every slight, every nasty glance thrown her way. She said she had a whole book of every bad thing Jack had ever done and why he deserved to die. At the end of it, she even had a list of what she'd do with his money after he was gone.

She had a separate list that Bobbie knows about and that creeps us both out, and another one in a slim, lime-green book that Bobbie doesn't know about, at all. In that one Elise claimed she had cataloged the indiscretions of virtually everyone she knew, and she made a point of saying that I was probably the only woman she knew who wasn't in it. The way she said it made it sound like just maybe Bobbie was, like she knew about Bobbie's one mistake.

"What do you suppose the police would make of the How I'll Spend His Money After He's Gone list?" Bobbie asks me. I've never told her about the lime-green volume because she would totally freak, and it could be that Elise was just bragging. Maybe she told every woman she knew that she was the *only one not in it*.

"If Jack was the one who was dead, it wouldn't look too good," I say. "But I don't suppose it will matter now. One of the other lists could be important, though. I mean, someone on one of those lists could have been the murderer."

"My money's on the husband," Bobbie says.

I tell her about his "alibi." And then I mention that there was something weird about Elise's house, something out of place or something that should have been there and wasn't, or shouldn't have been there and was.

"Uh…" Bobbie says "…I guess that would be Elise's body?"

CHAPTER 3

Design Tip of the Day

> The windows in your house are your eyes on the world. They frame the view of your house from both inside and outside and demand treatment. They should reflect your house's style, be it formal, casual or eclectic. Would you let the world see you without mascara? Don't let it see your windows without prettying them up, as well.
>
> —From TipsfromTeddi.com

Okay, before you meet my family, there's something you need to know. I was switched at birth. My parents insist this is not the case, but there is no question in my mind that I am an alien child. Now, by *alien* I mean either that my real parents were here illegally from some foreign country and there is no Long Island blood in me or that I was switched by body snatchers from another planet.

Either way, I don't belong here. Never have. This fact has escaped my mother (who, at sixty-eight, is still sure that with enough pressure she can convert me into a real Long Islander) and is irrelevant to my father (who is three years her senior and who I am convinced will love me even after my third eye makes its appearance).

My parents clearly intend to take up residence in my house, judging from the number of suitcases and amount of food my father has schlepped in. I will argue them out of this later. I hope.

At the moment, I am watching out the front window of my front-to-back split level home, the one I shared with Rio, while my father paces behind me repeating that he'll call Mel Rottman—*the best lawyer on the South Shore*—to talk to the police with me. Each time he says it, I assure him it isn't necessary.

My mother, however, isn't so sure that the innocent always go free. This is why she is telling me about a friend of hers who tried to get through customs by sewing undeclared jewelry into her brassiere and claiming it was her underwire bra setting off the metal detectors. It doesn't matter to June that the woman wasn't actually innocent. The point is that if a friend of hers could get frisked at JFK, I could wind up on death row.

Even when her stories are tedious, it's still amusing to watch my mother tell them because of all the cosmetic surgery she's had since my father's long-term affair with our housekeeper put her in the sanitarium and him in the dog house. He's footed the bill for more Botox, collagen and

Gore-Tex than Joan Rivers has tried to deduct from her taxes. What's really amazing is that even though the woman can't actually frown, grimace or pout, she can still give me "the look"—the one that says "you're a disappointment, Teddi. You're such a disappointment."

At the moment, I'm ignoring the look and wishing that one of my lovely children would entertain their grandmother long enough for me to finish filling out all the forms I need to send in for the decorator showcase at Bailey Manor before Detective Scoones shows up. Bailey Manor, for those who don't know, is a decorator showcase. Every year there's a benefit showcase and each lucky decorator or decorating firm that gets chosen gets assigned a room at a fabulous old mansion on Long Island that—provided they don't destroy any of the existing architecture—they can decorate however they think will best show off their talents. Bobbie knows someone who knows someone who is sleeping with the brother of the guy who is married to the woman who doles out the spaces, so I am doing the breakfast nook. I can't tell you how excited I would be if I had a stick of furniture that I thought was good enough to go in there or a way of getting some before Halloween, when it opens.

Oh, the irony of the timing of my father's retirement from the furniture business—just months before I opened my decorating business. And months after Rio's patience for being second in command there was exhausted and he began his scheme to drive me crazy so that he could put up our house as collateral for a loan to open an outlet center right next to my father's store.

"Maybe you should do the dining room," my mother says as she watches me fill in the forms. This despite having told her several times that I am lucky to have a room at all and that peons don't get to pick. She plucks a piece of lint off my sage-green silk sweater and adjusts the chunky necklace I made myself, telling me I look very nice, *considering*. I am going to assume that she means considering my day and not pursue it.

She and I both keep looking out the tall bay window of my living room, watching to see if it's a squad car that pulls up. A family of bikers rides by, all in helmets, the smallest on a pink bike with streamers and training wheels. I think they are the new people who bought the Kroll's house.

I remember riding around with our kids and, unlike Plastic Woman, it must show on my face since she says, "It's not too late for you to find someone decent this time and have another..."

"Way too late," I say, and then yell upstairs for Dana. "Come down and recite your portion of the haf tarah for Grandma and Grandpa." I realize that bringing up Dana's bat mitzvah is dangerous territory, where my mother has set minefields regarding the flowers, the food, the dresses, and hurry on. "Jesse, show Grandpa..." Nothing comes to mind, but I see that my father is fishing around in his pocket, which no doubt means he has some new techno-gadget he wants to show me.

"Wait until you see this, Jesse," he says as my ten-year-old bounds down the stairs. "I got a new phone for your mother to try." From his pocket he pulls out a PalmPilot, a key chain that beeps when you clap your hands and a spanking new phone.

"Dad, you have to stop doing this." I try to look annoyed with him, but it's hard. I mean, is it so awful for a man to spend his days in Best Buy, Circuit City or on the Internet buying the latest whatever? When you think about what else he could be doing? And he can afford it, so really is it so terrible that he shows up at my house a few days later with whatever he's bought, saying it a) doesn't work, b) isn't user friendly, c) doesn't do what the guy in the store—or the pop-up ad on the Internet—promised it would or d) isn't worth what he paid for it?

My it's-too-small-for-anyone's-fingers-to-use BlackBerry is *Bluetooth*. (He didn't even know what that meant, but before the salesman was through with him, he was convinced he needed it. I tried to make him understand it was a way computers and handhelds and phones could all communicate with one another and it worked like infrared, but when it didn't work for him on the first try, he lost interest.) My you-take-it laptop is Wi-Fi. (No, he doesn't know what that means, either.) My absolute-piece-of-crap phone sends photos across the country or across town so that my clients can see potential pieces of furniture or room settings as soon as I do.

"Video," he says, showing the new phone to Jesse. "That's

what they told me, but I got home and thought, who the hell am I gonna send video to? It's not like I have the store anymore to watch how they waste my money."

"The store" is Bayer's Fine Furniture (The Home Of Headache-Free Financing And Hassle-Free Furniture Buying), which my father opened in the late 1950s after he married my mother. I think he'd have actually kept it if only I'd agreed to come work for him. But there comes a time in everyone's life when they need to grow up and stand on their own two feet. At least that's what Ronnie Benjamin, the psychiatrist who helped me prove I wasn't crazy last year, says. She's helped me a few times since then, and it seems to me she's always right.

"Oh," Dana coos, her purple-polished nails reaching out for the phone while she confirms that someone at school has one that does indeed send streaming video, and her brother Jesse adds that the kid got it confiscated for broadcasting from the locker room before gym class.

"You can give the other one to Danala…" my father suggests "…if you can get this one to work."

"Mom can do it," Jesse, ever my champion, says. "And then I get Dana's phone, right, Grandpa?"

"And then there'll be one more person who won't take my calls," my mother accuses.

"I'll take your calls," little Alyssa says, smiling coyly at my mother. "If I get the phone I promise to never say, 'Oh shit, it's Grandma June.' I'll say 'Oh good!' I promise."

I'm supposed to yell at Alyssa for using the *S* word, but pointing that out will only lead to who she may have heard saying it, and I don't want to go there.

There is silence and then Dana starts to giggle. Jesse swats at her and then we all give up and laugh, except, of course, Grandma June, who huffs a bit before saying how we'll all miss her after she's gone.

If that sounds like a threat, don't be alarmed. I'm ashamed to admit that not only don't we take my mother's suicide comments to heart anymore, we don't even hear them. The days of her feeble attempts are, thankfully, behind us, or so we try to believe. My father gently gives her hand a pat, and I shoot her a not-in-front-of-the-children look. And just as I am about to try to video the kids with the phone, a car pulls into our driveway and my three children rush to the window like it's *Trading Families* and their new mother is going to get out of the car and come strolling up the walk.

The car is low and sleek and if I knew sports cars the way I know SUVs and minivans, I'm sure I'd recognize what it is. Detective Scoones, *Drew*, gets out of the car and adjusts his sunglasses. He has on pressed jeans and a casual sports jacket over an Izod sort of shirt in deep green, a favorite color of mine. I know it's not just me who can't breathe at the sight of him because my mother gasps and my daughter's jaw drops.

June beats me to the door, proving that when she wants

to she can move like lightning, and introduces herself, establishing immediately that 1) she knows all about everything that happens in my life and 2) that she is staying over to protect her grandchildren from whatever he might have in mind. Marty, his protective instincts in full gear, manages to mention the best lawyer on the South Shore twice before the man has both feet in the foyer. The good detective makes a point of taking note, nodding his head and muttering something about the lawyer's reputation.

He bothers to murmur compliments as he looks around at my house, noting that the dark green walls make the place look cozy and the salmon color of the bedroom, which he can glimpse from the hall, looks inviting. Yes, that is the word he uses. He says I look nice, too. *A lot better* might be what he actually says.

Dana and Jesse bound down the stairs, Alyssa lagging slightly behind, and he introduces himself to them, assuring them this is just routine and that their mother is in no way a suspect (as in: your mom's just helping the police out) and this is not any sort of date.

There are now seven of us occupying approximately four square feet of floor space in my foyer. I invite him into the living room and the group moves like we are bound by bungee cords. I motion for him to sit but after the kids jump onto the sofa and my parents take the club chairs, he remembers that he actually hasn't had a chance to stop for dinner and wonders if I would mind if he held the "interview" in a restaurant.

"Isn't that a bit irregular?" my elder daughter asks. Her tone hints that she thinks the handsome detective is up to no good.

"A bit," he admits with a smile that appears to win her over. "But pretty soon my stomach will be talking louder than my voice can cover."

When Alyssa starts to list all the Yu-Gi-Oh cards she has, I acquiesce because going to dinner with Drew Scoones is not exactly abhorrent. And because the alternative—spending an evening with my mother—has the potential of landing both of us back at South Winds Psychiatric Center. And then, too, there are a few things I'd like to tell the good detective that I don't want my kids to overhear.

Somehow we extricate ourselves, my father yelling down the walk after us to have a nice time and my mother fussing at him that we should do no such thing. Drew opens the car door for me, waits while I pull in my flowery skirt and wrestle with the seat belt. Then he closes me in.

As he slides into the driver's seat, he says, "I just wanted to check up on you and see if anything else might have occurred to you now that you've had some time to come to yourself."

"And you can't get in trouble for this?" I ask.

"For what? Eating?" he says, trying to push me into defining it as something more than that.

I fumble with a few words and then, more forcefully, say that I don't think there's anything else, though I have thought about what might be important. I don't tell him that I've also thought a lot about what might not be, like the rants in Elise's journals.

"Well, let's just grab a little something to eat, have a couple of beers, talk it out a bit," he says. "Sometimes a little memory jog can produce the smallest thing. It's always the smallest things that solve the biggest cases, you know.

"And you're sharp," he says. "Like about the dog knocking over the pills, and the alarm."

"You knew all that," I say, not about to be swayed by flattery. "Why pretend otherwise?"

He smiles shyly. "You never know. Sometimes it pays to be dumb."

"*Play* dumb," I correct. "Like on *Columbo*, when he asks all the murderers 'Why' and they come up with explanations that innocent people wouldn't bother with?"

"I've got a wrinkled raincoat in the trunk," he says with a shrug.

He pulls out of the driveway, his hand on the seat behind me as he backs up. If I sit any more erect, I'll be kissing the windshield. He drives up to Christiano's, a little Italian place in town that is supposedly the little Italian restaurant that Billy Joel made famous. Actually, I heard that after they'd put it on their menu and everything, one night Billy did a concert at Nassau Coliseum and refuted the whole rumor, just like that.

Everyone still believes it though. Sometimes people have a hard time letting go of mythology.

Anyway, they are nice to the regulars there, and I've been going there for years. The hostess's eyebrows rise when she sees me without the kids or Bobbie. I suppose it's Drew that's raising her eyebrows. She says something like, "Don't you look nice?" and gives me a covert thumbs-up behind Drew's back as she takes us to a secluded table in the corner.

On the way, we pass half a dozen families I know, and they all notice Drew, and frankly I enjoy every minute of it. They don't know that Drew isn't interested in *me*, but only in what I might know.

For that matter, I don't know that, either. I don't stop at any of their tables and I know that at least three of the women will call Bobbie before I get home and just casually mention that they saw me. *Is that Teddi's cousin from L.A. I saw her with? So what are you having for dinner? I was just at Christiano's. Yeah, I saw Teddi there…*

He asks if I have any more pictures of the Meyers's place, and I tell him that they are in my computer and that I can forward them to him at the precinct. He tells me his e-mail is on the card he gave me yesterday. I offer to give him my e-mail address, but he says he's already got it.

Once we've ordered (linguini with clam sauce for him, a salad, which I won't touch, for me), I ask if he ever thought I really was the murderer. He says they aren't sure yet that there's even been a murder. That's the second time he's evaded answering me about whether I'm a suspect.

"Do they know anything?" I ask.

"Well, they do know that she took a blow to the side of the head, just above the ear, and that the blow is what caused her death."

"So then they do know she was murdered." A waiter fills our water glasses and deposits a basket of warm garlic bread that smells divine and that I won't touch because who wants bad breath? We are silent until he leaves, and then Drew says that she could have hit her head on the edge of the counter.

When I look at him skeptically he adds, "Okay. The M.E. says it's consistent with being struck by a blunt object, like a metal pipe, or—"

"—a faucet." So then, it's true. I'm the one who bought the murder weapon. I paid for it. Well, technically, I suppose Jack Meyers has the bill, but I carried it in, I left it just where someone could pick it up and whack it into a living, breathing person's skull. Elise's skull.

"You okay?" Drew is half out of his seat, a hand on my arm. One of us is listing badly to one side. Apparently, it's me.

I put my hand on my chest. "My faucet killed her." I don't want to think it's amusement I see in Drew's eyes, that cops really are as hardened to matters of life and death as Jerry Orbach always made them seem. I think it is.

"I don't suppose you were wearing gloves when you brought it in?" he asks.

"Oh my God," I say, as I realize that my fingerprints are on the murder weapon.

He tells me to relax—as if that's possible—and explains

that my prints will serve to show whether or not anyone touched it after me, and whether they then wiped my prints off along with theirs.

"Not that we've found it," he says. "Yet. But we will."

I ask if he's going to fingerprint me, hiding my hands because of those two missing nail tips.

"Got 'em, sweetheart," he says. I've never been fingerprinted, not even after the whole Rio fiasco, and it must show on my face. "The bottle of Scotch," he says. "Can you believe the maid must have dusted the bottle? Yours were the only ones on it. They matched the ones on the glass you gave Jack Meyers. Of course, now we've got his, too."

I decide that they did that to isolate Jack's prints, and not because they suspect me. To be sure that this is the case, and because this is a murder investigation and there are things I know that the police should know, I decide I need to fill him in on a few things.

I take a deep breath. I do not like to carry tales, but… Our dinner comes and again we are silent until we are alone.

"You should understand…" I tell him off the bat "…that I am not a fan of cheating husbands. And that I might be overly suspicious and prejudiced, because of…well, my experience."

"I know," he says, and I get the feeling that this murder wasn't the only investigating he did this afternoon. He nods, like *yeah, I saw your file*. I nod, too. *Fine*. I have nothing to be ashamed of, except my naiveté.

"Okay, so you know that I think Jack probably did it, alibi

or not. I mean, even if it checks out, which I doubt it will, he could have hired someone, right?"

Drew's elbow knocks his knife off the table and he bends down to pick it up. He makes a fairly big deal of getting the waiter's attention to replace it, and it seems to me that it's all some sort of diversionary tactic. I think about how you're always hearing about hit men.

Only if Jack had hired a hit man to kill Elise, wouldn't he have put himself center court at a Knicks game where a gazillion witnesses would have seen him? And wouldn't the hit man have taken Elise's ring and some other stuff to make it look like a robbery? When I ask him this, Drew appears noncommittal.

"So you'd say that their marriage was not exactly made in heaven?" he asks.

"Elise got along with maybe three people, and Jack wasn't one of them. I don't know who started the cheating, but it was like they were in a competition. I know she slept with one of their neighbors, a man who Jack owed money to. And I know that he slept with one of Elise's friends."

He waits for me to continue, sensing that there is more, and of course, there is.

Not able to look him in the eye, I tell my salad that, "She kept a score sheet. I saw it once—"

His eyes are penetrating and I refuse to look at him. I'm not guilty of anything, but I feel like he's thinking that if I'd be friends with someone who would do that kind of thing, maybe I would. I suppose it's no more of a stretch than me thinking every man has the potential to do what Rio did. And yes, I know there's a lesson in here, but frankly I'm not really interested in it. My wounds haven't healed yet, and I'm not about to start picking at the scabs.

He asks if I know where she kept the list, but I don't. It wasn't in the notebooks.

And then it occurs to me what was missing in Elise's kitchen.

He asks if I can remember any names on the cheat sheet. "There were initials," I say, but I'm trying to decide if I should tell him about the notebooks.

He asks if that's all. There must be something about the way I say things. People always pick up vibes. He knows if he waits long enough I'll divulge more.

"There were grades," I say. "A, B...I don't know if they were for performance or you know, like importance or something." I have a feeling that my cheeks are redder than the checks on the tablecloth. I excuse myself to go to the ladies' room while he ponders what Elise's criteria might have been.

In the bathroom I dial up Bobbie on my old cell because I still haven't programmed the new one my father gave me. "I think all her Shit Lists were gone," I say.

"What are the bets Teddi Bayer and Bobbie Lyons are on them?" Bobbie asks.

"Seriously, Bobbie, there's incriminating stuff in there. People's darkest secrets."

"Just Elise's," Bobbie says. "Right?"

"Wrong. She had plenty of dirt on other people. She had stuff that other people did that somehow she knew about. People who bought clothes at Saks, wore them and then returned them. People who left restaurants without paying." Bobbie wants to know who, but instead of telling her I throw out a line to see if she'll bite. "People, happily married people, who had affairs."

Bobbie and I never ever mention her mistake. I don't think we could be easy around each other if we acknowledged it. I don't know who she cheated with and I don't want to know. I know she felt she had to even the score after Mike had the affair and that she did.

"So how did you wind up with a friend like that?" Bobbie asks. Does she mean a friend who was happily married and had an affair, or does she mean Elise? "Teddi? You there?"

"Elise wasn't a friend, she was a client. And I don't know if I should tell Detective Scoones about the notebooks. I mean, I'm pretty sure she made some horrible accusations that could ruin people's lives. Everyone would hate her for the rest of her—" I stop myself.

"—and even after that," Bobbie adds.

"They could just all be lies," I say, "but they could still do an awful lot of damage."

Bobbie asks if I'm sure the notebooks are gone. "Only one way to be sure," I say.

"You aren't thinking of going back there?" Bobbie asks,

and there is a slight quiver in her voice. I don't know which one of us she is scared for.

I tell her I've gotta go, the detective is waiting, and I close the phone while she's warning me that I could get into trouble.

When I return to the table Drew asks if everything is all right. Remind me never to play poker.

"So you were telling me about this list," he says. This is my chance to come clean.

"What would you do if you found it?" I ask.

He gives me that intent look that demands that I tell him the truth. But first, I demand an answer.

"Up to the Department, I guess," he says. Is that a warning? That he'd have to turn it over and it would be out of his hands?

I've already told him about the Jack and Elise Scorecard, so I reiterate that there were grades on it.

"And you said the grades might have been for importance?"

I explain that, first off, Jack had powerful clients and friends. There was a celebrity element. And then there was a one-upmanship sort of thing, a what-would-hurt-the-most, be-the-most-vindictive thing. Because I feel I'm withholding information, I wind up fumbling for the right words, hoping he won't ask me for an example, which, of course, he does.

"I'm not saying she did this," I say, making myself clear. "But like if Jack had a brother and they were sort of rivals and she were to sleep with the brother…"

He asks if Jack has a brother. I remind him it was just an

example. He asks if Jack knew about the list, but I have to admit that I don't know. He gives me a little smile and asks who was winning, and I'm not sure if he is joking or not.

"So your theory is that he was losing? Or maybe tiring of the game?" It's a good question, except I don't really have a theory. Just a suspect. And a burning need to get myself into Elise Meyers's kitchen one more time.

"Maybe it was the only way he could win," I suggest.

"Maybe," he agrees. "But why hit her on the head when there are so many less traceable, less obvious ways to do her in?"

I ask what he means.

"Well, poison, for one," he says. "A slow, untraceable poison that he could have, for example, put into capsules that she was taking anyway for some other condition."

I ask if they found poison in the capsules that were on Elise's floor.

"It was just an example," he says.

Yeah. Right.

CHAPTER 4

Design Tip of the Day

> Custom furniture is all in the details. Which means that if you can add some details to ready-made, you can customize your own. Fabric trims are available by the yard in any fabric store, and metal trims can be found in hardware stores or lighting fixture stores. Wrap the chair seat support in metal, hang some beads or chandelier tears from it and you've got a WOW look for only a few dollars and a little time.
>
> —From TipsfromTeddi.com

At home, my parents are playing cards on my hand-painted green-and-white-checked kitchen table with the cute chairs I covered and trimmed to match with green glass beads that hang just below the seats. My father tells me that Alyssa is asleep and my mother announces that someone named Howard has called.

"Twice," Jesse adds while I tell my parents that there really isn't any need for them to stay over.

My mother frets about how it will look if she "abandons me in my hour of need," but my father can take a hint and he all but pushes her out the door, saying he's sure I'll hear from her in the morning.

No kidding.

No sooner are they out the front door than Bobbie knocks on the back one. Jesse lets her in and she flips on my coffeepot and takes June's vacated seat at the table. This is Jesse's cue to watch TV in his own room, like his sister.

"I've got to get in there," I tell her. "Maybe the books are still sitting there."

"And if they are?" she asks.

"Then maybe the police missed them." I know this isn't the case. I was there before they came. I'd have seen them take them, wouldn't I?

"And if they did?"

I don't answer her. Bobbie's husband Mike would be devastated, even though his affair was what started the whole thing. Frankly, I don't know if they'd survive. I know that I've got to get those books before the police do.

Bobbie sighs the sigh of defeat. "I called Parkside Chapel. Jack's going to be there in the morning to make the funeral arrangements."

"I'll just look in through the patio doors," I promise her. "I won't even have to go inside. Probably."

She rolls her eyes at me and mumbles something about how I shouldn't get involved. And then she puts her hands out like I'm supposed to fork over something.

"What?" I ask.

"Tell me about dinner with The Handsome Detective," she says. "Tell me everything!" While I am going over everything in minute detail, which I don't mind doing because getting Bobbie's take on things is always worth the effort, I casually mention that while I was out with the detective, which I am very careful not to make sound like any sort of date, Howard Rosen has called twice.

Bobbie picks up my phone and tells Dana, who of course is talking on it, to hang up and go to bed. A short argument ensues, with Bobbie telling her to *for God's sake*, pretend to go to bed and use her cell phone, then hands the receiver to me.

"Call him right now," she orders. Bobbie has been trying to get me to date since the morning I came out of the lawyer's office an almost-free woman. "Men who can take you to The Polo Grill don't come along every day, Ted."

I don't want to ask what kind of man needs his sister to fix him up, so I don't say anything.

Bobbie raises her hands like two scales. "Christiano's..." She lowers her left hand slightly. "Polo Grill..." Her right hand plummets down and hits the table.

I put my hands up to weigh my options in response. "A sexy detective with very long fingers," I say, letting my left hand drift slowly down while Bobbie giggles. "An unknown quantity with an unlimited expense account." My right hand begins to lower. "Being responsible for myself and not having a man mucking up my life—" I raise both hands toward the ceiling "—priceless!"

Bobbie reminds me that every man is not Rio. She has completely forgiven and forgotten when it comes to Mike, and it only serves to remind me how important it is that I find Elise's damn notebooks before they wind up on the front page of *Newsday*. And she warns me that I am beginning to sound cynical when it comes to men.

I'm afraid that she is right, and so I reach for the phone to call Howard Rosen, meal ticket extraordinaire. This is supposed to prove I'm not cynical, but I'm not sure how.

You might think that my dialing a potential date would mean that Bobbie would leave, but then you wouldn't know Bobbie. She sits, her short, L'Oréal Féria–red hair framing her little girl face, her dark eyes sparkling, her chin perched on her folded hands, and she smiles while she waits for me to dial.

Howard answers on the first ring, before I've figured out what I want to say. He is funny and pleasant. I am morose and finally admit that it's been a bad day, which he apparently knows from talking to Helene. While he tries to convince me that the only way we are going to get her off our case is to go out once and report that it was awful, Bobbie gets up, kisses me on the top of my head and slips out the back door.

He tells me to get some sleep and that he'll call again in

a few days. If that's all right, he adds. I want to tell him it's not, but I can't think of any reason why not and it just seems simpler to agree. I picture myself at the altar next to a man with no face, saying "I don't have any reason not to."

I also imagine facing Helene after Howard lets her know that he called and I blew him off.

I tell him he can call and then kick myself up to bed, where I sleep more soundly than I expect to and wake only when the phone rings. Gayle Weiss, the neighbor who hooked me up with Elise to begin with, is calling to give me the details about Elise's funeral, which is scheduled for tomorrow.

"I just can't believe it," she says four or five times. "Elise Meyers! So what do the police say? Was it murder?" Gayle has one of those thick Long Island accents everyone likes to imitate, and she leaves the *r* off murder, making it *murdah*.

"I really can't say," I reply, knowing that isn't going to wash. "I mean, I don't think they've made an official determination yet. It only happened yesterday, Gayle."

"So they don't know the *murdahrah*," she says, as if using *r*'s costs extra. "She was hit over the head, right?"

I tell her that I think that was what happened. I am cradling the phone between my ear and my shoulder while I wander down the hall to make sure that my kids have got themselves up and off to school.

"And you and I know it was Jack, right?" Gayle says, without waiting for me to answer. "Listen. My David and her Jack are friends, so I can't really get involved, but—"

In the kitchen I find a note on the table written by Dana and signed by Jesse as well, telling me that they put Alyssa on the bus, that they hope I'm all right, that they let me sleep because of "you know" and that they'll come right home from school in case I need anything. I am so grateful my genes outweighed their father's that I send a kiss skyward while I give half my attention to Gayle.

"You know Marvin Katzmann? The jeweler?" she asks.

I stop fussing with the coffeepot to listen.

"The police should talk to him." I wait, my French vanilla decaf in hand. She says nothing more, which is so uncharacteristic I fear for her life.

"Gayle?" I say. "Why should the police talk to him?"

"I'm just saying," she says, "that they should."

"But—"

"I'm just saying," she repeats. "You wanna go to the funeral together? We could go to the diner for some coffee before the service."

I tell her that Bobbie is coming with me and she suddenly remembers an errand she has to run on her way to the funeral home because she and Bobbie are like two shades of green. Separately they are each fine but together they inevitably clash.

I call Bobbie's and get no answer. I guess I'm on my own.

I slip into what I suppose a cat burglar in Woodbury would wear at midmorning: a Ralph Lauren skirt I scored at T.J.Maxx and crisp white blouse, something no one would notice on Remsen Court. I rehearse my excuse if Jack is there. *I'm just coming to see if there is anything I can do to help?* The man doesn't like me or my decorating so I'm not too confident that would work. *I think I left something in the kitchen?* What if he tells the police I came back? They'll think I'm trying to cover my tracks or whatever it is that criminals do when they return to the scene of the crime.

By the time I drive to Elise's house the armpits of my blouse are drenched. My thighs are glued together with sweat. My makeup has deserted me. I park in the driveway of a home under construction and walk up to the doorway with a folder under my arm as if I am a prospective buyer or real estate agent or someone who belongs in a half-constructed house in The Estates.

I am examining the construction when I see Jack Meyers's car pull out of his driveway and head down the street. When I can't see the car anymore, I stroll across the street as though I want to see the long view of my new house. I back up some more. I back up to just past Elise's driveway. Is that a dog I hear? Oh! I'd better check. It sounds like it might be lost. I'd better just go into that backyard there and see if I can help.

And then I'm in Elise's backyard with my nose pressed up against the glass. I'd take to task the person who put bamboo vertical blinds on these windows if it weren't me. I was so right when I told Elise they would give her full privacy. I can't see a freaking thing.

I use my skirt to keep my fingerprints off the door handle and try sliding the glass door. Elise was always complaining that Jack never set the alarm and that one day someone would come in and rape and kill her and it would be his fault. In the better version of her break-in scenario the thief would run off with all Jack's sports crap. I just hope that Elise is right about Jack and the alarm, because otherwise I'm dead meat.

The door slides open easily. No siren sounds. I step into the kitchen and see the bloodstain on the tiles. Maggie May comes running to me and barks, runs back to where her bowl should be, barks again and begins making circles. "He didn't feed you, did he?" I ask. Maggie May was Elise's dog. I wonder what Jack will do with her now.

I look on the counter next to the refrigerator and, of course, there are no diaries. If there were, the police would have found and taken them. I know this is where she kept them because I argued with her about them clashing with the color scheme. That, as I'd realized last night at Christiano's, was what was missing yesterday—the discordant colors.

I figure you can't leave fingerprints on a dog, so I pet Maggie, who tries to bite my hand and then nudges me toward the door. She thinks I should leave and she's right, but I've come this far and the journals could just be upstairs, in which case they wouldn't be missing and I wouldn't have to tell the police. Keeping my hands behind my back so that I won't touch anything, I creep quietly into the hallway and climb the stairs. There must be five hundred of them, because when I reach the top, I swear to God, I can't breathe.

The door to the master bedroom is almost closed. With my shoulder I nudge it open, step into the room and lock eyes with Jack Meyers, who is sitting up in bed with his chest bare.

Every coherent thought goes out of my head. My heart knocks against my chest like it wants to leave without me. I swallow, gulp for air like I've been under water, and blink as if I can erase him that way. Finally, I say something about not wanting to disturb him in his mourning and thinking he wasn't home, and I start babbling endlessly as he extricates himself from the covers and stands, naked, about fifteen feet from me.

"I saw your car leave," I stutter. It's the best I can do.

"My brother and his wife have come to help with the funeral arrangements," he says, taking two steps closer to me. "He took my car."

"I left my notebook here yesterday," I say as he comes closer and I take a few steps back until I hit the wall by the door. "I mean, I thought I did. You know, with the confusion and all. But, hey, I don't see it, so…"

And then I see the lump of covers on the bed move and realize that old Jack is not alone.

My jaw drops. Even after her death, Jack Meyers still had to even the score with his wife.

"You didn't see anything," Jack says, and now he is only about a body length away. "Say it. You didn't see anything."

He comes closer.

"Say it!" Spittle hits my cheek and I inch left, feeling for the doorway, not without noticing that the whole episode is exciting him. I don't have much of a basis for comparison, but either my ex-husband was phenomenally well-endowed (and I think he'd have told me so—*many times*) or Jack really ought to put his robe on.

The woman in the bed coughs beneath the covers and I turn and run, nearly falling down the stairs, breaking a heel as I go. Maggie May, still hungry, whines at me and I grab her up and run through the kitchen, leaving the way I came. Only now I'm not strolling, I'm doing a four-minute mile while holding my breath. And a bichon frise I've just stolen.

I don't breathe again until I'm in the car. Not a minute later I'm pulling out of The Estates. It isn't until I'm almost home that I punch my speed dial and listen to my messages. My mother has called to tell me she hopes I slept all right. I am never telling her what I did this morning. The police have called to tell me I can pick up my shoe. I am never telling them, either.

I try Bobbie because she is the only person in the world I can tell, and she isn't there. She doesn't answer her cell, either, but she and Diane show up at my door around one o'clock with tuna melts on bagels and we eat them in the kitchen while I tell them about my morning.

At first I can't believe they're laughing, but, now that my

heart has slowed to near normal, I can see the humor in it. Black, sick humor, but we all laugh until our eyes are tearing. I keep holding up my broken-heeled shoe and Maggie May keeps making little circles next to us as if she, too, is in on it.

Diane makes sure to remind us often that she is an officer of the law and that we only discussed my escapade when she was out of the room.

When she finally has had enough Diet Pepsi to float the *Titanic*, she heads off to the bathroom and I take the opportunity to remind Bobbie that the Kate Spade journals are still at large. Of course, she doesn't know she's probably in them. And I am not going to be the one to tell her. And I'm not going to tell Diane, who thinks the world of her big sister, either.

Then Jesse's teacher calls, ostensibly to remind me to send in a permission slip but really to hear if it's true that I witnessed a murder.

I take five minutes to tweak my Web site because I've promised that every day I'll put on a decorating tip, and there are people who actually check the site each day. Bobbie helps with today's tip, which is to keep plumbing and lighting fixtures in their boxes until they are installed so as not to damage them or cause harm to anyone handling them.

Then my mother calls for the third time today for updates and to coach me regarding any questions the police might ask. Even Rio calls to tell me that I am probably endangering his children's lives and that he hopes I'm happy now. I tell him I've got the kids a dog. Score one for Mom.

And then the kids are home and they kiss me as though they've been in Siberia or I've been there. It is touching that death this close to home has made them realize that I am precious to them. Of course, it is short-lived. Dana says the dog is cute, but she isn't walking it. She and Bobbie's girls decide to walk over to the shopping center to play with the cosmetics, Alyssa demands to go with them and Jesse takes the dog up to his room to keep him company while he plays video games across the Internet.

Diane heads for home and the Lyonses and Gallos guiltily call in yet another pizza. Just as I am taking my first bite I hear from Howard Rosen, who makes me think I could be eating something a lot better than a whole wheat, thin crust Hawaiian pizza. I wonder where I'd be dining if I'd accepted a date with him. I wonder what he looks like. I wonder why I care, since I'm not interested in having a man in my life.

And thinking about a man makes me wonder about the handsome Detective Scoones, which in turn makes me wonder about Elise's books of lists.

If they weren't in her house and the police don't have them, who does?

CHAPTER 5

Design Tip of the Day

> Accessories set the mood in any room. The same beige couch and club chairs are formal with a French provincial coffee table, botanical prints and a crystal chandelier, but casual with an antique trunk, folk art figures and a Stickley lamp.
> —From TipsfromTeddi.com

In the morning, I choose a nice pair of black Ann Taylor pants that I got for a song out at the Tanger Factory Outlets after the season was over, and a deep blue blouse with a black shimmer. Its mood is accessory-dependent, so I am careful to wear only my watch, pull my hair back smoothly with a silver barrette and grab a plain, imitation-Coach black purse. Shoes are my nemesis. I can never decide which ones to wear and I finally settle on black Ralph Lauren loafers with a slight heel that I got at Marshalls a few years ago when I really could have spent more than I did on clothes and shoes because my father was paying Rio more than I knew and it turns out we could definitely have afforded it if Rio wasn't supporting a mistress on my father's dime. Enough of that. At the moment, looking in the mirror I think I look pretty presentable for the woman who discovered the body.

Bobbie, who is already in my kitchen fixing coffee, takes one look at me and asks if I'm anticipating a sighting by Detective Scoones.

A murder investigation, she warns me, is not a good place to flirt with danger.

The funeral home is on Jericho Turnpike, like most things in Syosset and Woodbury. Well, like most things on the North Shore of Long Island. On the South Shore everything is on Sunrise Highway, and in the middle there's Hempstead Turnpike, but people from the North and South Shores don't really count that because there's nothing really good on it—no good malls or upscale restaurants or anything.

At any rate, the funeral home has an understated elegance that complements the clientele who come in their black Gucci, their black Nanette Lepore, their black Dolce & Gabbana. All the designers are represented, sad faces topping their latest lines, tight smiles defying recent Botox injections, gossip hiding behind well-manicured hands.

Several people come up to me as Bobbie and I enter. All of them say how awful it must have been for me, all want any detail they can pry out of me. Jack Meyers avoids me.

The casket is open. This might not mean a lot in certain circles, but Jews, as a rule, do not have open caskets. The funeral home is abuzz. Gayle Weiss, who swoops down on me the minute Bobbie and I are separated, says that surely Elise would have wanted it that way. "She worked hard on that body. All those hours at the gym. She'd want people to remember how good she looked."

Pam Griffin, another of my clients and a friend of Elise's, coughs loudly behind me and whispers in my ear, "As hard as she worked on that body, her plastic surgeon worked twice as hard." I turn to gawk at her, and she gives me one of those butter-wouldn't-melt-in-my-mouth smiles. It's ten o'clock in the morning, she is drenched in Giorgio and has on enough makeup to attend the Academy Awards. She blinks at me innocently and tells me that the painters I sent showed up at the *ungodly hour* of 9:00 a.m.

Bobbie returns to my side. "You gonna look?" she asks. I shake my head but the natural flow of things moves me closer and closer to the casket, which means that I have to either turn and run, which won't go unnoticed, or actually see Elise this one last time.

Maybe one last look can erase the image of Elise on the floor in that Frederick's of Hollywood closeout number. They always say how people look so restful. So I stand politely beside the coffin, summon up my courage and look down.

Elise Meyers is being buried with her four-carat diamond ring, her gazillion diamonds necklace, her tennis bracelet and stud earrings that would choke a stud. I gasp, and Bobbie grabs my arm, saying something about the shock as she hurries me to the back of the chapel.

"He's burying her with all that jewelry?" she whispers. "Is he crazy? Are they going to take it off before they close the coffin, or what?"

I remember what Gayle Weiss said about Katzmann, the jeweler. "I have to call the police," I say, rushing out the door.

The strangest thing pops into my mind as I hurry past a woman standing just inside the doorway in dark sunglasses. *Orange juice*.

"Orange juice?" Drew says when I finally get him on the phone.

"No," I say. "The jeweler. You should talk to a jeweler named Marvin Katzmann." I can't tell him why. I can't tell him who told me. I do tell him Elise is about to be buried with all her carats. And that the casket is open. He says he knows.

I look up and see that he is standing beside a dark sedan parked just up the street. He nods at me. I see him talking into his cell phone. "Anything else?"

"Yeah," I tell him. "Turns out Jack Meyers does have a brother."

"Those examples will kill you every time," he says.

I say nothing. I've got the message.

"By the way," I tell him, because I know something he doesn't. "Jews don't generally have open caskets. Religious Jews, that is."

He says nothing.

"Jews who, for example, are religious enough to object to autopsies on religious grounds."

There's a pause while I make sure it registers and a reciprocal pause that acknowledges that it does. "'preciate those photos when you can get around to it," he says.

I admit I forgot to send them. "What exactly are you looking for?"

He laughs just a little. "Uh…evidence, maybe?" I watch him close his phone as Bobbie pulls me back into the chapel for the service.

"Elise Meyers," the rabbi says, "was a good person, a good neighbor, a good wife to her good husband Jack…." *Notwithstanding the poison and the murder and his sister-in-law in his bed*, I think. I wonder how much more evidence they need to arrest Jack for the murder of his wife. Such a juicy, Long Island story. I can see the headlines in *Newsday* now: Faithless Husband Arrested For Murder Of Faithless Wife.

Jack takes the podium but cannot bring himself to speak—probably on his lawyer's advice. Someone leads him away and the funeral director directs us to the cemetery, encouraging everyone to come to the internment.

"Not happening," Bobbie says, taking my arm and forcing me out of the pew. "I don't think I can watch Jack Meyers weep over his wife's grave knowing what we know."

Just as I am reminding her that we don't really "know" anything, Jack comes down the aisle on his brother's arm.

He stops beside me. I stare at him. He stares back. I wait, telling myself that he can't say I was in his house because I could say who was in his bed, right? He takes my arms in his hands and pulls me against him. His head is touching mine, his mouth just millimeters from my ear.

"I expect you to take back all that crap she ordered," he whispers. "Tomorrow morning would be good."

CHAPTER 6

Design Tip of the Day

> Collections personalize a house in a way nothing else can. They say: This is who I am. This is what I care about. This is my secret self.
>
> —From TipsfromTeddi.com

"Well," Bobbie says as we head up Woodbury Road to The Estates, where my crew of painters are, I hope, making Pam Griffin's dining room ceiling the sophisticated mushroom color I showed them, which will contrast beautifully with all the white woodwork we've added to the room. "We're not taking back one single item from Jack 'Freakin' Meyers's house. Not so much as a toothpick."

I remind her that we didn't buy toothpicks for Elise's kitchen. We bought bar stools, a table and chairs, an island that matched her existing cabinets, window dressings, lighting fixtures—everything but toothpicks. And frankly, I can't afford to take them back and eat the costs. Of course, I'm still owed a good sum of money on them, and not only do I think Jack will balk at paying, I think there's a good chance he'll be in prison before I can get paid.

"Maybe we can take just some of it back," I suggest. "Do the Bailey Manor showcase with it. It's not like I have something else I can use."

Bobbie says my kitchen's prettier than Elise's and if we're using anyone's furniture it should be mine.

I check the rearview mirror for the second time to make sure that the police are following Jack Meyers and not me. If we're being tailed, I don't see them. "We should use some sort of collection there," I say, still thinking about the showcase. Bobbie asks me if I mean salt and pepper shakers, or cuckoo clocks or something like that. I don't actually have in mind having the breakfast nook look like White Sale Days at Macy's Cellar, but I don't say as much. I just say it has to be something cooler, edgier, more upscale and, well, more collectible. I suggest maiolica ware, or maybe milk glass, and Bobbie offers to hunt around on eBay and see what might be in. I tell her we can't spend more than about ten cents.

"I know!" she says. "We could borrow all that Snoopy stuff from Gina at Precious Things."

"Or maybe Jesse will lend us his Star Wars figures," I say sarcastically. "I think they make a Chewbacca cookie jar."

"I think they've got *I Love Lucy* stuff on sale at Claire's!" Actually, I don't think that idea is half-bad. A pink and gray fifties-ish kitchen with jars of Vitameatavegamin could be adorable, if I had enough money to pull it off. Maybe we could borrow a collection of something for the couple weeks of the show. Of course, the only person with a collection I can think of is Jack Meyers, who isn't about to lend me sand at Jones Beach if I refuse to take back all the stuff I purchased for Elise. Not even then, despite the way I managed to make all those autographed basketballs and jerseys work in their house. Of course, I did have an incredible budget to work with.

Oh, they might have been the couple from hell, but it was the makeover job of my dreams.

"Remind me," I tell Bobbie, "to send any photos I have of Elise's house to the police when we get home."

"Why? Can they get your money for you?" she asks. We roll our eyes at each other because it beats crying and if there's one thing the last year has taught me it's that crying never balanced a checkbook or put a meal on the table. Well, actually it did put a few meals on the table, some from Bobbie, some from June and my father, but none that made me feel good about myself.

Bobbie turns her Ford Explorer into The Estates, a pseudo-gated community whose residents sprang for a little guardhouse but cheaped up on paying a guard. The thinking is, I suppose, that the station is enough to scare off the riffraff. Too bad for Elise the riffraff already lived there.

Vinny and Sal are working away at the Griffin place. They have drop cloths protecting the floor. They have matched the swatch to a T and I can see it is going to be perfect. Bobbie and I go down the hall to pull out the little lampshades with the taupe and white stripes and make sure they will match the walls. A companion fabric is going on the chairs and I still haven't decided which I want to use for the swags over the windows.

When we come back I find that Sal is holding my Black-Berry, pressing every button on it. He hands it to me with a shrug. "Where's that job we're supposed to do Monday?" he asks. Bobbie waits for me to tell the painter never to touch my stuff again. I wish I could say she didn't have a long wait, but the "Twelfth of Never" will probably come around twice before I have a confrontation I'm not forced to have.

Next week they will be painting Pam's guest room a deep rose color. Conventional thought would pair it with a pale blue-gray. I'm doing it with navy. Works great with the Aubusson rug she already has, and I'll use the blue-gray on the woodwork to tie it all together. I tell Sal he'll be here again. He acts like he never even requested the information. Too many paint fumes, if you ask me.

We still haven't found the perfect chandelier, so we head back home to scour the Internet and make sure our children are all accounted for.

The neighborhood Bobbie and I live in is pretty typical of Long Island. One or two models of houses are reversed here and there to look like more. You know, houses with the bedrooms over the garage on the left, next to houses with the bedrooms over the garage on the right. Since ours are front-to-back split levels, we've got sunken living rooms to the left of, or sunken living rooms to the right of, the front hall. The layouts of my house and Bobbie's are mirror images of each other, though they've been remodeled so many times over the years that now they appear pretty different. Mine is cutesy-poo gingerbread and hers is sleek modern.

I used to love coming home. Now every time I drive down Gregory Lane my heart stops until I see that my driveway is empty. Bobbie is attuned to this and says aloud that Rio's car isn't there. It's not like I expect him to steal the kids or anything as dramatic as that. We've had our drama. I just don't want to deal with him. I wish I could just make him go away. Forever.

Which reminds me of the reaction Drew had at dinner when I mentioned the possibility of a hit man. As we enter my house, I tell Bobbie about how he fumbled with his knife and changed the conversation.

I shout "hi" to the kids, listen for three "hi's" back, hear them with no postscripts. Alyssa comes running downstairs with Maggie May, and I get a big hello from both of them. Alyssa shows me her latest drawing, asks if she can have three cookies and if she can give a biscuit to the dog. I pat both heads—Alyssa's and Maggie's—say "sure" and head for my computer. Bobbie watches over my shoulder as I pull up the pictures of Elise's house. I dump my purse out on the big rolltop desk that houses my computer and most of the rest of my life and fish the card Drew gave me out of the morass. I copy in the e-mail address to send them to the police.

I pull up the picture Elise sent me and split the screen so that I can compare it to one of my "before pictures." While Bobbie raves about the improvements, I search for what hasn't changed. Something is off, but I can't put my finger on it. The pictures are from ever so slightly different angles so that I can't simply overlay them.

Bobbie plays with some swatches I have lying near the computer. She asks me who they are for and I mumble something about prospective clients because the truth is I couldn't resist the vintage Hawaiian barkcloth and I just know that someone is going to want a Polynesian theme eventually. The fifties and sixties are back big-time, only now they're known as *mid-Century* instead of *what-my-mother-threw-out*.

I enlarge the photos. Bobbie asks me if she can borrow my long slip on Saturday. I say sure and make the photos even bigger. Now I've got to move them section by section. She asks me if I've seen her "faces" bracelet, the one I got her at the craft fair at the Nassau Coliseum last year. I give up on Elise's kitchen and move into her hallway. Something there looks wrong.

Bobbie phones her daughters, tells them where she is if they need her and asks if they've borrowed her bracelet. I pull up the old living room photos. Bobbie goes to get us something to snack on from the kitchen. When she gets back, I am counting.

"You see these signed basketballs?" I ask her.

"I wasn't interested in them in person," she says, handing me a bowl of mint chocolate chip ice cream. "Why am I looking at them again?"

"Because—" I say, leaning back in my chair "—there's a slight problem with them."

Bobbie licks her empty spoon, a trick she has that makes her ice cream last longer for no more calories, and looks at the basketballs. "They're ugly?"

"How many do you see in the living room?" I ask her. She looks at both pictures and smiles.

"One less than in the hallway," she says and pats me on the back. "You are good! Now, what does it mean?"

And there's the rub. What does it mean? "Well, Jack wouldn't have parted with one of them," I say. "And he'd have killed—"

"—anyone that, say, got rid of one?" Bobbie finishes.

Drew, when I reach him by phone, is very interested in my little observation. He says it fills in a small piece of the puzzle, but won't say what. I imply that his source—me—may just clam up if he's going to be that way.

He does not think this is funny. He warns me about playing amateur detective in what is a murder case.

"So then you do know it's murder," I say. He is silent. "Are you going to charge Jack?"

"There's a bit of a wrinkle," he says, and I hear my call-waiting clicking. I ask him to hold on and press the flash button, connecting with Judith Brenner, a new client.

"I need to cancel our appointment," she tells me. I mouth as much to Bobbie and ask when she wants to reschedule.

"Well," she hedges. "I'm not sure I want to at all. I'm not blaming you or anything, but our house was broken into yesterday morning while I was at the gym and, well, you know, with the whole Elise Meyers thing—"

"You don't think I—" I start to say, and hold the phone so that Bobbie can hear her as well.

"Of course not," she says, but not very convincingly. "I did, naturally, tell the police that you and your friend were here last week taking measurements and all. I told them you couldn't possibly be involved, but my husband thinks it would be best if we just, you know, put the whole redecorating thing on hold for a while."

As in, *We'll get someone else who isn't involved in robbery and murder, if you don't mind.*

I tell her that I had some great ideas for the house that I'd love to show her whenever she's ready to proceed. I pick up her folder and pitch it toward the garbage as she says the equivalent of *Don't call us, we'll call you.*

I click back to Drew, who is waiting. "Does that wrinkle you mentioned have anything to do with the robbery at the Brenner's?" I ask him.

"How do you know about that?" he asks.

I tell him that she just called, because otherwise wouldn't

I look guilty knowing about the robbery? "I'm back to being a suspect, aren't I?"

He avoids the question by asking if I'm going to be home in an hour or so. "There's something I'd like to show you," he says, and then hangs up before I've agreed to be here.

"Oh my God," Bobbie says. "What if he asks you where you were?"

Maggie May looks at us and puts her head down on her paws.

I don't think telling him I was breaking and entering and that I kidnapped a dog is going to get me off the hook. "Do you think I'm really a suspect?" I ask her.

"Like anyone could suspect you of anything."

"Hey, they know all about me trying to shoot Rio," I say.

She reminds me I was under duress, that I was set up, that I was terrified and that I was never even charged with anything. Thanks, I suppose, to the fact that Rio's setup included a paintball rifle instead of a real one.

"Still, I pulled the trigger thinking it was a real gun," I say.

"And believing it was an intruder breaking into your back door."

"But doesn't it show that under duress I am capable of trying to kill someone?"

Bobbie has no answer. She gets the door when Drew rings the bell and he seems more than a little surprised to see her. "I'm Teddi's partner," she says, realizing that in these times such a statement makes it sound like more than business, so she starts to qualify it. But Drew cuts her off. It's clear he knows much more about me than I've told him. He tells Bobbie that he's here on official business and he needs to speak with me privately.

He raises an eyebrow at her suggestion that I might need an attorney, but if you've seen *Law and Order* once, you know that cops don't have a really high regard for lawyers. Bobbie shoots me a what-could-you-possibly-see-in-this-guy-besides-his-cute-butt look and yells goodbye to my kids.

Drew follows me into the kitchen, where he encounters Maggie May.

"New dog?" he asks.

"Watching her for a friend," I answer. And I think *you don't show me yours, I won't show you mine*.

He keeps walking through my kitchen, looks out the back door and suggests we go sit on the back deck. "I don't want your kids overhearing any of this," he says. "I should, by all rights, be doing this down at the station, but you're on my way home and I thought—"

"That you'd get more out of me here where my guard would be down." I really don't like the way he dismissed Bobbie, and he knows it.

"You and your friend should not start acting guilty," he warns me. "Not now when I've stuck my neck out for you."

I ask him what he's talking about.

"I shouldn't have told you about the case. It just seemed so obvious to me that it was—" He stops himself.

"And now it's not obvious?"

"You spend yesterday with your *girlfriend?*" he asks. He uses the same tone as my mother. She's had nothing but contempt for Bobbie ever since she took Mike back—this despite the fact that my mother moved back in with my father once his paramour/her housekeeper/my second mother moved out, but I don't get Drew's attitude.

"Most of it," I say. He waits for more. I look blankly at him and wonder if I really do need a lawyer.

He pulls a photo out of his jacket pocket and shows it to me. "You recognize this?" he asks.

I look at the picture of Bobbie's missing "face" bracelet. There is a tag tied to it with a bunch of numbers on it, clearly identifying it as evidence. I don't answer him.

"Please," he says. "Don't make me do this at the station."

"I bought the bracelet," I say. "Or one like it, at the craft fair at the Coliseum last fall."

He looks me dead in the eye and there is no play there. He waits. He waits some more.

"For who?" he finally says.

He's good. He's very, very good.

CHAPTER 7

Design Tip of the Day

A focal point is essential for pulling a room together. This can be an architectural element, such as a fireplace or window, a shock of color, such as an accent wall or a striking couch, or even an object, such as a sculpture. Often the right single item can command the attention of everyone in a room.

—From TipsfromTeddi.com

"I may not like him, but that doesn't alter the fact that the man is a hunka-hunka burning love," Bobbie says while she picks at her no-MSG, no-oil, hold-the-peanuts kung pao chicken at Empire Szechuan with the kids a few days later. "I'm not buying that you're just feigning romantic interest in him. Hell, he hates me, I'm happily married and I'm still interested in him. The crotch of a tree would be interested in him."

I tell her to knock it off because I don't like talking about my imaginary hot sex life in front of our kids, especially when the chances are that Drew Scoones is more likely trying to get information *out of* me than anything *into* me, if you get my drift. God, it's been a long, long time since the problem of talking about my sex life in front of the kids has come up.

"He is just so—" Bobbie begins, but my cell rings just as Kimmie, her daughter, finishes the thought for her, amid giggles from all the kids "—hot."

And, sadly, it's Looney Tunes and not the theme from *Dragnet* we hear.

"Hi Mom," I say, and even I can hear the disappointment in my voice.

"JDate," she says. "That's the answer."

I don't even ask what the question is. I am single on Long Island, so everyone knows the question.

"It's only thirty-five dollars for the first month and you probably won't need more than that."

Bobbie is trying not to let my mother hear her laughing.

"Teddi? Are you listening? It says right on the site that you can find a hottie. I think they're trying to sound hip, but it's for nice Jewish girls who can't find nice Jewish men on their own, and you know you qualify."

"First off, Mom, I don't think that not looking for something is the same as not being able to find it, and secondly, we're having dinner out with the kids and I really can't talk now."

My mother doesn't buy either excuse. "You can find someone on your own? Show me. Go ahead. Prove me a terrible mother who underestimates her daughter. Bring home a widowed plastic surgeon on your own and I'll apologize. In front of your father, even. On *Oprah*."

Bobbie can no longer hold back her laugh, only by now it's grown and it explodes out of her like a firecracker. Her daughters turn three shades of red and try to pretend they don't know her.

"Oh, like *her* husband's such a prize," my mother says.

"Mom, I really can't talk now," I say and close my phone because she won't stop as long as I am on the other end. Jesse gives me a look that says I should upgrade to the new phone and not tell my mother the number.

"Why didn't you tell her you've already got a *hottie?*" Bobbie asks and the kids, including Alyssa, giggle.

Trying to establish some sense of decorum, I reply, "Hottie or not—" and I gesture toward Alyssa, who for a little pitcher has mighty big ears "—Detective Scoones doesn't seem to think it's a coincidence that your bracelet turned up in Judith Brenner's house."

Bobbie's daughter Kristen stops playing with her food to ask if the handsome detective thinks her mother is a suspect and makes noises about what her father will do about any such ridiculous suspicions. Kimmie, her twin, who still hasn't forgiven Mike for cheating on Bobbie and for abandoning all of them last year for what turned out to be one of those male menopause moments, asks in earnest if Drew thinks her mother could have anything to do with our client's murder.

"Of course not," I rush to tell her, maybe a little too quickly. "I mean, I explained how we're in and out of all these houses measuring, consulting, dropping off swatches, checking on painters and contractors…."

"Did you tell them how careless she is?" Kristen demands. She is making little piles of steamed vegetables, separating her red peppers from her carrots and her celery from her bok choy. She spears a pea and adds, "She's always losing everything, like half her jewelry is missing at any given time, but the minute *I* lose anything she's like down my throat ripping out my lungs."

Bobbie defends herself and tells Kristen that when she pays for things she can feel free to lose them with no consequences, but as long as Bobbie's paying…which of course, leads to the comment by Kristen that Bobbie doesn't pay for things, Mike does.

Things are getting ugly when we all hear the theme from Looney Tunes once again, and Alyssa announces that Grandma is calling. Thankfully she is wrong, and it is Grandpa, who understands that I have a life and can actually hear me when I ask if I can call him back.

"Quick question," he says when I answer. This is code for *I can't work some gadget and I need you to walk me through it*. The problem with his quick questions is that the answers never are. Just the same, I tell him *sure* and then try to explain to him, slowly, *very* slowly, how he can receive e-mail via *Bluetooth* on his cell phone.

"You try the new video phone yet?" he asks. I promise him I will, soon.

"And I'm still getting like wavy lines and snow on my TV," Kimmie is saying while Jesse, bless him, entertains Alyssa with the magic tricks he's learning. Any qualms I had about how far he was straying from reality with all those *Harry Potter* books havc been overshadowed by the new confidence he's gaining as an amateur magician. It's amazing how on a soccer field Jess didn't know his right foot from his left elbow, but with a scarf and a wand he's a whiz. "That cable guy didn't make it even a little better."

I shoot Bobbie a did-you-know-about-any-cable-guy? look and she shakes her head. Apologizing to my father, I hang up with him and put on my stern face. This isn't hard to do when it comes to letting strangers in the house now that I am a single mom. Not that I shouldn't have been just as careful before. It's just that I figured, somewhere deep in my psyche, that Rio could protect us all even if he was at work. Now that I know he was actually screwing his jailbait girlfriend a good deal of the time he was supposedly at work, it makes the idea that he could protect me from afar even more ludicrous.

"Well, he came in a Cablevision truck, didn't he?" Dana asks, trying to vindicate her friends. Kimmie and Kristen exchange guilty looks and say that they had called Cablevision about the problem and that the repair man had come.

"What's the big deal?" they say almost in unison.

The big deal, I explain to them, is that they are lucky to be alive. Probably sensing what's coming, the couple to our left decide to take their chow mein to go. This doesn't affect Bobbie's demeanor or her volume, which is somewhat higher than mine.

"Okay, so some strange man shows up at the door and you just let him in," she says. "Right so far?" The girls shrug. "And you take him down to the basement?" she asks while a young family takes the table recently vacated on our left side.

"Uh..." Kimmie says while Kristen says he went straight to the master bedroom to fix the box there, which was stupid because the TV in her room gets the worst reception.

"Uh huh," Bobbie says, and she is gripping her chopsticks so tightly I think something, hopefully not *someone*, is about to be pierced and pronounced done. "You tried to get a strange man to come into your bedroom with you. Amazingly, that didn't work, so you took him into my bedroom."

Kimmie is turning a little red. Kristen just appears bored.

"Put your bangs back," Bobbie says, reaching across the table and swiping at Kristen's forehead. "I want to see where the Rape Me, Rape Me Now tattoo is. Next to the Murder Me one, perhaps? Too bad they're going to be hidden by the I Am A Freakin' Idiot one I'm having tattooed across both your foreheads before we go home tonight."

"Costs less to do Moron," Jesse says quietly to Alyssa. "Same sentiment, less letters."

"Said by the wiseacre who won't get raped unless he

winds up in jail," Bobbie says. The young family picks up their glasses and silverware and moves farther back in the restaurant while Jesse mumbles that he's sorry.

Alyssa announces that she has to use the bathroom and all three older girls volunteer to take her.

"Nice try," Bobbie says and signals the girls to sit down.

"What did *I* do?" Dana pouts. "This is like guilt by association or something." I'm impressed that she knows the phrase and I want to ask her if they showed *Good Night, and Good Luck* in school, but now doesn't seem like the best time.

Bobbie tells Dana that she would have done the exact same thing, and while I feel the urge to defend her, I think it's probably true. And if the fear of God—or a would-be-rapist—is the result of being lumped in with her friends, that's okay with me.

"It's a damn good thing he was just a petty thief," Bobbie says. "And that he was content with a handful of my costume jewelry."

Only that doesn't really make sense, does it?

"Did you stay in your mom's bedroom with him the whole time he worked on the TV?" I ask.

"The phone rang," Kimmie says.

"Yeah, Dad called," Kristen adds. "And we had to go downstairs for…" her voice trails off.

"…something," Kimmie says. They clearly don't remember what was so important that they'd leave a strange man they shouldn't have given entry to in the first place in their mother's bedroom.

"And he takes the junk jewelry and not the good stuff?" I say to Bobbie.

"Just lucky, I guess," Dana suggests.

"Maybe he's like one of those shoe fetishists," Jesse says. "Only he likes crappy jewelry."

Bobbie takes umbrage at the idea that any of her jewelry is "crappy."

"Takes the low-rent stuff and leaves the diamonds and gold," I say while Bobbie berates the girls. "Okay, but why?"

CHAPTER 8

Design Tip of the Day

> Often the problem with a room stems from too many elements fighting for your attention. If there is a fireplace, a television that can't be hidden and a to-die-for view all in the same room, the eye doesn't know where to look. Furniture-arranging in rooms with immovable elements can be a real challenge because it is easy to feel confused in such an atmosphere.
>
> —From TipsfromTeddi.com

My plan, when I accept Helene's brother Howard's invitation to dine at the Garden City Hotel, is to go out with him once, tell Helene that we simply did not click, and not have to hear about the man for the rest of my natural life.

A few days later, in the exquisite atmosphere of one of the finest restaurants on Long Island, it doesn't exactly go that way. It isn't love at first sight, but Howard is funny, warm and reminds me of a teddy bear, which is to say I wouldn't actually mind taking him to bed with me. That would, I suppose, make for two teddy bears in the bed, wouldn't it?

When sex was a regular occurrence—i.e., when I was married—I hardly ever gave it a moment's thought. Until his affair, Rio always wanted sex—and yes, his waning interest should have been a tip-off, but, silly me, I thought it was just consideration for my emotional state—the one he put me in. But I digress. The point I was trying to make is that when I wanted sex, it was available in the form of my husband.

It was safe (or so I thought). I mean, not just from the disease standpoint, but I wasn't risking my heart, my pride, my soul. (Okay, maybe I was, but I didn't know it at the time. Now I know.)

Howard makes me realize I want sex. I miss it. That incredible feeling of detachment from the problems of the world, of soaring outside oneself, of being treasured for however long the moment lasts. Howard is big, probably over six feet. He makes me feel petite and delicate. He looks like he enjoys life, smiling easily, laughing heartily, sighing with satisfaction.

Still, wanting sex and wanting sex with Howard are two different things.

"So—" he says, offering me a taste of his pappardelle with truffles, cheese and pancetta "—how would you rate this restaurant?"

The flavors melt on my tongue and I savor the moment. No children whose behavior I have to watch, no discussion about how much the dinner is costing, no concern about the wine going to my head when I have to drive home. I close my eyes and say, "Exquisite."

He says he's glad I like it and that he likes coming here because he's already done his review and can come as himself.

"Ordinarily, I have to dine incognito."

I admit that no one has ever said those words to me before and Howard laughs. I ask how that usually works.

"Well, I've gone out to dinner as a bum, as a very old man, as a real dandy, as a mafioso. First off, I can't have them recognizing me and doing for me what they don't do for their average customer. Secondly, I like to see how they treat people who aren't just like me."

"It must be fascinating," I say, and I'm thinking that I'd be willing to dress up as Bozo the Clown for another meal like this one.

"I've taken my gay lover out for an anniversary dinner, taken my mother out for a—"

"Back up," I say. I'm still on his gay lover.

"You should have seen the review that restaurant got. We were seated by the kitchen, they were out of nearly everything we wanted, there was cork in the wine and they wouldn't accommodate my brother's allergies. If he'd really been allergic to peanuts I'd have taken him home to his wife in a box."

"So it was really your brother," I clarify and he nods, admitting it can be fun to try to push a few buttons.

"When someone goes to a restaurant of this caliber, it's not just because he wants a good meal," he says, and he feeds me another strip of pappardelle off his fork. "It's an occasion, an experience. Even a meal as good as this can be ruined by a surly waiter."

At the word waiter, someone appears at his elbow and inquires about the pasta. Howard says that his boss thinks it is exquisite. The waiter's eyebrows rise as much as mine must at the appellation, but there is a noticeable shift in the dynamic.

"Can I get you anything else?" His attention is suddenly directed to me. Howard asks if I'd mind if he ordered some more wine.

"A white?" he suggests. When I hesitate he shrugs at the waiter as if to say he's got a cheap boss so it's no more wine.

"Oh, why not?" I say. "After all, you don't get a promotion every day."

"Very good, madam," the waiter says. "Shall I bring the wine list?"

Howard defers to me and as the waiter backs away I feel a gentle pat on my thigh under the tablecloth. "Nice work. You illustrated my point perfectly."

A wine steward appears with the list and hands it to me. Apparently word has been passed around that I am the one paying the check. I give Howard the honor of choosing the wine, since I am also going to give him the honor of paying for dinner.

After he orders what will no doubt be an amusing little vintage and the sommelier hurries off to allow the wine to breathe or whatever it is that wine does, Howard and I share a quiet laugh.

"And now," he asks, "has your opinion of the restaurant gone up or down?"

I admit that my affection for the restaurant has actually gone south. "It wasn't until they started fawning on me that I realized they hadn't been before. And while I don't like fawning, I don't like them paying more attention to me as your host than as your guest."

Howard tells me to look for a similar comment in a future review. "Very astute," he says warmly. My opinion of the restaurant may have gone down, but my opinion of Howard is rising steadily. Especially when he asks what my children are going as for Halloween and offers to lend Jesse a top hat and cape if he wants to go the magician route.

He asks me what decorating for other people is like. "I know that ordering for someone else's taste can be a trial," he says. "Someone I was dining with actually asked for ketchup over Béarnaise sauce. I had to come back and do the review alone."

I explain how I try to incorporate my taste into a client's preferences, and how I have to remind myself that I won't be living in the house, they will. We talk about my clients over salmon and crab paupiette and my favorite colors and styles over *fondant au chocolat*.

And, let me say, it sure beat arguing with children and eating warmed-up leftover kung pao chicken.

On the way home we talk about what it's like to be single on Long Island, and there is a longing in his voice that scares me because it mirrors how I feel. He says that Long Island is built for neat little families of four.

"But not a mom and three kids," I tell him and he agrees.

"Not a man and three dogs," he says.

"You have three dogs?" There isn't a stray hair on his suit. We have just Maggie May and I look like I've been processed in a lint factory.

"Okay, not a guy and a parrot and two goldfish."

"You have—" I start.

"Not a guy and a hot plate and an outdoor cat and a bird feeder."

"You're counting a hot plate as a member of your family?"

He smiles. "I have more meals with it than with anyone else."

I let it qualify just as we are pulling up to my house, where there is a dark sports car parked in the driveway and a man's silhouette on my front porch. He is not waiting at the door, but leaning against the post, watching as Howard runs around the front of the car to open my door. I think I can see Drew smirking, but it could be my imagination.

Under the stark porch light I awkwardly introduce Howard and Drew. "Detective Scoones of the Nassau Police Department," I say, pointing at Drew. "Howard Rosen, my uh." Cool, aren't I? A real master of words.

The men nod at each other. Let me say here and now that there is nothing more flattering to an almost-forty-year-old woman than to watch two grown men try to flex their muscles on her account. It takes the chill right out of the fall air to watch Howard try to assert some degree of possession while Drew does a lousy job of appearing unfazed. I love it, but the thing is, I just can't read Drew Scoones. I can't tell if he is pretending to like me or pretending not to.

Jesse opens the door and tells me through the lovely Victorian screen door that he didn't let the detective in because I wasn't home. Drew compliments him on showing good judgment, though he reminds my son that they have met before and that he did show Jesse his badge.

"You see Moron tattooed here?" Jesse asks him, lifting his hair off his forehead.

Drew looks at me, I tell Jesse "Enough," and Howard laughs as if he is in on the joke, just to make Drew feel like odd man out. I may actually be too old for these games, after all.

"I'll just wait for you two young folks to say good night," the good detective, who is probably ten years younger than either of us, says. And then he just stands there, casually leaning against the porch railing, watching Howard and me.

After an awkward silence I thank Howard for a lovely dinner, mentioning that the filet mignon at the Garden City Hotel was just perfection. Is that a tick by Drew Scoones's eye, I see?

"You had the shellfish," Howard says.

Jesse rolls his eyes and walks away while Drew covers his mouth and stifles a cough. I say something about how I saw the filet mignon and it *looked* wonderful. Howard says it's good at the Polo Club, which is how people in the know refer to the hotel's restaurant, but that he knows a place where it is even better.

"Maybe one night next week?" he suggests.

Drew asks if he's got a hotter date for the weekend. "Reserving the weekend for someone else?" he asks. The desire to kick him boils inside me and nearly spills over.

Howard explains that he will be away for the weekend. It takes everything I have not to say "Yes, so sorry I won't be able to join you for that," but I'm afraid he'll blurt out that he never asked me.

"Whenever you're done," Drew says. "I've got all night."

Howard checks his watch. He says it's getting late. I nod. He looks at Drew and asks if I'll be all right. Again I nod.

"It's just police business," Drew tells Howard. "Routine. Nothing to worry about. She's not actually a suspect."

"Actually?" I ask as Howard is backing down the walkway.

"Just a murder investigation," Drew says loudly enough for half the neighborhood to hear.

I don't have to tell him Howard is going to get the wrong impression. He knows.

He holds my own screen door open for me and follows me into the house.

"Sorry if I ruined your evening," he says and I give him an exasperated look. "What's that look supposed to mean? That I did ruin it or that there was nothing to ruin?"

I don't know the answer, so I ask him what it is he wants.

"The lab reports are back. I thought you'd want to know."

He saunters after me into the kitchen where I take off the cashmere shrug Bobbie lent me and try to pretend that I don't care whether he tells me or not, but he's better at this game than I am. Finally I relent and ask him to tell me.

"The pills we found around Elise Meyers? Poison. And they were in her system, too."

"So Jack Meyers doctored her pills and then decided he just couldn't wait? Is that it?" I ask.

Drew is studying my kitchen, probably looking for the remains of the night I shot Rio with his paintball rifle. I don't even want to think about what the other policemen have told him about that night and how they took me to South Winds Psychiatric Hospital and had me signed in. There are no signs of that night in the kitchen, but believe me they're on my psyche forever.

"You do know that it was all a setup, right?" I ask.

He cocks his head. "Are you saying she wanted it to

look like he was poisoning her and she was actually doing it herself?"

For a minute I don't know what he's talking about. "Oh, Elise. Right. I mean, no, not right. I mean—"

"Your husband. Right. A setup—"

"Poison."

"Paint gun."

"I painted the kitchen. I mean, I had it painted."

"It's more convoluted than it would appear."

"I'll say."

"I'm talking about the Meyers case," he says, as if that clarifies anything.

I agree that I was talking about that, too. He shakes his head at me like the jig is up.

"I did have their kitchen painted," I say, but it doesn't fool either of us.

"Maybe we should shoot the damn beast," he says, referring to the elephant in the room that we are trying to talk around. I agree that we should.

"From what I understand, your husband was trying to drive you crazy. To put the final nail in your coffin, he left his paintball rifle where you could find it, made you think that someone was breaking into the house and then came in the back door, where, upon his entering, you shot him. That about sum it up?"

I nod.

"You spent several days in South Winds, were released

and never pressed charges against the bastard because he wasn't breaking any laws."

I nod again.

"Your mother shot him in the leg at South Winds, and, for some reason the police can't fathom, he never pressed charges. Since then, Rio Gallo has received four speeding tickets, eleven parking tickets, had his car towed twice and been questioned in connection with two break-ins."

When I scrape my jaw off the table, Drew smiles and mumbles something about the law working in mysterious ways.

"I thought that was the Lord."

He shrugs. "Sometimes vengeance isn't just His."

"Well, Rio's still my children's father," I say, which is why I never turned him in for forging my signature on a loan application. I threatened to, and he and his lawyer know that I've got the document in my safe deposit box, but as long as he doesn't press charges against my mother and dutifully calls his children while keeping his distance, I won't turn it over to the authorities.

Drew nods. Who ever would have thought that the police were on my side? Even with Bobbie's sister, Diane, on the force, I never thought they'd be able to separate me from my mother, who they've taken to South Winds more than once.

"So, Elise Meyers," he says, putting the past behind me. "You know if she and Jack collected anything? Coins? Antiques? Maybe from, say, Iraq? Anything like that?"

I remind him that Jack, a sports agent, is into sports memorabilia. And I also remind him that one of Jack's balls is missing. From the look on his face he seems to know exactly where Jack's been hiding his balls, but all he says is, "Accounted for."

When I ask him in what way, he starts asking more questions about Jack and Elise's spending habits, if I know where they stored their valuables, if I know what might be in such a place, if one existed...all sorts of things that make me feel as though he's baiting a trap for me, which makes me wary, which, I'm afraid, makes me appear guilty.

"So did you check into Jack Meyers's alibi?" I ask. Does that seem like I'm shifting blame? On TV, when people start pointing fingers, it always means they're the actual culprit. "I mean, was he on his boat in Connecticut? Did you find out who his "client" was?"

Jesse comes down into the kitchen to complain that his sister is hogging the computer and ask why she can't just call the K's instead of IM-ing them. And Drew looks at his watch and says it's getting late and he doesn't want to keep me from my children.

I tell Jesse it's too late for either of them to be on the computer but Drew is already getting up and heading for the door.

He's really good at not answering questions. "So you'll be around?" he says.

"Is that like 'don't leave town?'" I ask.

Drew looks at Jesse, who, hands on hips, is daring him to say it is.

"Your mom is such a card," he says, and winks at me.

As I said, he's really good at not answering questions. Which means that after he leaves and I end the computer war by insisting that both Jesse and Dana go to bed (will they never learn that if they don't come seek me out I won't notice how late they are staying up?)I have to find the answers to a few questions on my own.

Like even though I don't know why he asked about Iraq or coins, I do know how to find out how much those sorts of things might be worth. In my bedroom I turn on my laptop, which, thanks to the Wi-Fi router my father gave me along with it, comes to life ready to tell me everything I could want to know. Except, of course, the really important stuff, like who killed Elise.

Ebay is naturally bookmarked, and I'm on and logged in with just a click or two. Nothing there seems worth Drew's interest so I tool around a little more. I Google Iraqi coins and artifacts, wind up on some museum site and find that there are some very rare coins missing from Iraqi museums looted during the early days of the war.

My buddy list shows that Bobbie is on line, so I IM her to ask if she knows why in the world Drew would be asking me about stolen Iraqi coins.

MAYBE HE THINKS THE SAME THIEF THAT STOLE MY STUFF STOLE STUFF FROM ELISE >:-(she types back to me.

OH YEAH, I reply. YOUR JUNK JEWELRY AND MUSEUM ARTIFACTS. THAT MAKES SENSE. I DON'T KNOW WHY I DIDN'T THINK OF THAT.;->

HE PROBABLY THINKS I STOLE IT, WHATEVER "IT" IS. ':-)

WHAT'S ':-) ? I type.

A RAISED EYEBROW.

GREAT. I'VE GOT A DETECTIVE SNIFFING AROUND AND YOU'RE DRAWING PICTURES!

I tell her I'll see her tomorrow at Ashley's Nail Salon, say goodnight, and close my laptop.

Ping.

Before I have my eyes closed, they are open wide. The noise, if I really heard a noise, is outside. When I don't hear anything else, I decide it was a squirrel on the roof and resettle myself.

Ping.

Okay, that wasn't a squirrel. It was a rock against my window. Looking out I see the end of my world as I know it. I raise the window sash and yell in a stage whisper. "What the hell do you think you're doing?"

My can't-be-soon-enough-ex-husband smiles at me in the moonlight. "Hey, Teddi," he says.

"Hey, yourself. Go away."

He says he just wants to see the kids.

"It's after midnight. The kids are asleep. Go away."

He says he thought Alyssa'd be asleep and that was why he didn't ring the doorbell.

"They're all asleep. I was asleep. Go away." I lower the window and almost smash it on my hand when a voice behind me startles me.

"I'm not asleep," Jesse says. "Why is Dad here?"

I tell him that I don't know, rather than say that he's probably drunk, or broke or looking for trouble. Or already in trouble.

"Are you going to let him in?" Dana, now lurking in the doorway, asks.

"No."

"Then I will," Dana says, turning on her heel.

I tell her that she will not, that she will go back to bed, that Jesse will go back to bed and that I will deal with their father. I say it with a tone that implies if they ever want to see their father again, they will do as they are told.

Jesse, who has become the de facto man of the house, pushes the bangs out of my eyes and gives me a long, hard stare. "Doesn't say Moron there, Mom. But I'm checking again in the morning."

I tell the kids good night and when Rio throws the third rock, I gesture to him to meet me at the front door, I grab my old chenille robe from the back of the bathroom door and close the kids' doors on the way down the hall.

Under the porch light Rio is as handsome as he ever was.

It just doesn't melt my insides the way it used to. In fact, it twists them in a knot.

"What do you want?" I ask him while Maggie May growls at him through the door.

"Teddi, you look great," he says, letting his eyes roam over me like my body is still his private playground. I ignore the comment and the look and ask him again what he wants.

"Why do I have to want something?" he asks, crouching down and trying to win Maggie May over with just his smile. Hey, once upon a time, it worked on me. "Can't I just miss you and the kids?"

I tell him he can miss us all he wants, but that we have an agreement and this little midnight visit is abridging it.

He tells me he misses all my big words, that he always found them sexy. Without a doubt, Rio Gallo is the biggest liar on Long Island, and, believe me, he's got a lot of competition.

"Did I get you out of bed?" he asks as he slips in the door. I remind him of the hour. "You've got that look, what do they call it? Bed-head eyes?"

He means bed*room* eyes, but I'm losing patience. "Go home to your little girlfriend," I tell him.

He assures me I have no reason to be jealous and pulls out his cell phone. "I'll call her and tell her I'd rather be with you. How's that?"

"Ludicrous," I say as he punches numbers into his phone and heads for the kitchen. "Where do you think you're going?"

"It's dark in the hall," he tells me. "You don't want me getting ideas, do you?"

I tell him I want him getting out. And I place my finger over the little camera lens in the phone that he has aimed at me.

"I'm calling the police," I say, "if you don't leave right now."

"I just wanted to remember you like this," he says, still trying to take my picture.

I pick up the kitchen phone.

"Gonna call your friend Detective Scoones?" he asks. Apparently, while the police have been watching him, he has been watching the police.

"I really don't think you want to find out," I warn him, punching in the first three numbers. Maggie is doing wild circles in the kitchen and I fear she will melt into a puddle soon.

"Give me five minutes, Teddi," he begs me. "I gave you twelve years, for Christ's sake. Can't you give me five minutes?"

I press in two more numbers.

"I left something in the basement," he says, deftly moving toward the den stairs.

I press in the remaining numbers.

"I'll be gone before they get here," he says, hurrying down the steps, Maggie on his heels.

I think about the police coming here in the middle of the night and how it would make the kids feel to see their father escorted from the house, and I hang up the phone. I don't know what he's looking for downstairs, but my vivid imagination has me as dead as Elise Meyers if I follow him down there. Instead I stand at the top of the steps and call down to him that they are on their way.

I can hear him rifling through things, moving boxes, cursing under his breath and I can't resist going down to see what he is up to.

"Did you hide something in my basement?" I demand as I descend the steps from the den to the basement. "Do I have stolen goods or something, Rio, because the police are very interested in...that sort of thing, these days."

Rio has pulled out drawers from an old chest, opened two old suitcases and is now rummaging through some bras I wore when I was pregnant with Dana and he and I were both mesmerized by my new size. My breasts increased much faster than my waistline and I felt positively Dolly Parton-esque for a month or two. We marveled, we measured, we documented and photographed.

"Reminiscing?" I ask him.

He gives me the standard line about the good times we had. The only good times I can remember involved sending all his belongings to his mother's house and suing him for divorce.

He reminds me that the police are on their way and asks if I don't want to get into something a little more alluring than my old chenille robe. Maggie makes a jump for the lace bra dangling from his fingers as we both hear footfalls on the stairs.

"Everything all right down here?" Drew Scoones asks. I

don't know who is more surprised to see him, Rio, who looks cut to the quick, or me.

"You really called the police?" he asks me, dropping my bra back into the drawer.

"Actually, she hung up," Drew explains as he finishes coming down the stairs. "But the caller ID was already registered and, well, here I am."

"Here we all are," is the only thing I can think of to say as we all stand there, just trying to look casual.

"Looking for something?" Drew asks Rio as he walks over and lifts my 34DD lace bra, looks at it, looks at my chest, looks at it again and politely places it back in the drawer with a mystified expression on his face.

Rio says he just stopped by because he thought he left something here, but it doesn't seem to be around. He's jiggling his leg and the tapping noise fills the basement.

"Guess you'll be taking off then," Drew says.

Rio, who never knows how far to push, says that he'll be leaving in a little while.

My detective shakes his head almost imperceptibly. "Now."

My ex-husband makes noises about peeking in on the kids.

Again Drew shakes his head. "Your car's parked on the wrong side of the street," he says. Rio always used to do that, park on the left side of the street like traffic laws didn't apply to him. "Wouldn't want to get a ticket."

"You ever hear of harassment?" Rio asks Drew. "'Cause another ticket could be just one too many, if you get my drift."

Drew suggests that Rio drift out the door. I get an I'll-be-back look from my nearly ex-husband, and then he is gone.

Drew perches on the edge of the dresser. "You have any idea what he wanted?"

"To beat the system?" I suggest.

"Your husband used to handle hot cars, didn't he?"

I remind him that Rio is no longer my husband. Or at least he won't be in two more months.

"You've got a regular Grand Central Station going here," Drew says. "Men coming in and out at all hours of the night." He traces the drawer pull with his finger, but doesn't open the drawer.

"Were you at the station house?" I ask. "Or do they call it the precinct?"

When he says he wasn't, I can't help asking, "Then what are you doing here?"

CHAPTER 9

Design Tip of the Day

Sometimes it's best to consult with an expert. While experts charge, they can save you time, money and aggravation. Never underestimate the value of someone trained to help.
—From TipsfromTeddi.com

"It's so nice to see you," Ronnie Benjamin says a few days later when she opens her office door to find me in her waiting room. She beckons me into the office I redecorated for her in warm shades of camel and brick and asks how I've been as I sink into the ultrasuede wingback chair across from her desk.

I tell her that considering that in the past ten days I've seen a dead person, possibly escaped murder myself by moments, that my best friend may be accused of the crime by a sexy detective I might be falling for instead of the man I'm dating, whom my mother would no doubt like, and that my ex-husband threw rocks at my window two nights ago, not bad.

"There are people," she tells me with a laugh, "who lead dull lives."

I admit I don't seem to be one of them. "I just want to be sure that I'm not losing my grip," I tell her. "I want to be sure it's not paranoia that has me thinking that everyone is watching me and acting suspicious."

She asks who is watching me.

Who isn't? "When Rio was at the house, the detective—the sexy one—showed up even though he wasn't on duty and I hadn't completed the call to the police. He claimed that it was caller ID, but I think he somehow is monitoring my phone."

"Because…?"

I can't really say that he has the hots for me, can I? "I guess because he thinks that Bobbie is somehow involved in the murder. And then there's the fact that she's keeping stuff from me. And I think that Drew—the detective—knows something, and she knows he knows, and I don't know what anyone knows."

Dr. Benjamin sits back in her chair, folds her hands primly across a belly that really could use a crash course in Pilates and smiles serenely. "You know," she says, "the world keeps changing at such an incredible pace. Every day there are major advances, leaps of achievement. It's nice to see that one small part of the world is the same as I left it."

"Meaning that I haven't made major advances or leaps

of achievement." And I'm actually going to pay her for these words of wisdom that cut me to the quick?

"Meaning," she says, "that you are as healthy and engaging as you were a year ago. That you have all the enthusiasm and angst-ridden joie de vivre that makes you the unique person you are."

All I can manage is, "Oh."

She sighs and tells me to go ahead and ask it but that the answer is "no."

"You don't think I'm paranoid?"

She shakes her head. "Paranoia is the inability to distinguish a real threat from an imagined one. It is based on irrational and unreasonable suspicions that have no basis in fact. From what you've said—Rio showing up, the police showing up—I think your concerns are reality-based. Tell me, what makes you think that Bobbie isn't being wholly truthful with you?"

I explain about how she and Drew keep exchanging glances as though they both know something and have agreed to keep it from me.

Dr. Benjamin asks why I'm really sitting across the desk from her. I don't bother asking what she means.

"I'm interested in a man," I admit. She shrugs, gives me a look that asks *What's wrong with that?* "For one thing," I tell her, "less than a year ago, in this very chair, I swore I'd never let a man in my life again."

"And now you've got over that," she says.

I shift uneasily in my chair, glad I was able to convince her to get rid of the awful leather one I spent last summer sticking to. "I'm not sure I have," I admit to the hem of my jeans.

Dr. Benjamin waits. She always likes to let me trip myself up. Finally she asks if seeing Rio stirred old feelings.

I can't help but laugh. "Yeah—like wariness, mistrust, frustration. It's not Rio."

She admits she's relieved and asks what the problem is, then.

I explain that Howard is a wonderful man, easy to be with, funny, generous. That he offers to take me nice places, feigns interest in my work and is even pleasant to my sullen, unfriendly children. That he's a man my mother would actually approve of.

"And this is a problem because…?" she asks. I examine the diplomas behind her, which I've reframed, matting them with a sueded cream inner matt and a deeper brown outer matt. They look wonderful and I'd rather look at them than at her when I admit the truth.

"Because he's not the man I'm attracted to. I mean, I want to be, and he doesn't repulse me or anything. And if I hadn't met this other man, a man who infuriates me and puzzles me and is annoying and actually thinks that my best friend could be a murderer and that I could possibly be complicit, I might develop some feelings for him. I mean sometime in the future. If it wasn't for this other man…"

"But you feel you shouldn't be interested in the— I take it this is the detective investigating the murder you discovered, right? Is he married?"

I shrug. "I don't think so. It's not what worries me. I mean, that's a big thing, and I wouldn't ignore it. I don't think he is. But that, as I said, isn't it."

She gives me her patented *get-to-it-Teddi* look.

"I think he's dangerous. Not in the same way as Rio, but still… I think I'm interested in him because he isn't the man I should be interested in. And I think I'm not interested in the man I should be interested in because he is. Howard, that is. I *should* be interested in him. He's nice. He's kind. He's gentle and safe."

"Maybe you don't want gentle and safe."

Well, duh—that's why I'm sitting in a psychiatrist's office. "Drew's drop-dead gorgeous. My daughter thinks so, too. Even my mother thinks so."

"Rio was gorgeous," the good doctor says, like I haven't made that connection myself.

"Caring about looks is not only shallow," I tell her, "but can blind you to other, more important characteristics, like honesty, like considerateness, like the capacity to love."

"I'd agree. All handsome men are in Rio's mold. They all, without exception, need to be written off, mistrusted, shunned."

I can do without the hyperbole.

"What interests me, Teddi…" she says after she's sure

she's made her point "...is what Rio was doing in your house the other night."

I tell her that he said he was looking for something, that he rooted around the basement for a while, but that he left when Drew showed up.

She nods, but I can see she isn't satisfied. "My real question concerns why you let him in your house."

It's a question I've been asking myself. I keep getting the same answer I get when I ask why I'm so drawn to Drew Scoones. "I think I might possibly like danger?" It comes out a question.

"Your detective friend," she says. "Does he represent danger to you?"

I know that Drew is on the side of law and order. I know that he will come to his senses about Bobbie's involvement in Elise's murder. I know that as soon as he solves this case I'll never see him again.

"Yeah," I admit. "To my heart."

CHAPTER 10

Design Tip of the Day

Don't be fooled into thinking the details don't matter. Would you go out with your hem coming down? Would you attend a formal wedding without your hair combed and your nails polished? Would you wear red shoes with your green slacks? Fix the fringe on that area rug, replace the burned-down candles in that candelabra, arrange the photos on the mantle. And by the way—give the green pants to Goodwill!

—From TipsfromTeddi.com

The beauty salon where Bobbie and I have our nails done is over the top. If Bobbie didn't nag me constantly about how important the image I present to my clients is, I'd never set foot in this place. Not that it isn't lovely. In fact, it's too lovely. I'm not comfortable being treated like visiting royalty. I don't need three different kinds of creamer for two different choices of decaf or three types of regular. I don't want cookies from the bakery or bagels from the bagelry with cream cheese or butter, thank you very much.

I'd be happy with the bargain place down in Hicksville, but then I wouldn't get to rub newly exfoliated elbows with the movers and shakers who I'm hoping will hire Bobbie and me to decorate their houses. I wouldn't know that having "tracks put in their hair" means getting extensions, or that "threading their chins" means getting stray hairs taken off, and I would be even more out of my element than not having read *The Secret Handbook of Long Island* makes me.

My mother approves of this salon. That ought to tell you how much I don't belong here. Anyway, Kim is trying, at the moment, to salvage my fingernails so that I don't embarrass Bobbie the next time we see a prospective client, which, with the cloud hanging over our heads, doesn't seem to be an imminent danger. Thank goodness I've got Sal and Vinny over at Pam Griffin's house and that, at least as of this morning, she's pleased with their work. And as soon as Pam pays me I can finish repaying my father's loan and declare myself an independent woman.

Kim is *tsk*ing over my hangnails and berating me for missing my last two appointments, which she assures me is the reason my nails look like they've been caught in the Cuisinart.

I'm wishing Bobbie would show up to fill the chair next

to mine so that we can talk to each other and maybe then Kim won't talk to me.

"I haven't seen your nails this bad since—" she stops herself because there is no polite way to refer to the demise of my marriage "—you know when."

"Where's Bobbie?" Ashley, the best pedicurist on Long Island, asks me as she hustles by, carrying a customer's shoes, handbag and keys for her, while the customer waddles behind her, toe separators making walking in paper sandals difficult. Ashley guides her to a chair where her toenail polish will be dried and hardened by mechanical means, and she offers her coffee and a cookie or two. "She's late for her two o'clock," she tells me as if she's been waiting for hours for Bobbie to show up.

Kim rolls her eyes at Ashley because she knows that I will call Bobbie and probably mess my nails. She grabs the cell phone I have placed on the edge of the table and opens it for me before I can do permanent damage to her job.

"Is this new?" she asks.

I nod. "It does video," I say and several people say "Oh." I don't tell them I still haven't tried it out. Several people make jokes about how they hope Bobbie's not in some compromising position while I tell Kim to hold down the number three until it shows that it's dialing.

"What?" we all hear Bobbie snap since Kim has her on speaker phone. We don't see anything. "Kristen's barfing again and I've got to pick her up at school, so make it fast."

"You could have called," Ashley yells toward the phone while I tell Bobbie not to worry about it.

"Ashley cancelled my appointment," she says. I look at Ashley, whose expression says she clearly did not. Ohhh. Shades of last year, when my appointments changed seemingly by themselves. I remind myself that Dr. Benjamin says I am not paranoid as I wonder, for just a second, if someone isn't trying to set Bobbie up.

Meanwhile, Bobbie is telling me that there is a message on my machine from Jack Meyers, who wants us to pick up the stuff Elise ordered and give him a refund.

"She picks up your messages?" Kim mouths to me. I shrug. There are a million reasons Bobbie could have been in my house. She could have run out of coffee or wanted to check to see if we had any appointments this afternoon. Or she could have been curious to see if Howard had called me, or the *hunka-hunka* detective. I don't ask.

"I don't have money to refund to Jack Meyers," I tell her. "I don't even think I'll be able to cancel the rest of the order."

"Why not? Didn't you and Howie trip the light fandango last night? I thought that would surely get us a discount with Helene at the very least."

"You're seeing someone?" the woman at the next nail station asks. I'd ignore her, but it's clear she thinks that since we share an appointment time we're soul mates. I smile shyly.

"I've been thinking about possibly using some of the Marrakech stuff for Bailey Manor," I tell Bobbie.

"He was that bad?" she asks, ignoring my suggestion in favor of my date with Howard.

The woman in the next chair waits for me to answer as though she is the one who has asked the question. As if she has a right to know the answer. I tell her that Howard was not bad at all, but I'm just not really interested in seeing someone.

"Oh, you should!" the woman beside me gushes, shaking her finger at Parvin to indicate she does not want the shade of nail polish Parvin has picked out and brought to the table. "It's like riding a horse. You have to get back on." She points at another bottle, which Parvin indicates is the same color but opens anyway.

"Give me a horse over a man anytime," the shampoo girl says as she leads a customer past us toward the sinks. "And while you're at it, make it a gelding."

Several customers *ooh* and wave their hands to indicate the girl is steaming. "Someone's been burned," a woman whose hair has more shades of gold than the Sherwin-Williams chip rack says.

Meanwhile Bobbie says she's at the school and I tell her I hope Kristen feels better. I also tell her I'll go to our appointment alone this afternoon. I'm afraid that if I put it off, Grace Blanchard might cancel it before I can sell her on using me despite what happened to Elise. And the robbery at Judith Brenner's house.

Once my nails are semidry, and with Kim warning me that I am going to smudge them, I take off for Grace Blanchard's house. If I get this job, it will be a miracle because, for one, it was a referral from my neighbor Gayle, who never does anything nice for anyone, and also because it's in Oyster Bay Cove, which is totally snooty upscale and those people only use decorators with *names*—big, important names.

I do smudge my thumb as I buckle up, and I lick it to try to make it better, which tastes lousy and doesn't help and I know this because I've tried it a million times before, but that doesn't stop me. Then I try to check my BlackBerry for the address without doing further damage. Fat chance.

Pulling in to Grace's neighborhood, I find her block easily, check the house number twice as I drive down the perfectly manicured lane, gawking at houses that are meant to look ungarishly enormous, as if the owners know they aren't supposed to flaunt their wealth but can't resist the urge.

"Two seventy-seven," I say aloud, as I drive down a block with only a dozen or so houses, wondering where the other two hundred and sixty-five addresses on it are. And then I stop, dead, in the middle of the street.

In front of 277 Cornucopia Drive sit three police cars and a private security car. The front of the house is roped off with yellow police tape.

Again.

And I know damn well that the police are not going to buy that this is yet another coincidence. I sit in the car shaking my head. I just can't believe it. I've already had my mind play tricks on me, or my husband play tricks or whatever…

This is too much. I'd swear this doesn't even look like Grace's house—that's how far gone I must be, because I remember it being more of a neo-Federal, with more brick in the front, like the one I passed a couple of houses ago.

I put the car in Reverse just as a police officer starts walking toward me. Pausing, I roll down my window and ask if that house is the Blanchards'.

The officer asks if there is something he can do to help me, gesturing toward the house. "Crime scene," he says.

"Okay," I say. "But it's not the Blanchards' house, right?" I show him my BlackBerry with the 277 address and tell him it must be a mistake, right?

He hasn't got a clue, which makes two of us.

"That's the Blanchards' house, right?" I say, pointing two doors down. "It's a mistake, right?"

He confirms that the house tied up with yellow ribbon is not Grace Blanchard's, and I could kiss him.

"See? It's not a coincidence," I say. "It's not anything."

I hate that police officers always look at me like I'm dangerous and shouldn't be out alone.

"Detective Scoones isn't in there by any chance, is he?" I ask, pointing at the crime scene. "Because I'm thinking that maybe it isn't *not* a coincidence."

Even I roll my eyes at my statement.

The policeman asks me if I am all right. I ask him if anyone is dead in there. He asks how I know Detective Scoones. I ask him if it was a robbery. He thinks I should probably step out of the car. I think I should back up, and I do, while the officer watches me, stunned, and talks into his shoulder.

I think what he actually says is "backup." Of course, he's talking about something entirely different, but I shout, "Yes, sir," out the window and keep going down the block until I'm far enough away to back into a driveway, turn around and peel out of there.

In my rearview mirror I can see him getting into a squad car.

It's time to call Drew. By the time I hear his voice on my phone, the officer's lights are flashing. I pull over to the side of the road, tell Drew it's me, and hand the cell phone to the officer through the car window. He gestures for me to get out of the car.

"Talk to him," I say, gesturing toward the phone. He tells me to keep my hands where he can see them. They are covering my mouth at the moment and, what with my polish smeared, my hair coming out of the pseudo updo I tried to do as I drove and my hyperventilating, I'm quite the picture of a psycho case. Don't forget—been there, done that, got the straitjacket.

I can hear Drew trying to identify himself loudly enough for the officer to hear. "Detective Scoones," I say, pointing at the phone. "I won't move. Please. Talk to him."

The policeman describes me—not unfavorably, I have to admit. In fact, I actually start to preen. They establish that I am the Teddi Bayer who Drew assumes I am. Only then the policeman starts to describe how I went backing down the street, how I was babbling incoherently and, well, let's face it, putting me in a rather bad light with a guy whose opinion matters to me. Just professionally, of course.

I mean, I wouldn't want him to think I've gone round the bend or that I'm acting suspiciously.

I ask if perhaps I could talk to the detective, and he hands me the phone. I tell him about trying to go to my client's house and finding the police there.

"But here's the interesting thing," I tell him. "The house they were at is the address that I had in my BlackBerry, but that address isn't really my client's. Don't you think that's kind of coincidental? Like it *was* my client, but it wasn't?"

Drew tells me to give the phone back to the officer, who nods several times, doesn't argue and tells me I'm free to go. He closes my phone, hands it back to me and reminds me to fasten my seat belt. Then he leans into the car and says—and I really think you could describe it as maliciously—"Detective Scoones will be waiting at your house, so go directly home, ma'am."

You'd think the worst part of that would be the hint that I am in jeopardy. Or maybe that I now have to miss the appointment with a prospective client, but no. The worst part is being called ma'am and thinking that the officer looks almost young enough to date my daughter.

CHAPTER 11

Design Tip of the Day

They say that music soothes the savage breast, but I say water calms the harried one. Think how many doctors' offices have fish tanks, how many sleep machines feature the sound of ocean waves. If you're blessed with a water view, play it up for all it's worth. If not, all is not lost. There are always koi ponds or water gardens that can be dug in view of the right window. And short of that, there is the option of an indoor fountain or aquarium.

—From TipsfromTeddi.com

Detective Drew Scoones is waiting at my front door when I get home. "Where were you?" I demand, like Elise's is the only case Drew Scoones has to solve and, like a robbery in Oyster Bay Cove, must necessarily be related to Elise's murder.

The man looks amused while I open the door and nearly trip over Maggie May.

"May I remind you that a woman is dead, my friend has been burgled and a policeman just told me not to make any sudden moves?"

"I thought there was some mistake about the house and that it wasn't your friend," he says.

I tell him that I meant Bobbie, and he asks if she reported it to the police. Something in his tone implies that he thinks she wouldn't.

"It was after the fact," I explain, telling him that we didn't know about it until the girls admitted letting in a Cablevision guy who probably wasn't one. Drew makes some notes and says he'll check it out, but he's chewing on the side of his lip.

"The girls know how stupid what they did is?" he asks. I assure him they were read the riot act. He offers to talk to them. I tell him I'll ask Bobbie and he lets it go.

"So how come you weren't investigating the robbery in Oyster Bay Cove?" I ask.

"Because I spent the morning in Connecticut confirming *your* main suspect's alibi, which, you'll be interested to know, is ironclad."

"Ha," is all I can think of to say while I find a biscuit for Maggie May and throw it down into the den so that she doesn't sit in front of Drew with the stupid collar Elise put on her and I haven't thought until this moment it might be a good idea to remove.

"I know whose dog it is," he says when Maggie won't take

the bait and does her I'm-so-happy-you're-here dance around my feet.

"You really think Jack was in Connecticut," I say, as if that will make him forget I stole a dog.

"Not only was he in Connecticut, but he was with someone prominent enough for the restauranteur to recognize her. And he saw them go across to the motel, saw Meyers get a key, and saw them go into a room."

"Well, that part I believe," I say, fussing with the coffeemaker because having Drew Scoones sitting at the counter in my kitchen is very unnerving. I imagine Dr. Benjamin asking me whether it's *a* man in my kitchen or *this* man in my kitchen that has rendered me incapable of opening the new bag of coffee without resorting to a steak knife. "Why didn't he just tell you who he was with?"

"Because this particular woman is particularly well known," Drew says, grabbing the bag from me and unsealing it easily.

"I could have done it," I say, taking it back and scooping some coffee into the maker while I talk. "So she didn't want to be known as a home-wrecker? Is that it? I thought athletes lived for that sort of excitement. Don't all football players have like five kids by five different women?"

Drew shrugs as if to say what's sauce for the goose may not be sauce for the gander. And then it hits me.

"She's married."

"You didn't hear it from me," he says.

"She's a client, and she's married and she's well known," I say slowly, trying to put all the pieces together. I know most of Jack Meyers's clients—I hung pictures of him with them on the walls, put their signed memorabilia in cases, listened to him brag about the endorsements he'd got them and how much his commission was on everything from golf clubs to orange juice.

A flash from Elise's funeral crosses my mind, along with this vague idea of orange juice. The woman in the back of the room with the sunglasses reminded me of a nice, tall glass of orange juice. And now I have it. Duh. Tracey Summers, the tennis star who lovingly pours orange juice for her family every morning just after Al Roker does the weather and before Katie Couric introduces yet another expert who can fix what's wrong with my life.

The lightbulb over my head must be blinding Drew because he is looking everywhere but at me. "That information is classified, you realize," he says.

"And pretty useless," I add, putting some Ho Hos on a plate and pulling out coffee mugs. "I mean he could have hired someone to do it, right?"

"He could have," Drew agrees.

"But?"

Drew waits for me to answer my own question.

Right. It's the old center-court-at-the-Knicks-game alibi.

"There are also some financial irregularities that have cropped up in the course of the investigation," he says, and his eyes roam my body as if I've got Jack's funds stashed on my person.

"Why are you telling me this?" I ask him. I mean, it seems odd to me that he keeps feeding me these little tidbits of information like I'm supposed to make sense of them. I'm just waiting for him to put on that wrinkled raincoat he claims to have and say "One more thing" and then arrest me.

"The truth?" he asks. Yeah, like he's capable of telling it.

I nod and go to refill our cups, only neither of us have taken more than a sip. "I think you know something that could crack this case wide open."

"And I'm not telling you because…?" I ask him. Let him say it's because I like having him around, sniffing at my skirts. I dare him. Or because I'm hiding something.

"'Cause you don't know you know it."

"Oh," is all I can muster. Now am I supposed to say *Tell me what you know?* Or will that seem like I'm trying to get information out of him to cover my butt? And then I remember what my neighbor Gayle said about talking to Elise's jeweler.

"What?" he asks. I swear I must have a neon sign on my forehead since I can't think a single thought without it showing there.

"Did you ever talk to that jeweler, Marvin Katzmann?" I ask.

He pulls out his notebook and writes down Marvin's name. "Your friend Bobbie say why?"

I tell him it wasn't Bobbie, but the look on his face says *yeah, right*. I still can't believe he thinks Bobbie is somehow involved in Elise's murder.

"You think Katzmann's a fence?" I ask. His eyebrows rise like he thinks I've seen one too many episodes of *Law and Order*.

"If it wasn't Bobbie, what neighbor told you I should talk to this jeweler?" he asks.

"Right," I say. "How would Gayle Weiss know a fence?"

"Do you always do that?" he asks. "Skip ahead so that you're answering something I haven't asked yet?"

It would be so cool if I could bring myself to smile and say *Nothing, why?* That way he'd be stuck saying *huh?* And I'd get to say *Weren't you going to ask what I'm doing tonight?*

"The truth is that the captain is thinking these robberies are connected and that Elise's murder was most likely a foiled robbery attempt."

I ask if the guy wouldn't have taken that rock off her finger if his motive was robbery and not murder.

"Not—" he says, and stares at me very hard "—if he—or she—was interrupted."

It takes me a minute to realize that he means *by me*. That I walked in on the murderer. "Is that what you think? That Elise caught someone robbing her house, he killed her, and before he could get the ring off her finger, he heard me come in?"

Drew corrects my statement to allow for a murderess and says that's the theory the department is going with now.

"Do you always do that?" I ask. "Not answer a direct question?"

He flips his notebook closed, finishes a swig of coffee and dismounts from the stool. "I'll check on your friend's jeweler tip," he says as he heads for the hall.

I see him to the door, where he stops for a moment, his hand on the knob.

"How long have you known Bobbie Lyons?" he asks, and a chill runs through me.

"Long enough to know that you are barking up the wrong tree, mister," I say. "If it wasn't for Bobbie, I'd probably be locked away in an institution and my ex-husband would be raising my children with his underage lover, so you really need to focus your energies in some other direction, if you get what I mean."

Drew puts his hands up in surrender. "Okay, okay," he says as he opens the door. Then, he turns as he's going down the porch steps and adds, "Way I heard it, you pretty much saved yourself."

It's hard to hate a guy who gives you credit.

After he leaves I grab my keys and take Maggie for a walk. She and I are getting to be great friends. I tell her all my theories about men and murder and she enthusiastically agrees with everything I say, for which I reward her handsomely with dog bone cookies that Alyssa and I bake ourselves. She seems to like all the dried corn stalks people have tied to the lampposts and tries to decorate them in a way only dogs can, but she's a bit leery of the pumpkins beginning to crop up on porches. I assure her she will not have to go trick-or-treating with the kids on Halloween.

After a long enough walk to burn off the top half of an Oreo, she and I return home, where I've once again forgotten to set the alarm. You would think, wouldn't you, that a woman who found a dead body in a kitchen not three miles from her own home would remember to press four buttons on a key pad. I can't seem to remember it to save my life. Literally.

"Do not tell the kids about this," I warn Maggie May. "Or there will be no more peanut butter bones for you."

Maggie looks up, bends her head way back and shows me that her lips are sealed. I tell her what a good dog she is, make her do a little dance for her biscuit and then head toward my office to check e-mail.

I watch as my e-mail program downloads forty messages and automatically sends twenty-two of them to spam. Six of the remaining ones are forwards from Bobbie, four about sales at various stores. Two are jokes about PMS and what it stands for: Psychotic Mood Shift, Perpetual Munching Spree, Potential Murder Suspect.

Seven are forwards from my mother. Usually these are warnings about deodorant causing cancer and other urban legends, advice from police about how to avoid being a victim (not one of which, by the way, suggests not keeping uninstalled faucets where nervous burglars can find them), etc. I used to just delete them, but she got wise and now she quizzes me on them to make sure I've read them.

I open the first one and there is a strange message from a man who says that he is six-two, forty-seven years young and likes to travel. He isn't bad looking (he says) and earns a good living as a periodontist. He isn't sure he's interested in a permanent relationship but wouldn't shy away from one with the right woman.

Oh, and he thinks I'm very attractive and would like to know how old my picture is.

I reach for the phone but since it isn't there—God only knows where I've left it this time—I decide to open the rest of my mother's e-mails first to see if there isn't some explanation other than the one that's crawling up my spine and setting my teeth on edge.

I've never tried a dating service before and feel funny trying to compress my life into a few paragraphs. Like you, I'm divorced. It hurt, but I'm over it now. In case you're wondering, she was the one who cheated. It was a classic B movie with a twist—came home and she was in bed with my best friend. Only my best friend was a woman. It's behind me now. I can't say it didn't scar me, but after fourteen years, I guess it's time to move on. She said I had no bedside manner, but what did she expect? She married a surgeon, and she got a surgeon. But she was the one doing the operating and I was the one who got cut up.

I can't help snickering as I read, and I click another.

You are much too beautiful to be lonely. I would leave you alone only at temple, where I would be sad to sit with the men while you sit upstairs with the women. Is that a wig in the picture? It looks very natural. You already got three children so we would have a head start—

I hear something and sit up straighter, straining to be sure. Maggie's ears are up and her teeth are bared so I know I'm not just imagining things. Now it could be Bobbie or one of the kids, but they should be in school and she should be home with Kristen, and, besides, Maggie doesn't bark at them. I was an idiot not to check the house when I found the alarm wasn't on.

The closet of my office is stuffed to the gills so there will be no hiding in there. To leave my office I'd have to go out into the hall, which means I'd risk being seen. It seems to me the only place I could possibly hide is under my desk, so I cram myself into the kneehole with my big, hot cpu, my UPS backup, my 80-gig external hard drive, which automatically backs up my files every night, my Linksys router, my cable surfboard and a million wires.

And then I get a great idea. Carefully I unfold myself,

throw out an arm to turn the monitor off and then fold myself back in, taking my wireless keyboard with me.

THERE IS SOMEONE IN MY HOUSE, I type as silently as I can. IF I GET KILLED, TELL MY CHILDREN I ADORE THEM AND WOULD DO ANYTHING FOR THEM. WOULD **HAVE DONE** ANYTHING FOR THEM.

The footsteps get closer, Maggie wilder, the CPU hotter.

"You gotta get used to me, Maggie," a familiar voice says and I recognize Italian loafers on the feet standing by the desk. He starts to sing "Maggie May" with an exaggerated hoarse voice. It might work for Rod Stewart, but it doesn't work for Rio Gallo.

I could reach out, grab his foot and send him flying and I truly itch to do it, but then I'll never know what it is he's looking for.

"She'd hide 'em from the kids," he tells the dog as he stands in front of my desk going through my files while I am roasted alive at his feet. "But most of all we've got to hide it from the kids...Ku ku ka choo, Mrs. Robinson," he sings, trying to imitate Paul Simon almost as badly as Rod Stewart. He succeeds.

Finally I can't stand it anymore and I yank his right foot right off the ground. Down he goes like a ton of bricks and I scramble out of my hiding place ready to defend my actions.

Only Rio isn't yelling at me. He isn't shouting, whining, cursing. He's lying on the floor and I'm the one shouting and cursing. Mostly I'm yelling "no," though the s-word does keep punctuating my sentences as I kneel down next to him and pray that what I've wished for almost every night hasn't happened.

"If you are dead, Rio Gallo..." I tell him, resisting the urge to punch him in the chest "...I will never forgive you. I will kill you all over again and I will—"

His eyelids flutter open. Rio has very long, dark lashes and the movement is incredibly sexy. Or would be if I didn't know him.

Of course he asks what happened, and of course I lie and say that he must have fallen and I found him lying in my office. He clearly doesn't know I nearly killed him because he's doing his little defensive backpedaling about needing something and coming when I wasn't home so that I didn't have to see him.

"How did you get in?" I ask as he struggles to sit up. For all my wishing the man ill, I'm really not enjoying seeing him clearly in pain.

Not enjoying it very much, anyway.

"What do you mean?" he asks, stalling for time and finally admitting that Dana gave him a key.

I tell him that I don't believe Dana would give him a key and he hems and haws a bit when I demand to know when and under what circumstances.

"I saw her at the mall a couple of weeks ago," he finally says. "And I told her how you wouldn't let me get my stuff and she gave me her key to pick my shit up. She thought you'd want me to get it out of the house."

"What is this mysterious 'stuff' you keep searching for? Have you got drugs in my house or something?"

Rio give me his usual mortally wounded look. "If you must know—" he says and shrugs a little like his clothes aren't sitting right "—I was looking for your old love notes. Remember how you used to write me those cute little dirty notes and stick them in my pockets and stuff? And how, when I'd go up to Neversink on those paintball weekends, you'd write me a note for every day with like pictures and hearts and stuff?"

I don't know which of us is more embarrassed—me for having ever written them, or him for having kept them.

"I wanted to get them before you found 'em and trashed 'em."

"I wouldn't—" I start to say and then stop myself. *I would.*

"So Dana injudiciously loaned you her key two weeks ago," I say. "How did you come to still have it today?"

Rio complains about the pain in his back and asks if his head is bleeding.

I tell him, "Not yet."

"I miss you and the kids," he says. "Aren't you ever going to forgive me and let me come home?"

"No," I say simply. "Not ever. You made a copy of Dana's key, didn't you?"

"When I got here that day, you were home," he says. "I

thought it would be better if I came some other time when you weren't here and you weren't any the wiser. If you know what I mean."

I tell him I know exactly what he means, which is a good part of the reason he will never again be part of my life. And then I hold out my hand, palm up, and ask for the key.

"Sure, sure," he says, which tells me that it isn't the only copy.

"Shit," I mutter. Money isn't exactly growing on trees and I don't want to think about how much it's going to cost to have all the locks replaced.

"Some coffee'd be nice, Ted," he says as he fishes the key out of his pocket and hands it over.

I reach into my desk and pull out one of the dollars I keep stashed there for the ice cream man or whatever other emergencies the kids come up with. I hold it out to him.

"Try the Plainview Diner." And then a thought occurs to me. "Where's your car, anyway, Rio? I didn't see it in the driveway."

"A friend drove me over," he says, taking the dollar and walking out of my room. I glance out the window and see a yellow Corvette parked across the street. As Rio leaves the house the driver's window opens and the engine roars to life. Rio gets in the passenger side, surprising me.

It's not like Rio to let anyone else be in the driver's seat.

The car pulls away just as the school bus rounds the

corner and I am so grateful that the kids didn't have to witness yet another scene between their father and me. Especially one that puts me under my desk cowering in fear.

I meet Alyssa's bus and pop her into the car with the excuse that we need to buy Maggie May a new collar when what I really need is to get out of the house.

"It should be a princess collar," Alyssa tells me. "And we should get me a princess bracelet that matches it so everyone knows that Maggie May is my dog."

She's lucky she's only six, or I'd give her the do-you-walk-her?-do-you-feed-her?-what-makes-her-yours? speech. In the meantime I have that ready to go for Jesse and Dana, should they ever refer to Maggie May as theirs.

Later, after we've argued about whether pepperoni comes from pigs or cows since we are no longer eating beef because of mad cow disease, and no longer eating chicken or turkey because of avian flu and not having lamb because the farm factories are intolerable (thanks, *National Geographic* special), and we've argued about who will do the dishes and why I insist on using real plates instead of paper ones so that I can pretend we are having a real dinner instead of a pretend one, and we've argued about who can use the computer first and who last, and I've convinced everyone that sleep is not a negotiable item, I sit alone in my bedroom.

Don't get the wrong impression. I don't miss Rio. I mean, not the Rio he turned out to be. I miss a man seducing me with just a look. I miss Lys's father sitting on her bed and telling her that as long as the monsters had enough Oreos they wouldn't come out of the closet to bother her. I don't miss cleaning out the Oreos from her closet.

What I really miss is being married. Being part of a couple. Having someone who cares about my kids as much as I do, and even if I remarry some day I know that a second husband won't be able to love my children like his own. I am so sad to admit that. The magical moment is gone forever. And life will never be uncomplicated again.

I miss believing that Rio could fix my troubles. And then I remind myself that the biggest trouble I had was him.

The phone rings and the caller ID tells me that it's Howard. I don't really want to talk to him, but if I let the phone keep ringing it will wake up the kids.

"It's late," I tell him.

"I'm sorry," he says and I tell him it's all right and that I can't sleep anyway.

He says he'll talk me to sleep, and I let him try.

"Once upon a time," he begins, and I feel some of the tension begin to leave my body. "There was a very nice man. He was tall, and sometimes he had a mustache. But sometimes he didn't. And sometimes he had a southern accent, though usually he didn't. One thing that was always constant about him was that he liked to eat and he liked to have fun.

"Well, there aren't too many employers looking for men who like to eat and have fun, and so he became a...sumo wrestler. No, no, that didn't work because he also liked to drive fancy cars and sumo wrestlers can only fit in vans."

"I have a van," I say.

"Ah," he says. "If only he'd known you back then. But he didn't, and so he became a food tester for the king of Glockenschpeil. But the king only liked Fluffnutter sandwiches on graham crackers and so he..."

Howard's voice is lovely, soothing, and after a few minutes he tells me to close my eyes and go to sleep and he hangs up.

I hold the phone and tell the dial tone that I may have interrupted a murder. That a minute or two one way or the other and it could have been me lying on that floor—though I'd have been better dressed than Elise. That today, when I heard that noise in the house, I thought it was Elise's killer coming for me.

I put the phone back into the cradle and lie in the darkness thinking about how the world is full of accidents and random moments and coincidences and it's hard for me to believe that there is any master plan. Take for instance the robberies and how it seems like all my clients were victims and then today that house down the block from my client... It reminds me of how things would happen, or seem to happen, last summer, when Rio was setting me up so that I would pick up the rifle he left in the kitchen, seemingly at random, but—

I am off the bed in a shot, running down to the kitchen to pull my BlackBerry out of my handbag. Somewhere in

Menu I find the Intellisync Application and click on View Log. There I find Big Guy (my desktop computer), B&M (Bobbie and Mike's computer), Bobolink (Bobbie's Palm), Big Guy, Peanuts, Big Guy...*Peanuts?* Who the hell is Peanuts?

So. I've been hacked. Someone has purloined the addresses of my clients from my BlackBerry and is committing the robberies to make it look like I'm the culprit. Or that Bobbie is. Someone even found—or more likely, stole—Bobbie's bracelet and planted it to make her look guilty. I think of the cable guy in the house with Bobbie's daughters and realize that he might be Elise's murderer. It makes my skin crawl.

And still the question remains. Why? On all the detective shows I've ever seen, other crimes are committed to hide the real motive for one by lumping it in with others.

I refuse to let paranoia overwhelm me. In the morning, I'll think about calling Ronnie Benjamin for another appointment. For now, I'll check that all the doors are locked and I'll look in on my children. And I will not take upstairs the knife that I am fondling in the kitchen because I know that statistics show that weapons in the house are often turned on the occupants. Okay, I have no idea what statistics show, but if Elise was killed with her faucet because it was at hand, I'm sure as hell not going to have a knife at hand in my bedroom for someone else to take away from me and use.

He could smother me with a pillow.

There is no chance I am sleeping tonight.

I check on my precious, sweet, lovable children, reminding myself that I was on the brink of sending them all away to boarding school just a few hours ago, and crawl into my own bed and take the phone under the covers with me. I wonder if Drew has the night shift. I wonder if he has a girlfriend. I wonder why I'm wondering that when I should be wondering who would want to frame me or Bobbie.

Duh.

Rio, who wants his old life back. But how would my being arrested accomplish that? And Rio would never kill anyone. Okay, he does hunt, but not every hunter would whack a woman he doesn't even know, right?

And then there's the hacking into my BlackBerry. Would Rio know how to do that? Not likely.

But *someone* did.

I turn on the light and dial the police.

CHAPTER 12

Design Tip of the Day

> Nothing compares with seeing a room done in a style you like—not a photograph, a layout in a magazine or some computer-generated simulation. If there is a model home in your neighborhood, check it out. Haunt the showrooms of the better department stores where couches are placed in faux rooms instead of rows. By all means, if there is a decorator showcase within driving distance, GO SEE IT. You can find not only wonderful decorating ideas, but wonderful decorators who are on your wavelength.
>
> —From TipsfromTeddi.com

As soon as all the kids are on buses, Bobbie and I drive over to Bailey Manor to see our spot. On the way I tell her about calling and leaving word for Drew about the hacking, and I reassure her that he will be able to put the pieces together and see that we are being framed.

The drive is lovelier than usual, which is saying a lot because driving through Lattingtown is a little like driving through a storybook forest. Streets with names like Chicken Valley Road meander through groves of tall trees, which are turning crimson and gold. Scarecrows lean against lampposts swathed in cornstalks, and pumpkins the size of tractor tires sit smiling on porches as though they own them.

The sun trickles in here and there, spattering the leaves. I imagine living here and wonder if I would dress differently, serve different meals. If life here is really a world unto itself, where children behave and husbands come home to martinis and ask their wives what they did all day and they don't mean it as an admonition.

I imagine that inside these houses classical music is playing. I almost hear it, but it can't drown out the theme from Looney Tunes that drifts out of my handbag.

Bobbie snickers, digs out my phone and opens it for me. "Hi, June," she says. "How are you? Teddi's driving the car and I want to live to see another day, so—"

"Don't imply my daughter's a bad driver," my mother says. "Besides, it's not like I don't know. Put me on speakerphone."

Bobbie finds my mother endlessly amusing. That's because June isn't her mother.

"Did you get my forwards?" she asks me.

"The one in the plaid shirt," Bobbie says. "Now that was a hottie, June."

My mother says she's addressing me. I tell her *she* may be

speaking to *me*, but *I'm* not speaking to *her*. And then, naturally, I speak to her, but just to ask exactly what she's said about me to these men.

"You wouldn't sign yourself up," she says. "So I had to do it for you. And they asked for a bio, so I just put down the truth."

"As you see it," Bobbie says.

"Well, of course as *I* see it. As anyone with two eyes can see it. I said that *I*—meaning *you*, Teddi—was divorced after a terrible lapse in judgment and that I now wanted to come back to the fold. That you—only I said *I*—came from a wonderful, successful background with two loving, wealthy parents and you were looking for a relationship as lasting as theirs. Meaning, of course, your father's and mine."

"Of course," I say, though it's hard to keep a straight face.

"And of course I said that you were lonely, and—"

I ask her not to tell me anymore, because I really can't bear to hear the promises she's no doubt made.

"Tell me, June," Bobbie says. "Did you use the lipstick font to say 'For a good time, call Teddi Bayer'?"

I notice that my mother doesn't say no.

"We're at Bailey Manor, Mom," I say. "I have to go, but I want you to go on that site, that JDate or whatever, and remove my name. You got that?"

My mother is saying something about paying for the whole month and getting her money's worth when I hit End and turn into the gravel circular driveway of Bailey Manor, where I park my car next to a lavender van with Delia's Design Service written in that gorgeous Vivaldi font.

Bobbie grabs my hand and squeezes it. "Excited?" she asks me and I nod because I can barely speak. I feel as if my life is starting now. Everything else was the preface, the preamble. My real life starts now.

A security officer taps on my window. "You can't park here," he says, and points to an area in the distance. The way-far, ruin-your-good-heels-when-they-sink-into-the-grass distance.

Okay, so my real life will start after a good five-minute hike.

"You think that Helene will take back any of the Meyers's stuff?" Bobbie asks. "I mean, you *are* seeing her loser brother."

I tell her that he is not a loser and that he kindly talked me to sleep last night.

She sticks her finger down her throat and says "Barf," the same way she did when I told her that I'd chosen "Wind Beneath My Wings" for her ring on my new cell phone. "But, it could be worse. He could be one of your mother's fix-ups."

The sad part of that is that he could be. My mother would like him. And the sad part of *that* is that my mother's approval is the kiss of death as far as I am concerned. And, to take it ad nauseum, the sad part of *that* is that I haven't learned my lesson from the whole Rio fiasco.

"What's Helene's story, anyway?" Bobbie asks me.

"Same old, same old," I say, which means that her husband cheated on her, she demanded a divorce, he's with a young sweet thing and she's all alone and bitter.

"If life was fair," Bobbie starts.

"Brad Pitt would have already left Angelina Jolie for me," I end. This is a running joke for us and goes back all the way to Erik Estrada, who is probably in a retirement home by now, but who should have been mine in the mid-eighties.

"Someone ought to take the stick out of her butt," Bobbie says. "You know, let her hair frizz, chip a nail, dribble crumbs down her cleavage."

I stare at Bobbie, whose hair is perfect, whose nails are short and dark and could be used in a Revlon nail polish ad and who barely has cleavage, but, if she had, would surely be crumb-free.

"I am *keeping* a husband, not *looking* for one," she says when I look her over without saying anything. "Totally different rules."

"Intimidation keeps a husband in line," she explains. "It scares the shit out of a date."

I'd love to laugh at her, but the two most intimidating women I know, Bobbie and my mother, are both still married, while I, the least intimidating woman on the planet, am not. I know, I know. My choice. And the right one. But sometimes I think, maybe if I'd been more intimidating Rio never would have dared try all the tricks he did. Maybe I'd have scared his girlfriend away.

"Don't go there," Bobbie tells me. "Some men are keepers and some men are bottom feeders. A mistake to hook them, a bigger mistake not to throw them back."

"I wonder what Helene's husband was like," I say, and Bobbie sneers.

"If her taste in husbands is anything like her taste in help..." she says, letting the rest of the sentence dangle.

And then, because we are who we are despite aspiring to be better people, we dish a bit about Gina. Well, Bobbie dishes and I try not to laugh because I'm not a mean-spirited person. Or because I really don't want to be. Though I'll admit that the Charlie Brown and Lucy figures on top of Gina's computer are a little juvenile.

"And she glued magnets to their mouths so they can kiss," Bobbie says as her Stuart Weitzman boots sink into the soil and she curses the guard who made us move the car. This, I realize, is not a good time to tell her that I've left the admittance letter in the car, without which we can't get in.

I send her ahead without me and run back to the car for it, search around the car, realize it's in my bag with the self-measuring tape measure, a Fendi notebook Bobbie gave me so that I would look successful and professional and more pens than I could lose in a week. Not that I won't try.

At the door, Bobbie is arguing with someone I take to be the woman in charge. She's got on the sort of smock that salesgirls in the makeup department at Saks wear, black pants that narrow at the ankle and puddle toward shoes that she could not possibly have navigated the gravel drive in.

She's holding a clipboard, eyes closed, and shaking her head back and forth.

Bobbie grabs the letter out of my hand and waves it in front of Clipboard Woman's face until she opens her eyes to see what the breeze is all about.

"Happy now?" Bobbie asks while I try to smooth things over, introduce myself, babble about how I'm doing the breakfast nook. CW gives me a half smile, grimaces at Bobbie and hands me a map of the first floor with the breakfast nook indicated.

Before I can finish telling my dearest friend about catching more flies with honey, she grabs the map, storms off into the house and shouts, loudly enough for everyone in the vicinity to hear, that I should screw the flies and shove them down Dale Carnegie's throat while I'm at it.

If I knew the name of that disease where you can't control your utterings, I'd tell the people with their jaws dropped that Bobbie suffers from it.

We pass a woman on her knees picking up pieces of what must have been quite a work of art in the vessel tradition, otherwise known as a vase. She stares up at Bobbie like she's never heard the word *screwed* before. "Oh, like you're having a great day?" Bobbie barks at her.

I trail in her wake, smiling apologetically at each person we pass.

"What is wrong with you?" I finally ask when I can catch up to her.

"Your friend called," she says, waving her cell phone at me. "While you were getting the stupid letter from the car? And he wants me down at the station this afternoon. Seems he found the ankle bracelet Mike gave me five million years ago."

"Mike gave you an ankle bracelet?" I say. It seems so un-Bobbie-like. "Really?"

"Yeah, really. And guess where it turned up?"

She doesn't have to tell me. "277 Cornucopia Drive." When she confirms it with her look, I tell her that it just proves my theory.

"Well, Scoones seems to think it proves his," she snaps back.

"I'll go with you."

Bobbie shrugs like it doesn't make any difference and stares at her map. "According to this, we're standing in the breakfast nook."

We both look around. *Nook* is something of an overstatement. The breakfast closet maybe. The breakfast breezeway. I look up at the ceiling. It's a good twenty feet up, so there's no way I can do a ceiling treatment unless I do a dropped ceiling which is so not in my budget.

"Trompe l'oeil windows," I say, pointing to the long wall. At maybe seven feet, *long* is an exaggeration. "Looking out on a seascape. Beach, back of beach chairs, striped umbrella billowing. Reeds over there." I point. I can see the whole thing. Who wouldn't want to look out at the ocean over their orange juice? Especially in the winter.

"Real shutters," Bobbie says, and I agree.

"Definitely. Wicker furniture. Striped cushions that mimic the umbrella."

I pull out the tape measure from my bag, along with the notebook and a pen, which I hand to Bobbie.

"Sisal placemats. A sisal rug." Bobbie writes down every word I'm saying. "I can do the painting. We can take the shutters off your bathroom windows and put them back when the show is over.

"We need to avoid the Florida look. No turquoise, no peach. This is East Hampton, not Palm Beach."

"No shells," Bobbie says as she writes.

"No fish, no sea horses. Think the Cape. I take back the wicker. Painted white furniture. Slightly distressed."

"Yes," Bobbie squeals as though she's having a Clairol Herbal Essence moment. Oh, wait, it's like an orgasm. I forgot people have them.

"This wall," I say, pointing at the opposite wall. "Narrow white shelves. Very distressed. We could build them with planking. On the shelves, eight-by-tens of beach scenes. Black and whites. Kids building sand castles, a profile on a hazy day."

"Jack Kennedy in a golf jacket," Bobbie shouts. People turn their heads.

"Yeah, like that," I say. "A woman in a jacket with her hair blowing across her face."

"You really are talented," Bobbie says, twirling in my little closet of a space as if she can see exactly what I'm talking about.

I think she's right. Maybe. Just maybe. I am.

With all the measurements down in the book, we leave Bailey Manor with a handbook full of rules about what we can and can't do to the premises.

"Your own little handbook," Bobbie teases. "Your prayers have been answered."

CHAPTER 13

Design Tip of the Day

Sometimes redecorating comes down to rearranging—taking a piece from one room and placing it in another. This is one of the reasons I recommend that you coordinate the colors throughout your house. You never know when an incidental piece from one room could transform another.
—From TipsfromTeddi.com

At Jack's house, Bobbie tells me to go in by myself. "It'll seem more professional," she claims. "And he can't expect you to haul much stuff out of there alone."

I remind her that the last two occasions on which I entered the Meyers's house alone were what you might term disastrous. Even Bobbie can't argue with that, though she drags her already-ruined Stuart Weitzman boots on the pavement as though it's "the last mile."

Jack Meyers lets us in with a grunt, glaring at both of us

like we're what's wrong with his life. It's possible that Bobbie was right about it seeming to Jack like we are outnumbering him.

"You got platinum balls, I'll give you that," he says to Bobbie and I'm really relieved that she caved in and agreed to come in with me.

I explain that we are in a bit of a hurry, leaving out that we have to deliver Bobbie to the police before getting home for our children, and he says something about it being too bad we don't have time for a tea party.

"Out," he says. "I want it all out. Call me sentimental, say it pains me to see the ideas she had stopped in their tracks, the way she was. Just get the crap out."

He points down the hall toward the kitchen while he veers off into the living room where he is apparently intent on wrecking the house.

"You must really be grieving," I say sympathetically, pretending that I don't have any recollection of the blow job his sister-in-law was giving him the day after Elise was killed. "It must be awful."

He looks at me like I've lost my marbles and pulls the cushions from the couch, throwing them toward a growing pile in the center of the room.

"Ask him what he's looking for," Bobbie whispers as I tiptoe out of the room before Jack picks me up and throws me on the mound. She pushes me back toward the living room, instructing me again to "ask him."

"Jack," I say. "Is there something I can help you find?" *Those Iraqi coins Drew asked me about, perhaps?*

The are-you-crazy-look gets replaced with a do-you-have-a-death-wish look. Considering where I am, I smile tentatively and step carefully out of the room without turning my back on Jack.

"By the way, Jack," I say, measuring with my eyes how far it is to the front door and gauging how quickly we can make an escape. "I noticed that one of your basketballs is missing, and I was wondering—"

You know how in the old movies actors' eyes would get all bugged out when something surprised or shocked them and it looks so funny and silly? Well, people do it in real life, after all. At least Jack does, because his eyes are huge, his mouth is frozen open and he is charging into the hallway. Bobbie and I bang into each other at the front door, but he isn't coming after us. He's coming to stare at his balls.

He counts. (Personally, I didn't think a guy needed more than two, but I figure now isn't the time to tell Jack that.) He twists his head this way and that to check signatures (or maybe see if an exorcism is in order). He throws off one of the floating Lucite covers and I cringe as it hits the floor and shatters. I bought a little bitty one of those for the Derick Jeter–signed baseball my father bought Jesse and it cost almost as much as the baseball.

He utters a string of expletives that would make Howard Stern blush while Bobbie and I fiddle with the doorknob.

He orders us to stay where we are, and while we are contemplating whether we can get out alive, the cell phone on the shelf in the entryway begins to play "Take Me Out to the Ball Game."

Staring us into paralysis, a feat I didn't think was possible, he grabs up the phone and stomps toward the kitchen with his head turned so that he can keep an eye on us.

Some people have a sweet tooth. It makes them reckless when it comes to candy. You've probably never heard of a stupid bone, but I have one and it makes me reckless when it comes to my own safety. So while Bobbie's all for getting out of the house while Jack the Ripper is in the kitchen, I've just got to hear what he's saying and figure out what he's tearing the house apart to find.

Bobbie leans forward a little and whispers it's a woman on the phone.

And then it occurs to me what he's looking for, searching the house for—the *list*. No doubt Tracey Summers is on that list. Miss Orange Juice herself, and who knows who else?

I jerk my head toward the door and we turn the knob slowly. So slowly it makes my insides shake until I think I'll wet my pants. And then, door open, we run to the car like we're running over hot coals, jump inside, lock the doors and knock over the garbage pails on our way out of the driveway.

"Oh...my...God," we say about half a dozen times as we drive down the block and out of The Estates. "Oh... my...God," we say again.

We tell each other that we have to calm down because we're going to look mighty suspicious at the police station, which somehow, instead of sobering us, gives us the giggles.

By the time I pull into the Guest Parking at the police station we have lost it completely.

"Guests?" Bobbie asks. "Like of the state?"

I remind her this is only the county police, but I do it a little too loudly and get a nasty look from an "only the county" police officer.

Inside the station we sober quickly. I ask for Detective Scoones, and Bobbie cops an attitude that says she couldn't care less. Maybe the police are buying it, but I'm not.

Drew comes down a long corridor and I'm struck by how good-looking he is in real life. I thought I'd embellished a bit in my imagination, but I hadn't. He doesn't smile.

After picking up an envelope from the desk, he asks Bobbie to follow him into his office. I ignore the fact that the invitation doesn't include me, and Bobbie and I trail behind him down the hall.

He gestures for us to take seats. Bobbie asks if she isn't supposed to be in some sparsely furnished room with only a metal chair and a light shining in her face. Drew ignores her, opens the envelope and slips out a small gold chain with two hearts pierced by arrows on it.

"Yours?" he asks. She nods and he suggests she take a close look. I look with her. This tacky thing is hers? One heart is engraved *Mike* and the other says *Barbie*.

"It's not hers," I say. "She's not Barbie."

"It's mine," she says, not looking at me. "I used to go by Barbie."

"Just shows what you don't know about people," Drew says. He isn't looking at me, either. "You didn't list this on the missing items you reported taken."

"You filed a report?" I ask. "Barbie" ignores me.

"I forgot all about it. I haven't seen that thing in fifteen years."

Drew asks where she kept it. "Barbie" indicates she has no idea.

"We checked with Cablevision." Drew fingers the ankle bracelet and, next to me, Bobbie flinches. "They have no record of a complaint or of anyone sent to repair your reception."

I remind Drew that the thief was just using Cablevision as a cover and wasn't really a repairman. And I say that every time I call for service they don't remember I've ever complained before.

Drew and Bobbie just try to outstare each other.

"Do I need a lawyer?" Bobbie asks, grabbing the ankle bracelet out of Drew's hand.

He holds the envelope open and indicates that Bobbie, or Barbie, should drop the jewelry into it. After she does, he asks, "Do you have something to hide?"

"Okay, this is beyond stupid," I tell them both. "If she were the killer, would she be so careless as to twice, I repeat, *twice*, leave a piece of jewelry that is clearly hers at the scene of the crime? Can't you see that this is a setup?"

"I can see that it appears to be a setup," Drew says. "Barbie" says nothing.

"I had no reason to kill Elise Meyers," she finally says.

"In addition to the fact that she could never kill anyone," I say. "She is a good, decent, wonderful, best friend."

Drew asks me to wait outside for just a moment. I start to refuse, but Bobbie nods like she wants me to, and so I go.

Five minutes later they come walking down the hall. Bobbie looks visibly shaken. I have to say that Drew doesn't look much better.

"Are we free to go?" I ask. I want it to come out kind of snooty, but it falls flat.

Drew nods and Bobbie and I turn to leave.

"I'll be in touch," he says, but I'm not sure if he means Bobbie or me.

When I turn to look he is talking to the desk sergeant. Bobbie stares at her feet as we walk out into the parking lot.

"Let's go shoe shopping," she says cheerfully, like it's the best idea she's had in weeks.

"What?"

"I need Bailey Manor shoes," she says, lifting up her left foot to show me the damage this morning has done to her Stuart Weitzman's.

Sometimes the woman reminds me of *Courageous Cat and Minute Mouse*. Remember how they always had the right sort of gun for every occasion and Courageous Cat would say something like, "I'll just use my scaling-the-left-side-of-a-mountain-that's-covered-with-ice-and-about-to-melt gun." Bobbie's got going-to-the-grocery-store-in-Plainview-in-the-rain shoes, which differ from her going-to-the-grocery-store-in-Woodbury-in-the-rain shoes.

Next thing you know she'll need going-to-court shoes, and after that…

CHAPTER 14

Design Tip of the Day

Question: How do I know how much paint or wallpaper I need for a room? I just don't trust the salesman's estimate!

Answer: Go online! Put *calculating paint needs* into Google and you'll get 618,000 sites, almost all of them with charts or interactive calculators! Same for wallpaper.

—From TipsfromTeddi.com

Sometimes I think that if Bobbie weren't happily married, she'd be happier with Howard than I am. Not that I don't like the great meals, the pleasant company, the late-night phone calls. It's just that Bobbie's the one who pines for the fancy restaurants Howard takes me to, lusts for his Mercedes-Benz and doesn't mind talking deep into the night.

I'm more the neighborhood-Chinese-or-Italian-restaurant, car-where-the-windshield-wipers-don't-cost-an-arm-and-a-leg-to-replace, crawl-into-bed-with-the-kids-at-nine-'o-clock kind of person.

Except tonight. Tonight I am having a ball because Howard and I are—get this—incognito. Howard sent over a gray wig, a schoolmarm sweater, a blouse and a pleated skirt and told me to meet him in the bar of some nice Italian restaurant a few minutes away in Commack. Kimmie, who is in all the school plays, helped me with some makeup, and Dana and Jesse nearly died laughing when I came out of my bedroom.

They all sent me on my way with admonitions not to drive too slowly, not to forget where I live and to take an extra Depends.

I've never been to Il Giardino, but it's the kind of place you feel at home in the minute you walk in. I forget that I am an old lady until the maitre d' helps me out of my coat and insists on my sitting while I wait for my "gentleman friend." I catch a glimpse of myself in the mirror and think that for a dowdy old broad I sure do have a lot of sparkle in my eyes.

Howard saunters in when I am halfway through my glass of port, which I've ordered because it seems like something an older woman would drink. He carries a cane in the crook of his arm and gives his hat and coat to the maitre d' before sidling up beside me and asking lecherously if anyone is sitting on the stool next to mine.

I see the bartender and the maitre d' exchange amused glances and I tell Howard he's welcome to the seat. He is wearing a tweed sports jacket with suede patches on the elbows and a bow tie. He looks pretty dapper for an older man.

"Can I buy you dinner?" he asks me and I smile my gratitude like he's saved me from sharing a can of cat food with Sylvester. When we are shown to our table, he takes the seat next to me on the bench, rather than across from me, and sits a little too close.

The waiter brings us complimentary antipasto, and Howard asks if that's usual. "Only for special customers," he says with a wink, then adds, "Of course, all our customers are special."

Howard seems to make a mental note. I ask how his day was and he says this dinner is the highlight.

I whisper to him that I wonder if we are fooling anyone. Howard answers, just loud enough for the waiter to overhear, "I think they know we're married, my dear." His voice shakes just enough to sound elderly.

"It is fun to pretend," I say, and my voice catches in my throat. I let myself rest my head on his shoulder for a moment, close my eyes, and imagine that we've been married for a very long time and will be together for the rest of our lives. In my old-lady's clothes and wig it's a funny feeling—like looking back from the future.

When I open my eyes I imagine I see Jack Meyers's face. He is seated with a man whose back is toward me and who has hidden him from my view until now when he reaches down to pull something from his briefcase. I strain to be sure it's Jack, which Howard takes for nuzzling and pets my head awkwardly as I all but bury my head in his lap.

It is definitely Jack Meyers. Not only is it Jack, but what the man has taken out of his briefcase is Elise's lime-green Kate Spade journal. I can feel Howard trying to right me, but I'm too shocked to respond.

"Change seats with me," I demand. Howard slides over slightly, expecting me to get up and go around to the other side of him if I'm so desperate to change positions. "No. You get up and walk around," I tell him. "And do it unobtrusively."

After a short discussion under our breaths about how he's just fine where he is and what's the matter with me, anyway? he wipes his mouth with the napkin, rises and goes around the table while I slide over into his space.

"Musical chairs?" the waiter asks, and I say something about the air blowing on me which satisfies both the waiter and Howard, who asks why I didn't just say so.

I resist calling him a moron and tell him that of course that isn't the reason—that Elise's murderer is sitting in this very restaurant with his blackmail manual on the table between him and whatever it is you call a blackmail victim.

Howard appears unimpressed and tells me I don't know what I know. Meanwhile, we aren't the only diners bickering. So are Jack and the man across from him. In fact, Jack's face gets redder and redder as the man taps on the cover of the journal, shaking his head.

"He's trying to blackmail him," I insist. "He's got Elise's

dirt on everyone and now he's trying to collect. I wonder if she was blackmailing people, too. That could have given someone a motive to kill her."

"I thought this guy was your murderer," Howard says. He seems bored with the whole discussion, which makes me wonder what I'm doing out with a guy who could find ambiance so interesting and murder so dull.

"Doesn't rule him out. Maybe she wasn't letting him in on the action."

Jack's dining companion comes to his feet abruptly and puts up his hands. "I can't do what I can't do," he says. "I can't give you what you want."

I shoot Howard an *I told you so* look and for just a second Jack has a clear view of me. I quickly lift the charger plate in front of me and pretend to be looking at the label. Next to me Howard's body shakes a little and I realize he's smirking. He covers the laugh with his napkin, but I know what he's thinking and I don't care. I'm used to people not taking me seriously. I sit up a little straighter, knowing that it usually turns out to be their mistake—witness my soon-to-be ex-husband.

Beyond the edge of my plate, which the waiter is trying to take from me as he sets down my dinner, I can see Jack thumbing through Elise's notebook. He heaves a deep sigh and takes out his cell phone.

"Another mark," I say. Howard swirls his wine, making circles on the table with the base of his glass. "He's calling another victim he's going to blackmail."

"Try your squid ink pasta," Howard says. "Tell me if the truffle sauce overpowers it."

I look down at what he has ordered me as an appetizer. There are black strings in a puddle of beige sauce. "*You* try it," I tell him. He does, with his eyes closed, like he's having sex with it.

Jack is gesturing with his free hand while he whispers into the phone. He checks his watch. He looks at me for a moment and I reach for my wine glass. My hand shakes so badly I nearly spill my wine, but he dismisses me without recognition. I guess I look like just another old lady to him.

He calls for the check and I reach for my purse. "We have to follow him," I tell Howard, who doesn't budge. He is savoring something that looks like they forgot to cook it. He says something that sounds like *carpaccio perfetto*.

Jack rises. I tell the waiter we need our check. Howard casually countermands my order and asks for another turn of the pepper mill. I hiss at him that we have got to leave.

"I'm working," he tells me. "This is my job. We can play cops and robbers some other time."

I want to like Howard. I really do. But he's making it very hard.

"Look," he says, taking my hand in his. "If you are right about this guy being a murderer, the last place I want to take you is in his vicinity. If you're so sure about him, why not call your detective friend?"

Because my detective friend will mock me. He will say

you saw Jack Meyers in a restaurant and he made a phone call and that proves exactly what?

Jack grabs his journal. I grab my purse. Howard grabs my arm. "I am not going to let you go after some murder suspect." His voice is very quiet and very determined. He is also very big and very strong and I get the sense that he will physically stop me if he has to.

"You're right," I say. "I'll go to the ladies' room and call the police."

He rubs my arm where he's grabbed it. "If anything happened to you," he says, and lets the rest of the sentence trail away.

I smile adoringly at him, knowing full well that there is no way I am letting Jack Meyers out of my sight, and that the man is an idiot if he thinks I am. "I'll be back in a minute," I say and I half blow him a kiss.

And then I am out of the restaurant so fast the tablecloths flap behind me. As I pull out of the lot I see Howard rushing from the restaurant and I shrug at him as if to say that it was beyond my control. His face is contorted in anger or anguish, I can't really tell which, but the last thing I see in my rearview mirror is him jumping into his Mercedes S500.

Jack is two cars ahead of me, weaving in and out of traffic as if he owns Jericho Turnpike. I keep up with him, and Howard's black Mercedes keeps up with me. A mile or so from Syosset, Jack turns into the Alaskas, so called because the streets are all named Nome, Fairbanks and the like. It's dark, and he makes a turn and is gone.

I make the turn after him, and only after it's too late and I've rear-ended him do I realize that he has turned off his headlights. I feel a smack from behind, and then another. Front doors open in the houses on both sides of the street. Apparently, four car pileups aren't a usual occurrence in the Alaskas.

Jack is out of his car screaming at me. Howard is opening my door and asking if I'm all right. The driver of the fourth car is sauntering our way and it isn't looking pretty.

"What the hell were you doing?" Jack yells at me. "Following me?"

Howard tries to keep me in the car, but I get out just as Drew Scoones reaches the three of us.

"Great. Police," Jack yells. "You see what she did?"

"What were your lights doing off?" Drew asks, but I can see that he's checking out Howard checking me out for bruises and breaks. He hands Howard a flashlight, which Howard shines in my face.

"I know you," Jack says, wagging a finger at me. "Don't I? He reaches out and tugs at my wig, which slides off my head. He gurgles like he's choking, and out comes, "You!"

Both Howard and Drew step between Jack and me, which isn't easy since Jack is just inches from my nose.

"She's stalking me," Jack says, pointing over Drew's shoulder. "I want her arrested for stalking."

Drew bites the inside of his cheek while he waits for me

to respond. Howard shines the flashlight at his dented car and broken headlight and looks positively mournful. To his credit, he doesn't say a word.

"If anyone should be arrested—" I say, pointing at Jack Meyers "—it's him. He's a blackmailer and he was on his way to his next victim."

Howard rolls his eyes. Drew pretends to believe me but is so transparent that Jack doesn't even feel the need to deny it.

"He's got a book in his car, a journal, with very delicate information and he's using it to blackmail people."

The police must have taken the journals just after Elise was killed because Drew seems to know what I'm talking about. But from the expression on his face, he's surprised that Jack has them. I am, too, since I was sure the police must have taken them.

Jack says I'm ridiculous. Well, what he actually says is that I'm crazy, but I don't hear that word anymore. After last year I am selectively deaf to it. I don't miss his tone, however.

"Well," I say to Jack. "It's easy enough to disprove. Just get the journal from your briefcase and show it to the officer." Jack doesn't move.

Howard runs his hand over his car hood and walks to the rear of his car, where he examines his car and Drew's. On a man as big as Howard it's hard to miss the sagging of his shoulders.

"Go ahead," I bait him. "Get the journal and prove I'm wrong."

Jack looks at Drew as if to ask whether it's necessary. Drew tells him it could clear things up. Howard, at the rear of his car, tries to open his trunk and curses under his breath.

Then he comes toward us with the flashlight and shines it on the rear of my car. "Just a broken taillight," he says and we can all hear the irony in his voice. His Mercedes is a mess, and my old Toyota is barely dented.

Jack asks Howard to shine the light on his rear, so to speak, and I've done a pretty good job on it. Howard says something reassuring to me and Jack asks if we are together. Before Howard can stumble through an answer, Drew asks about the journal.

Jack goes back to his car door, which he's left open and reaches in. Two patrol cars pull up, no doubt responding to calls from the neighbors, and Drew tells them that he's got it under control. He reaches for the journal from Jack, who hands it over reluctantly.

Opening it, Drew's lip twitches. I explain how Jack was in the restaurant with some man he was clearly blackmailing and that the man refused to meet Jack's terms and how he'd probably wind up dead or with broken knees.

Meanwhile Drew is biting his lip. "To be attacked by the Shaq," he reads, "is to be whacked by a hack."

Howard and I stare first at Drew and then at Jack.

Drew continues. "Your body's wracked, your bones are stacked. Face it boy, you're jacked, your flacked."

"What?" Jack asks, shrugging as Drew rubs the sides of his

mouth to cover the fact that he badly wants to laugh. "It's good stuff. Sports poetry. Nobody's doing this kind of thing."

"Maybe it's a code," I suggest.

"I think you've been jacked and flacked," Drew says to me. Howard snickers.

"So who was that man you were with?" I ask Jack, not that it's any of my business, which he reminds me before admitting it was a literary agent who was declining to represent him.

"And where were you going now?" I ask.

"I don't have to answer you," he says. "You're nobody. You're the crazy woman who rammed the back of my car. You're the one who should be answering questions, honey, not me."

"You turned your lights off," I say.

Drew looks at him like I've made a valid point. "Technically, your actions caused a chain reaction," he says.

Jack doesn't take this well. "That woman—" he shouts, pointing his finger at me "—is stalking me. I want her arrested and prosecuted to the full extent of the law."

I deny that I am stalking him and say that I just happened to be in the same restaurant tonight. Sheer coincidence.

"In disguise?" he says. "Who goes to a restaurant in disguise? A little early for Halloween, isn't it?"

It takes a long time to explain how food critics work, especially with Howard chiming in every now and then that of course, this is all hypothetical, and he isn't admitting he's a food critic, or taking off his disguise to show his face.

It ends pretty much as you'd expect.

"She's crazy," Jack says. "She belongs on some psychiatrist's couch or in Bellevue or something. I'm telling you, the woman's crazy."

CHAPTER 15

Design Tip of the Day

> One good piece of furniture can make a room. Splurge on a great couch, a fireplace mantle, an antique rug. Let that quality piece dominate the room and get the rest of the furniture from IKEA or a discount store.
>
> —From TipsfromTeddi.com

I am lying on the tufted leather couch in Ronnie Benjamin's office. Even on my worst days I have never actually reclined in her office before.

"That bad?" she asks me.

"I think I may be obsessed," I say.

She says something about our making progress, as last year I thought I was *possessed*.

I tell her I'm not kidding. She reminds me that neither is she. "Tell me what makes you think you're being obsessive."

I tell her how I can't let go of Jack and Elise and what I think I know and how it's going to ruin my life.

"Take a deep breath," she tells me. "Before you hyperventilate."

"It took me a long time to get back on my feet," I tell her.

"But you did it," she says from somewhere behind me.

"I did." I take her through a litany of the last year of my life.

"After I got out of the hospital, I had to pull myself together for the kids," I remind her, as if she needs reminding.

"I had to help them deal with the divorce without letting them know just what a scum their father was and how he tried to drive me crazy just so that he could get his hands on some money."

"Where is this going, Teddi?" she asks me.

"And I had to find a way to support them because I knew that Rio wouldn't be able to after my father fired him, and I couldn't value myself if I let my parents give me money."

"Yes," Dr. Benjamin says. "You can be proud of yourself. You made it through. You actualized yourself. Why do you feel the need to revisit this?"

"Because I think it may be at risk. *I* may be at risk. And I can't seem to stop myself."

"I see," she says, and I imagine that behind me she is steepling her hands.

"You don't see. I caused a four-car accident yesterday," I say, which is only slightly stretching the truth, since really Jack caused it. "And I was chasing a murderer at the time."

Dr. Benjamin releases a deep breath noisily.

I assure her that I am not making this up. "Do you know

how hard it was to borrow the money from my father to finish my degree at Parsons? To be obligated to him and my mother at nearly 40 years old? At a time when I ought to be thinking about taking care of them, and they have to take care of me?"

Dr. Benjamin says that she knows exactly what it took. "Guts, Teddi. Something you have in abundance."

"Yeah, well, I just don't want those guts splayed on the floor."

"So what are you doing to prevent that?" she asks.

"Prevent it? I seem to be courting it. What kind of crazy woman goes running after a murderer?"

"What kind does, Teddi?"

"Elise Meyers's death was not some robbery gone bad. I know it with every fiber of my body. And Jack Meyers was involved. I know that, too."

"Let's say you're right. Why not just leave it to the police?"

"That's what I'm asking you. Why can't I just leave it to the police?"

"Did you finish paying your parents back?" she asks.

I tell her that I'm just one payment away and ask what that has to do with the price of tea in China.

"You're a woman who takes her responsibilities seriously, wouldn't you say?"

"I guess," I answer, and she harrumphs.

"How are the kids?" she asks.

"They're fine. Dana misses Rio, so I let her see him on

occasion, often enough for her to feel that he cares about her, but not often enough for him to insinuate himself in her life. Jesse has no use for Rio. He's trying to become the man of the family, but a ten-year-old boy shouldn't have that responsibility, so I play down the need for one. It's amazing how self-sufficient I can pretend to be."

"And Alyssa?"

"Jesse and Dana have both picked up the slack where Alyssa's concerned. It worried me, at first, them watching out for her, spending extra time with her. But I can see that it's good for them as well as for her. They've discovered that there is a world outside of themselves."

"So we can agree that you take your responsibilities seriously, then?"

"I guess."

"Like pulling teeth," she whines.

I agree that I take my responsibilities seriously. Anything to get back to my obsessive need to solve the murder of a woman I didn't even like.

"So," Dr. B says. "You missed witnessing the murder by what, a few minutes?"

I take an uneven breath. "I guess."

"And?"

"And what?" I don't know what she's getting at, but I know she'll make a point eventually.

"Had you got there a few minutes earlier..."

I see it now. "...it could have been me. But—"

She doesn't let me finish.

"That alone is enough, but let's go one thought further. A few minutes earlier it could have *been* you. And if it had been?"

And there it is. Dr. Benjamin's golden nugget. I sit up on the couch and turn toward her.

"I'd sure as hell want someone obsessed with finding out the truth."

She smiles at me and nods toward the clock. Our hour is up.

CHAPTER 16

Design Tip of the Day

> Always know who you are dealing with when ordering goods or services over the Internet. If you are not buying from a major retailer, but from a vender on ebay, check the seller's history, available on the same page as the merchandise offered, to be sure that they are worthy of your business.
> —From TipsfromTeddi.com

Howard really is a nice guy. He sent flowers after the accident and suggested a mechanic who could repair my car for a "reasonable sum." In all the time since the accident he hasn't once mentioned what it must be costing to fix his Mercedes, which, as you may recall, he checked on only after he checked on me. And he did run to my car, as opposed to sauntering on over. And he's called every night, which someone who shall remain nameless has not.

On top of that, he has been insistent about taking me on another restaurant assessment, despite the fiasco the last one descended into. And, now that I've finally agreed, he has suddenly developed an interest in my work, as well.

Which is why we're stopping at Bailey Manor instead of heading straight for Panama Hattie's, a four-star restaurant with prices to match, that Howard wants to review.

"We're closed," says the same woman who checked Bobbie and me in the other day. And then she sees Howard, looking larger than life in a Texas oilman getup, making a show of checking his watch. He touches his glued-on mustache and raises just one eyebrow, and as he does she relents. "Five minutes," she says.

"I've got *nine* minutes to six," he drawls and swaggers past her like he knows the place isn't supposed to close before six. When we are out of her earshot I ask where it says that. "Only makes sense," he says. "Whose closing time is five fifty-five?"

I show Howard my breakfast breezeway and start describing how I'm going to decorate it. He looks somewhat skeptical as he puts out his arms and touches the corresponding walls at once. I admit it's small but tell him that's precisely what makes it doable for me. He tells me I'm beautiful when I'm excited and I let myself believe he really thinks so and isn't just handing me a line. And I let myself be flattered that he'd bother if he is.

He stands behind me, and I can feel the welcome warmth radiating from him as he points over my shoulder at the wall where we are envisioning a window. "Will the windowsill be real or tromp l'oeil?" he asks, and with his body touching mine I know he's really asking if I'll sleep with him tonight.

"Real," I say, and my body leans back only the slightest bit, seeking out that warmth in the cold of the manor and maybe implying that the answer is yes. "With a row of small vases with a daisy in each."

He burrows his nose in my hair and says it smells good. I brush it back and say we should be going, but he takes my hand and leads me down the corridor, insisting we should see what the other decorators are doing.

I follow him reluctantly, looking at my watch because the witch who runs this place will probably lock us in if we stay a minute after 6:00 p.m. Howard hurries through the rooms with me trailing after him, asking him what he's looking for. It seems to me that all the men I know are looking for things—Rio is looking for pieces of our past, Drew is looking for a murderer, Howard is looking for—

"Where are the bedrooms?" He glares at me like I've hidden them.

I tell him I suppose they are upstairs and he winks at me and heads for the stairs.

"I'm not going up there," I tell him. It's late and I'm still the kind of woman who is afraid of getting in trouble. Hard to believe, since I find myself in piles of it all the time.

"Come on," he says, trying to coax me up the steps. "You know you want to."

And it's true, I do. I'd give my eyeteeth for a shot at

doing a bedroom in the decorator showcase, and what I really want to see is that I could have done the rooms better. I peek over my shoulder and since there is no sign of the showcase coordinator, I slip up the stairs behind Howard.

He says something patronizing like "that's my girl," and dips into the first doorway on the right.

Both of us stare at the room. Each article on its own would be enough—the stuffed giraffe in the corner, the zebra rug on the floor. The bedside table made from an elephant's leg. The gazelle's head on the wall. Silently we back out of the room—Howard shell-shocked, me smug.

He gestures for me to stand where I am, runs down the hall a bit, pokes his head into room after room and comes back for me with a smile. "I found something you'll love," he says, taking my arm and guiding me to the room at the end of the hall.

The bedroom is tastefully done. The bedspread is damask. The bed is a four poster, which requires a step to climb onto, and is piled high with pillows. The whole room is done in shades of one color. Now, if the color was, say, forest-green, or terra-cotta, or blue, or…any color but taupe, I could love this room. But every room in my mother's house was, and is, taupe. My mother's hair is kind of taupe. My room growing up was taupe. Once, as a rebellious teen, I put up framed posters in my room while my mother was off on one of her sojourns to South Winds. When she was released, she came home and ripped them from the walls. Eventually, as a spiteful joke, I got taupe matting and framed it—just solid taupe in a taupe frame.

She loved it.

"Nice," I say, rather than explain all this to Howard, who is staring at me intently with what I think is lust in his eyes.

"Just your color," he says.

I can't see that the point is worth arguing, so I just look around and smile.

"A woman as beautiful as you shouldn't be lonely," he says, and he tries to slide my deep cowl-neck sweater off my left shoulder. Being neither the time nor the place, I simply assure him that, no, I am not lonely. In fact, I seem to have men coming out of my ears this week.

"I'm lonely, too," he says, only now he's mauling the sweater.

I tell him more adamantly that I am not lonely and I take two steps back, which lands me smack against the wall, where Howard traps me with a hand on either side.

"You made a mistake. So did I—" he begins.

"You're making one now," I tell him, slipping under his arm and glaring him into place.

He stares at me for a while trying to find a subtext that isn't there. Finally he spits out, "Fine. I'll take you to dinner."

"Fine," I agree, as unhappy as he is at the sudden shift in our relationship. I want to say he should just take me home, and I would, really, if I hadn't heard that dinner at Panama Hattie's costs close to a hundred dollars a person and is actually worth it. And if this behavior didn't seem so out of character for him.

The gatekeeper rolls her eyes at us as we come down the stairs. She points at her watch. Howard doesn't care, since he doesn't ever have to see her again. But I do, and I apologize profusely, telling her that my shoe got stuck upstairs and we had to get it out of the carpet without damaging it, to which Howard adds that the zebra had me in its jaws. By the time we get to the car we're both laughing.

"Here's what I think," he suggests after we're buckled up and he's pulling out onto Jericho Turnpike. "You should close your eyes and pretend you're typing a note to me."

I ask why in the world I'd want to do that.

"Some people find it easier to be honest and open when they don't have to stare into someone else's eyes."

I remind him that he's driving and that I can't look into his eyes because, hopefully, they are on the road, but I know what he means. I have the most intimate and revealing conversations with my kids when I'm driving the car and we don't have to stare into each other's eyes.

"Humor me," he says.

I close my eyes. He's right. It's easier to talk to him without seeing his cowboy hat and mustache. "I don't like feeling pressured," I say.

"I don't like playing games," he replies.

I tell him I'm not playing any games and he humphs.

"I'm looking for a woman. You're looking for a man. You

want to be wined and dined. I'm in a position to do that. You want to be told you're beautiful. That's easy. You are. You're afraid you're getting old. You're not. You have a black negligee that hides nothing but your appendix scar."

My eyes fly open. "Excuse me?"

"I want to kiss that scar. You want me in the general vicinity—"

I tell him to stop the car. He tells me he's in the middle of traffic and I should close my eyes again. I tell him to pull the freakin' car over and stop or I'm going to leap out into traffic. He puts a hand on my knee. I reach for the door handle.

"I'm pulling over, I'm pulling," he says, putting on his blinker and cutting off two cars as he gets into the right lane and makes a turn sharp enough to send me nearly into his lap.

"Look," he says, and exasperation drips from his voice. "If you're not interested, what the hell are you doing on JDate anyway?"

I cover my mouth with my hand and swallow hard while the pieces all fall into place. "Have you been communicating with me on JDate?"

"Are you trying to pretend you didn't know it was me?" he asks, incredulous. "There's nothing to be embarrassed about. I knew you were joking when you asked me to measure—"

I put my hands up. "Stop!" I close my eyes, open them to glance at him and then look away, out the car window.

There is a giggle building up inside me, working it's way up from my stomach and I'm swallowing hard to try to keep it down.

"You were serious last night?" he asks, trying to figure out where he fits in the equation. "Oh, God. And now you think I was serious and you're afraid? Is that it?"

I'm holding my hand over my mouth and convulsing. Howard asks if I'm going to be sick and opens the window next to me. Which is good, because I'm getting light-headed holding in this giggle.

When I can talk at all, I manage to force out, "Just how big did you tell my *mother* your penis is?" before dissolving into laughter.

Howard doesn't think it's funny. He begs my pardon.

"I have never been on JDate," I tell him. "My mother is looking for a nice Jewish man for me. You've been having e-sex with a sixty-eight-year-old married woman."

Now Howard looks like he's the one going to be sick, and he opens his window and gulps in air. "Oh, my God," is all he can say at first, then he adds something about me having no idea.

"Oh, but I do," I say. "She's been my mother for thirty-eight years."

"Aren't there laws against her doing that?" he asks as he loosens his tie. "My mother, may she rest in peace, would never—"

I explain that my mother doesn't know from laws. "This

is nothing," I tell him. "Last year she shot my husband and came damn close to shortening his measurements."

"Your husband?" he croaks out, and I notice little beads of sweat on his upper lip.

"He's not my husband anymore," I say, surprised that Helene hasn't filled him in on my sordid past. He admits he vaguely recalls reading about the paintball episode in the paper.

I glance at my watch and realize our reservations were for half an hour ago.

"Under the circumstances," he starts, and I think he's somehow blaming me for the fact that he and my mother have apparently been carrying on an e-ffair.

And it occurs to me that I'm the one with the right to be pissed. "And what—" I ask him, sitting up rather primly as he puts the car in Drive and pulls into a driveway to turn around "—were you doing trolling on JDate last night? Looking for someone better?"

Howard ignores me, ignores the No Left Turn sign and pulls out onto Jericho Turnpike heading in the exact opposite direction of Panama Hattie's. Serves me right for flaunting my dinner plans in front of the kids while they were having pizza. Of course, they weren't too jealous when we pulled up the menu on the Internet and in a page full of cheeses they couldn't find Velveeta.

"Shit," Howard says, and he slams the heel of his hand against the wheel while a siren sounds behind us and a light flashes in the rearview mirror. "Unmarked car. Something so fitting about that, don't you think?" he asks as he pulls to the curb. "People with hidden identities?"

"Why are you acting like this is *my* fault?" I say just as the officer taps on Howard's window and leans down into the car.

"Can I see your license please, sir," an all-too-familiar voice asks.

"You have some ID?" Howard asks while I shake my head and try to warn him that this is not a man to toy with.

The officer whips out his wallet and displays his detective shield and ID card.

Howard looks at the ID and then looks at Drew Scoones. "Aren't you…?" he begins.

Drew ignores his question and dips his head until he can meet my eyes. He asks Howard for his license and comments on the fact that on his license he doesn't have a mustache.

"You two are really into Halloween, huh?" Drew says. "Hoping for a little trick or treat?"

Howard is too steamed to answer.

"Did you see the sign as you were coming out of that development?" Drew asks.

"Sign?" Howard repeats as I unbuckle my seatbelt and reach for the door handle. "Stay in the car, damn it. I'll handle this."

"Ma'am?" Drew says. "Is there a problem?"

I can't help it. All I can think of to say is that the man next to me had e-sex with my mother. Worse, I say it.

Howard gasps and reaches for me as I open the door

and get out of the car. "Get the hell back in the car," he shouts at me.

Drew tells Howard that that is no way to speak to a lady. Howard says that he's not sure I am one. Drew starts writing up a ticket, but I put my hand over the paper.

"He's had a rough night," I say softly. "Can't you just let it go?"

Drew looks down into the car. "You want to apologize to the little lady, Tex?" he asks Howard, who sits fuming, his mustache hanging at an odd angle. "Let's hear it."

"I'm sorry, Teddi," Howard says, and it sounds as though he really means it. "I'm a little rattled about, well, you know. Would you get back in the car? Please?"

I start to head back around the car, but Drew puts a hand on my arm. "I could bring the lady home, if she prefers."

"The 'lady'?" I say, and Drew nods like a cop. Or maybe a Texan. He's having altogether too much fun mocking Howard.

Howard says it's not necessary, glares at me and tells me again to get back in the car. It occurs to me that there isn't much of a chance for a relationship with a man who won't be able to look my mother in the eye in this lifetime, so I tell him goodbye. All the way to Drew's car I can hear Howard pounding the steering wheel.

"Why are you every place I am?" I ask Drew when we are settled in his bucket seats. He throws the ticket pad into my lap and I see that it is an order form for equipment. "So were you just harassing my date?"

He tells me that my date made an illegal left turn. I ask if I'm supposed to believe it was a coincidence that he was there to catch him doing it.

"I thought you'd want to know that I spoke to a hacking expert," he says in that way he has of always avoiding answering me.

"And…?"

"Apparently there is no way to track Bluetooth activity. It slides in under the radar."

I cross my arms over my chest. "You followed me on a date, pulled the man over, threatened him with a ticket and had me come into your car so that you could tell me you know nothing?"

"I didn't say that," he says, and a smug smile creeps up that handsome face.

"You know something!" I shout and he says something about how he knows a lot. Like where I am at any given moment, I suppose.

"I spoke to your jeweler friend," he tells me, knowing full well Marvin Katzmann is not my friend. It turns out, he says, that Jack Meyers's sudden influx of money came from selling Elise's diamonds and having them replaced with CZ's. Which, of course, explains why he allowed her to be buried with her jewelry on. He wanted it under eight feet of dirt.

I tell him about how Jack reacted when I mentioned the missing basketball and he tells me to stay the hell out of the Meyers house and away from Jack. He tells me, too, that he's on it and that, contrary to any opinions I might have about the police department's effectiveness, they are handling the case.

"And Bobbie?" I ask.

"Bobbie may not be exactly who you think she is," he tells me.

I tell him I would trust Bobbie with my life. I am about to add that I'd trust her with my children's lives when he says, "Yeah, well, you trusted Rio Gallo, too."

It's a low blow, and he knows it when I slam the car door behind me, hurry up the walk and enter my house alone.

CHAPTER 17

Design Tip of the Day

Things aren't always the way they seem, and isn't that lucky for the creative decorator. A fancy, full-length tablecloth can make a cardboard side table look like a million dollars. A tromp l'oeil painting can put you in Paris or at the beach without leaving your community. Just make sure no one can see the *man behind the curtain* when you work your magic.

—From TipsfromTeddi.com

I spend the night painting the most glorious scene for the window at Bailey Manor and get the finishing touches—a small, naked-bottomed child with a pail and shovel at the water's edge—done around 3:00 a.m. Then I post a tip on my Web site, send an e-mail to my mother telling her that if she doesn't get me off JDate today, I will personally come to her house and yank her wires out, and one to my father telling him that he'd better do something about my mother.

After I get the kids off to school in the morning, my father calls and asks how I like the new video phone. I tell him I took video of Maggie May dancing and will send it to his computer. I also tell him he's got to stop my mother and her JDate exploits.

He suggests I involve her more in Dana's bat mitzvah preparations. I suggest he consider having his head examined.

"It'll keep her out of your hair about this JDate business," he says.

"I won't have any hair left," I warn him.

He tries to convince me, but I don't really hear him because I'm busy doing our ritual dance. You've heard of a maypole, where everyone dances around a center post. In our family we have a Junepole—my father and I dance around my mother, who insists on being the center of everything.

After a few minutes we hang up, having accomplished nothing more than establishing the fact that, despite how difficult my mother is, my father still loves her, and I still love him.

I pour myself a second cup of coffee while I wait for Bobbie to show up so we can head for Bailey Manor and dial up Precious Things, figuring it would be a good idea to give Helene my version of what happened before her brother does. I just want her to know that it was not my fault. Not that I'm saying it was Howard's, either, exactly. I plan to tell her that my mother, who Helene knows is crazy, is at the bottom of it and leave it at that. Only Gina is the one who answers and she tells me some cockamamy story about how Helene won a trip to Las Vegas and is away for a while.

"Is there anything I can help you with?" she offers. "Helene said I should take care of you."

I ask if Helene is very mad. Gina claims she didn't say, but I know better. She's no more in Las Vegas than I'm in Timbuktu.

"So, then, I don't suppose she'd be willing to lend me some furniture for the showcase," I say.

Gina asks what happened between the two of us and while I could let her simply take Helene's version, it seems like an opportune moment to explain that it was all my mother's fault and ask her to pass on my apologies. Gina says she will but that she doubts that Helene will see me for a while.

"I'd just lie low," she advises. "Not show my face for a little bit."

So much for borrowing anything for the showcase, which is what I tell Bobbie when she and I get into my car to head over to Bailey Manor. I'm surprised her stomach doesn't still hurt from laughing so hard last night when I called and told her all about Howard and my mother measuring their parts in cyberspace.

I tell Bobbie it looks like she will have to deal with Helene from now on and that I should have known better than go out with a business associate's relative. And then I ask her what's really on my mind.

"Why does Drew Scoones keep telling me that I don't really know you?"

Bobbie doesn't seem surprised. She doesn't seem outraged, perturbed or disposed to answer my question, either. She puts down the visor and checks her lipstick in the vanity mirror.

"Bobbie?"

"They think that Kristen has anorexia," she says.

Now if I say that she's dodging the question, it'll seem like I don't care about Kristen, and if I let her change the topic, then I won't know what she and Drew won't tell me. My concern for Kristen wins out. "*Who* thinks?" I ask.

"The school," she says, and she launches into a recap of the meeting she had with the school nurse and the school psychologist when she picked up her daughter the other day.

I'm not the kind of person who would ask if she is just making all this up to avoid my question. But I guess I am the kind of person who would think it because I can barely pay attention, despite the fact that Kristen is practically one of my own.

She asks me if I've noticed a change in Kristen's eating habits. Actually, now that she mentions it, Kristen has seemed pickier than usual. Though, with Kristen, it's hard to tell.

"Bobbie, about Drew—" I start.

"They think she needs psychological help."

I say that's probably a good idea.

"You know that people die from anorexia?" she asks me. "Remember Karen Carpenter?"

I tell her she should definitely get Kristen all the help she needs. And then I say, "Drew Scoones says I don't know you at all. Is he right?"

Bobbie tells me that of course he isn't right, that we've been friends for twelve years and that I know more about her than anyone except Mike, her husband.

I ask what she and Drew talked about at the police station.

"Mike is going to want to take Kristen to Dr. Hepstein—"

"The hypnotherapist he had the affair with?" I squeak without thinking.

Bobbie reminds me that Phyllis Hepstein specializes in eating disorders. Silly me. I thought she specialized in breaking up marriages. Though I guess she only dabbled in that, since Mike is back with Bobbie.

"There must be a hundred doctors who specialize in eating disorders on Long Island. I mean anorexia here must be more common than the cold."

Bobbie accuses me of not caring. If the shoe were on the other foot, she'd be accusing me of sending up a smoke screen so that I didn't have to discuss whatever it is she's hiding from me. Bobbie can do that with aplomb. Must be guidelines in that damn handbook.

I admit that Kristen has eating issues. "Have you seen her naked?" I ask. Bobbie shrugs, as if to say *Kristen is twelve. I don't bathe her.* I ask if she's seen Kimmie naked and she nods. I think it's not a good sign that Kristen won't let Bobbie see her, but I don't think she looks unusually thin. At least not yet.

"Let me ask Ronnie Benjamin for a recommendation," I say, but Bobbie says it's premature. I don't know what to make of it.

At Bailey Manor the door matron looks disapprovingly at me and tells me she hopes I'm not planning on staying beyond six o'clock again, sending Bobbie into peels of artificial laughter. Drew is right. She is hiding something from me. I ask for permission to park outside the door while we carry in a painting and she grudgingly allows it. I know the window is really good when she can't stop herself from smiling at it and telling me it's lovely.

Bobbie tells her I painted it myself, that I'm incredibly talented and that she won't believe how terrific the breakfast nook is when I get through with it.

I remind Bobbie that I won't get through with it without some more furniture, and Bobbie offers to try Helene. While I rearrange chairs on the *Titanic*, otherwise known as moving around the vases that I've filled with that acrylic water and placed artificial daisies in because I have no actual furniture to move about, Bobbie dials up Precious Things.

"Hi Gina," I hear Bobbie say. "I'm over at Bailey Manor with Teddi and we just saw the smartest thing in one of the sitting rooms. The decorator has a discreet sign that says that furniture was donated by Sit Yourself Down and there is a contest going on in the store to win the furniture."

I can tell from the expression on Bobbie's face that she is making all of this up.

"I guess that Sit Yourself Down figures that will get people in the store and once they see what she's got there, they'll place orders. Isn't that a great idea?"

She shoots me an I-don't-know-if-she's-buying-this face.

"So I wanted to talk with Helene about possibly doing the same thing here with an item or two. Like just a couple of bar stools, or—"

"Well, when she gets back," Bobbie says. She mouths to me that Helene's mother broke her hip in Florida. "No, I can see how you wouldn't want to bother her with this now. Maybe you could just—"

"I thought she was in Vegas," I say loudly enough for Gina to hear.

Bobbie passes on the news that Helene *was* in Vegas when she got the call about her mother and how it's always the daughters that come running and never the sons, and it lets me resent Howard just a little bit more.

CHAPTER 18

Design Tip of the Day

> Rather than wallpaper an entire room, you can get an even more decorated effect by putting pattern only above or below a chair rail. This is especially effective in a dining room and can be made easier still by stretching sheets between floor molding and a three foot mark and then putting up a chair rail to cover the staples.
>
> —From TipsfromTeddi.com

It is amazing how many dinners I get asked out to and don't get to eat these days. First there was the Panama Hattie with Howard fiasco, and now Drew is twenty minutes late to pick me up and I'm guessing he isn't showing up at all.

"Can I?" Dana asks in that tone that implies that not only should I know what she is talking about, but she's already asked more than once. I apologize and ask what it is she wants permission for. "You didn't hear a word I said, did you?" The accusation is all the more stinging because it is true.

"You know," I tell her, "that when you are asking for a favor or permission to do something, using that tone of voice is probably not your best choice."

"It's *my* fault you weren't listening?" she asks, and her voice squeaks with indignation.

I want to explain to her that I'd be much more likely to say "sure" if she were even a little sympathetic about my inability to concentrate on her problems while having so many of my own. But what kind of mother puts her own needs first? Of course, my daughter's problems are usually of the I-have-nothing-in-my-closet-to-wear variety while mine are the my-best-friend-is-being-set-up-as-a-murderer kind.

"Jesse's old enough to watch Alyssa, and, besides, shouldn't she be your responsibility and not ours? I mean, you can go out, even though you aren't even divorced from Dad yet, but I—"

"You are so on the wrong track," I tell her. "And you are heading for a serious crash."

"I don't even know what you're talking about," she shouts at me, arms flailing. "You aren't even making sense."

I stare at her silently long enough for her to calm down. I point to the living room couch where I can talk to her and watch out the window on the off chance that Drew actually does show up.

"Darling," I tell her, "I feel a life lesson coming on."

As you can imagine, she rolls her eyes. I assure her that if she has no desire to get ahead in life, I can just skip it.

"But you won't give me permission until I hear it, right?" I remind myself that all twelve-year-olds are obnoxious and I remind her that the chances are I'll say no even if she hears me out. "Of course, the chances are that next time I'll say 'yes' because you'll actually take my advice to heart."

Neither of us really thinks that's going to happen, but I launch into my speech anyway, advising her to learn how to handle people and phrase her requests in the way that best insures the response she wants.

"You know how it works already. You use it every time you want Jesse to do something for you and you tell him that he probably wouldn't know how to do it right, anyway. Then he has to prove to you that he can, and he winds up doing it for you."

"I don't do that," she says as her cheeks redden.

"You do, and you do it well. Now, if you want Alyssa to do something you just tell her to do the opposite, right? Like when you tell her she should try to stay up as late as she can, even if she's very, very tired, she shouldn't put her head down on that pillow, even for a second."

"I only do that when it's late and she—"

"Now," I say, "you have to figure out how to get me to say what you want. Think of the different response you'd get if you started your request with 'why can't I…' or if you started it with 'do you think it would be all right if…'"

"Are you telling me to play you?" she asks, just as I see Drew's sports car pull into the driveway.

I stand and smooth out my skirt, adjusting the low-slung belt Bobbie showed me how to wear. "This is not a date," I tell my daughter.

"Right." She smiles at me and fusses a little with my hair. "This isn't Alyssa you're talking to," she says as she pushes me toward the door.

I open it and a very serious Drew faces me through the screen door. He apologizes for being late, but I wave it away. "We have to talk," he tells me, his eyes on Dana. When I open the screen door he shakes his head. "Not here."

"I'm going out now," I yell toward the stairs. "Dana's in charge."

Jesse appears at the top of the stairs "I don't need—" he starts as Alyssa comes out of her room to echo him. I repeat the fact that Dana is in charge.

"And…" I add, because in some respects Dana is right and Alyssa is my responsibility and not hers "…Dana is going to get paid for babysitting tonight."

My daughter's eyes glisten and she grows about four inches before our eyes. "How much?" she asks.

Before I can tell her that she's pushing it, Drew pulls a twenty out of his pocket and hands it to her with a wink. "Try to save the calls for emergencies," he tells her.

She wishes us a good time, but Drew tells her and the others that this is strictly business.

"Your mother is a big help in this investigation," he tells

them. "Whatever happens, you remember that in the end it will all be all right, and that will be due to your mom."

There are three solemn faces staring at me with newfound respect as Drew holds open the door and we leave the house.

Drew says nothing in the car until we arrive at Pastaeria, a local Italian restaurant with the best veal parmesan heroes on the island. "Takeout all right?" he asks.

I nod.

"I don't want anyone to overhear us," he says.

I nod again. "We could skip dinner," I offer, but my stomach rumbles and he hears it.

He tells me he's already ordered, he'll just run in and get it and then we'll go to his place. "If that's all right with you."

I feel like a bobble-head doll as I nod again and he catches my chin. "It *will* be all right in the end," he tells me. "If it's not all right, it's not the end."

I'm so not convinced.

Drew has a nice apartment. It's surprisingly clean. I don't have the nerve to ask if anyone else lives there, but a trip to the bathroom reveals no Tampax, no Midol and no moisturizer of any kind. I'm convinced he lives alone when the soap in the dish turns out to be Lava.

He's set up our dinner in the dining room. It's a barren, cold room, and I can't help decorating it in my mind. I guess it shows, because he apologizes for the sterility of the place. "I never really noticed it before," he says. "But I guess I'm learning some decorating stuff from this case."

I tell him it looks fine, that it's a nice table and chairs, but I admit he could use a few things on the wall. And a rug. And a chandelier that wasn't provided by the builder. And a side piece, which could even be just a shelf fastened to the wall—maybe with a wine rack beneath it. "And if you put shelves on this wall," I say, "surrounding the doorway and even over it, you could make them look built in by putting up fabric behind them and closing in the sides. Very classy."

He looks where I point, then busies himself with distributing the hero sandwiches and the silverware. "This isn't a date," he says, like he's afraid I'm redecorating and moving in.

"Good," I say. "Because I'm not ready to date."

He asks what I think it is I'm doing with Howard Rosen. I offer the Howard debacle as proof I'm not ready. "This is strictly business," he says.

I tell him I know that. "You're pumping me for information."

"I'm not *pumping* you," he says, then mutters something that sounds like he wishes he were pumping me.

We're silent for a while, playing with our food without taking a bite.

"You want some wine?" he asks. "I've got some in the cabinet. Temporarily, of course, until I get that wine rack."

I remind him this is supposed to be business.

"I'm just getting you drunk so you'll spill the beans," he says with a half smile, but he doesn't get up.

I tell him wine makes me sleepy. He tells me he's got a bed.

"Everybody's got a bed," I say.

"That include Howard?" he asks.

I shrug. Of course Howard's got a bed. He's all but seduced my mother into it. Or maybe it's the other way around. "What am I doing here?" I ask him. "What is it you want to tell me that no one is supposed to overhear?"

Drew looks uncomfortable. He looks out his window, he looks at his dinner. He doesn't look at me.

"Is it about the case?" I ask.

He says he's told me everything he can about the case. "More than I should have." He pinches the bridge of his nose. "Much more. That's what I want to talk to you about."

"I don't know anything else," I tell him. "And I don't play games well. If you think I know something, go ahead and ask me. You don't have to—" I was going to say wine and dine me, but my veal-parm hero is cold and my real-life hero is hot, and, besides, there's no sign of the wine he offered.

"What I've told you, the very fact that you're here—it could compromise the case, the department, my job."

I offer to go to the corner and call a cab to take me home.

He tells me that would be a good idea, but he starts to play with my hand while he does.

"I'll take you home," he says, but neither of us gets up

from the table. "Soft," he says as he continues to stroke the back of my hand. It makes my heart thump as hard as if he were passionately kissing me.

"Joy Brown says I can't get serious with a man until I've been divorced for a year," I say, and my voice quivers.

"That's okay," he says, and his hand is making its way slowly up my arm, massaging my shoulder, teasing my neck. "This isn't serious. It's business, remember?"

My father would call it monkey business, and my mother would send this young man packing. I ask Drew how old he is.

"Older than your kids and younger than your dad," he says as he slips my cardigan down my arm.

"But closer to my son's age, right?" I ask. He tells me he understood there was to be no math at this dinner, and he stares at me intently. I start to tell him that I'm thirty-eight, but as soon as I say, "I'm," he says, "perfect."

And he stands up and offers me his hand. And my head is screaming for me to protect his career and my heart—okay, mostly my heart—but I take his hand, stand, and let him lead me right past the couch, past the door, past the bathroom with the Lava soap and into his bedroom.

The comforter on his bed is navy blue with thin cranberry stripes. It reminds me of a prep school tie and I know I'll never look at a similar tie again without replaying this moment in my mind.

I stand frozen to the ground but he fixes that by gently

lifting me up and setting me down on the bed. He eases off the Jimmy Choo sandals I borrowed from Bobbie and slips out of his deck shoes before sitting beside me.

"You have a way of getting under a man's skin," he says, playing with the ends of my hair.

I croak something brilliant, like "I do?" because a so very handsome, so very much younger man is sitting so very close and trying so very hard to seduce me.

And he really doesn't have to try so very hard because, truth be told, I am so very willing.

I lean back on the bed and expect him to make his move, but he's full of surprises. He lies back, too, but next to me, linking a hand in mine. "That crack in the ceiling," he says looking up, "is the wrinkle by my mother's eye."

"That one?" I ask, pointing past him so that my upper arm brushes his lips.

He laughs and guides my arm until I'm pointing in the other direction and his arm just skims my breast. "That one," he says. "And this one," he adds, pulling my arm up and over my head, "is a butterfly tattoo on a woman's behind."

He pins my other arm above my head and holds both hands in one of his. With his free hand he traces the side of my face, my neck, the curve of one breast.

"You have any tattoos, Teddi Bayer?" he asks, tugging gently at my neckline. For the first time in my life I am sorry that I don't. It makes me feel old and matronly and incredibly dull. I shake my head sadly. "Good. I wouldn't want this marred."

I am on a roller coaster and I never want the ride to end.

He puts his hand on the zipper to my jeans. "Trust me?" he asks.

"Not for a moment."

"Smart," he says and unbuttons my waistband. "Trust me now?" he asks, his hand on my zipper.

I struggle to swallow. How many years since I played this game? How many years since I didn't know just what would happen next?

"You like kissing, Teddi Bayer?" he asks, his lips poised millimeters from mine.

"Shut up," I tell him, stretching my neck to meet his mouth.

He gives me only a peck.

"Don't interrupt my interrogation," he says, a finger against my lips.

"I forgot that this is police business," I admit.

"Well, don't forget it," he warns me, asking again if I like kissing.

I tell him I do.

"And touching?" he asks, his hand resting now on my breast. "Do you like touching?"

I tell him I do. Very much.

He asks if I'd prefer to take my own clothes off, or have him do it for me. He says it as if there is no choice of whether, just by whom. I lie limp in answer, my eyes closed. The truth is that I don't think I could make my fingers work any better than my tongue can form words at the moment.

He relieves me of my sweater and jeans so easily that I have to lie to myself about the number of times he's done this before. He tells me he is glad that there is no tattoo on my breast, and kisses the rise there. He tells me he is glad that there is no tattoo here, and here, and here and he kisses each spot, easing off my bra, my undies.

When I open my eyes he is shucking off his own clothes and I am grateful he hasn't asked me to undress him. I watch shamelessly and he catches me. I feel my face redden and he laughs at me as he takes off his own watch and leans over me to take off mine. I try to stop him, but he prevails without words. He unplugs his phone from the wall. It is just beginning to get dark outside and the room is bathed in twilight blue when he lays down next to me again.

"You're more beautiful than I expected," he says. "I mean, this would have happened anyway, but it's like an incredible bonus, like I hit the jackpot, like I got the upgrade, somehow."

I think of the women he's no doubt been with—younger than me, firmer than me, women who haven't borne three kids and still, six years after the last one, carry five extra pounds along with their stretch marks, and I reach for the comforter and wrap it around myself.

He looks confused and possibly hurt. "That must have come out wrong. I thought I said you were stunning to look at." He clamors under the covers and reaches for me.

Sex with my ex-husband was good. Really good. It's just that somehow what I'm doing with Drew isn't sex. It's something better, on a higher plane. Something more magical, mystical, not of this world. My head is spinning with new tastes and scents and sights. He strokes my inner thighs, strays higher, lower, his lips busy elsewhere. He asks nothing of me in return, no *my turn, Teddi*, no moving my hand where it might not want to be, no guiding my head, nothing but pleasuring me, pleasuring me, pleasuring me.

Somewhere far, far away, music plays. Lovely, soft music that fits like someone is scoring my life. I am soaring, and Drew is the wind beneath my wings. Then the words to the actual song float in my head, coupled with heavy breathing in my ear, the bed creaking, and my own moans getting louder and louder.

The music gets louder along with my moans.

"Yes!" I'm yelling, covering my mouth so the kids won't hear me, realizing the kids are miles away, yelling again, realizing that there are neighbors on the other side of the wall but yelling "yes, yes," again and again anyway.

Only then I'm jumping out of the bed and running naked into the living room, Drew right behind me, following the sound of my phone ringing somewhere in my purse.

"Is it your kids?" Drew asks, as he, too, searches for my bag.

"It's Bobbie," I tell him. "When the kids call it plays "I Want Candy" by Bow Wow Wow."

"Christ, just let it ring, then," Drew says, trying to grab me like I'm a greased pig getting away.

"She wouldn't interrupt us unless it was a national emergency," I say. My kids are dead. Worse, Rio took them. My house is burning down.

I grab the phone too late and press in Bobbie's number. My father's had a heart attack. My mother's shot someone else. But it's none of those. "I'm fucking being arrested," she shouts through the phone. Drew can hear her. I know he can, but his face is stoic. "The cops are here, they just found Elise's faucet in my basement and I'm being arrested."

CHAPTER 19

Design Tip of the Day

Throw pillows can be recovered often to change the look of a room. Slipcovers in pastels welcome the spring, in deep turquoise shout summer, in russets and golds say autumn is near and nothing says winter like ivory.

—From TipsfromTeddi.com

Here's a tip I ought to post on my Web site: *It is hard to be haughty when naked.*

It's even harder when you realize you've been had.

"It's not—" Drew says, coming toward me, apparently not the least bit embarrassed by his own nakedness. Of course, he's got a great body and that isn't what he should be embarrassed about anyway.

"—a date. I know. You told me. It's business." I have to go past him to get to my clothing, and I don't want to go anywhere near him. I grab a place mat off the table and cover myself as best I can.

Drew says something about my being delicious or quite a dish, and puts out his hand. I think he actually believes we can go back to what we were doing when the phone rang.

"I would really like you to move out of the way so that I can get my things," I say as calmly as I possibly can, considering that in the full light of the dining room my stretch marks are probably glistening. I edge my way toward the couch, figuring a sofa pillow will hide more than the place mat. He says something about a fan dance.

"Teddi, there is a simple explanation for this," he says, and the jerk has the nerve to snicker as my place mat covers only half of the areas I consider vital.

I tell him I know the explanation. He told me beforehand and I just wasn't listening. "It's business."

"You think this was—" he starts, and he manages to look hurt and angry at the same time. He gestures for me to go ahead to the sofa. "What are you thinking? That I was supposed to keep you 'busy' while the feds arrested your friend? Is that it?"

I tell him I think he was doing the same thing I was doing, "looking for information. Looking to play a mild physical attraction for all it was worth. Using sex to get what we want in the end."

He tells me I don't mean that. He is between me and the bedroom and I demand that he get the hell out of my way. He refuses until I hear him out, stationing himself in the hallway to his bedroom.

"Oh, what? Are you going to try to tell me this was love? That what happened in your bedroom was magic?" I take a few steps to the right and he mirrors me so that I can't get down the hall. "I can't say you didn't warn me. *'It's just business,'* you said."

"That wasn't a warning, and it wasn't what I meant, and you know it," he yells at me as we both move left and right and he finally wedges himself so that his back is up against one wall and his legs are up on the other, effectively closing off the hallway.

"I want my clothes," I say, trying to look dignified as I hold a sofa pillow to my chest and pray that it reaches my thighs.

"Get 'em," he says, taking a long slow look up and down my body before shrugging.

"Fine." I smash into his legs, and he loses his balance enough for me to push past him and hurry into his bedroom. The blanket is on the floor. The lamp is in the corner under a pillow. My clothes are everywhere. You'd think we either had a great time or tried to kill each other. I find my lacey underpants under the bed.

Drew watches from the doorway. "You're being ridiculous," he tells me.

"Oh, that'll change my mind," I say, thinking this man is no wiser than Dana in the get-what-you-want-from-Teddi department.

"You're making a mistake," he says.

I tell him I've already made it.

He agrees and points at my panties. "Inside out." I think, *no—that's my guts, my heart, my self-respect.* For heaven's sake—I'm almost forty, five pounds overweight and no smarter than I was a year ago.

"I may be stupid for this—" I tell him, waving toward his bed "—but I only hurt myself. Can you say as much?"

He insists he hasn't hurt me, hasn't betrayed me or played me, that I'm the one who's hurting myself thinking that, not him.

"And Bobbie? Is it her imagination she's been set up and you and your cronies are stupid enough to arrest her? Is that somehow her fault, too?"

"Actually," he says, "I think it's yours, technically. If you hadn't rammed your way into this investigation, hadn't told everyone from the police to the lamppost that Elise Meyers's murder was not some robbery gone bad, I truly doubt that it would have come to this."

I ask if I was supposed to let the police be stupid and he tells me that I was supposed to let the police do their job.

"There is a lot more to this investigation than you know, Teddi. A lot more to Bobbie than you know, but for your sake, I promise—"

I stare at him, incredulous. "You want me to trust you? After tonight? After telling my children that everything will come out all right thanks to their mom, and then arresting the woman they think of as their aunt? After seducing me? And don't pretend that isn't what this was, even if I was willing. You were the one who brought me here—and under false pretenses from the start about having to talk to me privately. You did whatever it took to keep me out of the house and busy so that your men could go to my best friend's house and find evidence that they themselves planted, and you want me to trust you? You are out of your freakin' mind."

"There are things you don't know," he says, and now that I am dressed he is slipping into his jeans, sans underwear, and stepping into his shoes. "Things I am not at liberty to tell you. Things that not only endanger the investigation, but you and your stupid friend."

I tell him it's not my friend who is stupid, it's the entire Nassau County police force. I remind him it's not the first time I've dealt with them and what they don't "get" could fill the Long Island Sound.

He grabs up his watch, thrusts his wallet in his pocket and picks up his keys. "You do not know everything," he says through gritted teeth.

"And you do?" I say, as he gestures for me to precede him out of the bedroom.

"More than you think," he says, and I sense he wants to tell me something, but can't. Or won't. "More than I want to know."

"Like what?" I ask, daring him to prove this wasn't just some distract-and-destroy mission.

He tries to swear me to secrecy. I tell him maybe, if it's worth keeping to myself. He warns me that I'm out of my depth and from here on out I have got to play by his rules. "Or what?" I ask. "You'll have me arrested, too?"

"I don't want to find you the way I found your client," he says, and he looks a little sick when he says it, which is good because the idea of being dead doesn't exactly make me feel too good, either. "Swear this goes no further. Not even to Bobbie."

I tell him that Bobbie and I don't have secrets. "Two words," he says. I know what they are going to be. "You do."

I promise reluctantly as he opens the front door and we walk toward his car. He waits until we are inside and on the road.

"The Department knew there was trouble in the Meyer household several days before you walked in and found Mrs. Meyers dead," he says. "That 911 call wasn't exactly unexpected, except it was the wrong Meyers that was dead."

I tell him I don't know what he means.

"The money from that missing basketball? It was offered to someone in the Department posing as a hit man."

"I tried to tell you," I say, but he puts a hand on my thigh. I pull away and hug the door.

"The hit man wasn't hired by Jack," he says.

"Elise was trying to arrange her own murder?" I say. "To implicate Jack?"

He shakes his head and his tongue plays with the inside of his cheek. "Guess again."

"Elise knew she was dying and—"

Again he shakes his head.

"Elise hired a hit man to kill Jack?"

"Bingo. And the lovely woman wins this beautiful genuine simulated pearl necklace..."

So Jack was poisoning Elise and she was trying to have him killed. "So who killed Elise? I mean you don't really think that Bobbie—"

"Listen to me, Teddi, and listen carefully. This case is bigger than you think. There's plenty more that you don't know. There's even, believe it or not, plenty that I don't know, at least not yet."

He pulls into my driveway, cuts the engine and turns in his seat to face me. He takes my face in both his hands. "You matter to me, Teddi. More than you should. Trust me when I tell you that I will take care of this."

"I told you. I can't. Not with Bobbie in jail."

"Bobbie can take care of herself. In fact, she is taking care of herself."

I ask him what that means.

"It means she's got more to hide than you know about."

I tell him that's ridiculous.

"You mean to tell me you know about her and Jack Meyers?" he asks me. He knows it's a mistake the minute he says it because, like everything else, it's written all over my face. "You okay?" he asks when I take a minute to compose myself.

Finally I tell him that he's mistaken. "And even if you weren't, I have to—"

He loses it and interrupts me. "Goddammit, Teddi, stop worrying about Bobbie. She can take care of herself. This is not *Murder, She Wrote*, and you're not Jessica Fletcher."

Things aren't bad enough? He has to compare me to a woman old enough to be my grandmother? He couldn't have compared me to, say, Cybill Shepherd in *Moonlighting*? To Laura Holt from *Remington Steele*?

I tell him I know I'm not Jessica Fletcher. I storm out of the car. "I assume you'd have drawn the line at sleeping with her," I say as I slam the door behind me.

The kids are waiting up for me and from the looks on their faces they already know what happened with Bobbie. Maggie May dances around my ankles while Jesse asks how I am going to fix it.

Before I admit that I'm in over my head, Dana does it for me. "For the zillionth time, I told you she can't fix it," she snaps at him. She tells me that he's convinced I am going to be the hero of this drama because Detective Scoones has said as much.

The man has the ability to rock my world in more ways than I want to think about.

I look over Jesse's head and see Mike and the girls coming up the back deck. I order Maggie to sit while I let them in and put on coffee for Mike and me and pull out the chocolate syrup and milk for the kids.

I look at Mike and all I can think is that he started it. If he hadn't taken up with his hypnotherapist friend, the one he swore he knew in a previous life, Bobbie would never have slept with Jack Meyers.

Oh.

There it is. My denial notwithstanding, I guess I do believe it. And I hate Mike for starting all this. I hate Bobbie for needing revenge. I hate Jack for being so slimy that Bobbie could do it with him without risking being emotionally involved.

And I hate Drew most of all, for telling me.

I busy myself with the coffee and chocolate milk so that Mike can't read my face.

"You should have seen her," he says, and I can't tell if he's proud or dumfounded. "She reminded me of your mother going off to South Winds. I mean, she was telling the girls not to forget their permission slips, telling me what was in the freezer, going off like it was a freakin' vacation."

"A brave front," I say, thinking she's better at hiding her emotions than I thought. "That's our girl."

Mike repeats the bit about dinners in the freezer, as though I'm supposed to do something about them. I, of course, offer meals at my house. He looks at me like I'm missing the point.

I admit that, having got Elise as a client, having found her body, having had relations with the police (and I blush when I say that and pray no one is the wiser), I feel this is somehow all my fault.

Jesse relates to Bobbie's family what Drew told them as

he left, and Mike sounds just like Drew as he warns me to stay out of the whole mess.

"It's not your fault," he says. "You had nothing to do with it except the bad fortune to be in the wrong place at the wrong time. Bobbie doesn't hold you responsible and to tell you the truth, I think she's enjoying her little five minutes of fame."

"You mean *infamy*," Kristen corrects.

"She was so weird," Kimmie says. "Like she told me to try out for the school play because I had her talent for acting. And she told Kristen if she lost a pound while she was in jail she'd force-feed her when she got home."

Something Drew said occurs to me. "Who exactly arrested her?" I ask.

Mike says he thinks it was the local police. But I'm sure Drew said something about the feds.

Of course, he also said to stay out of it…

After a sleepless night, I open the door to send the kids off to school in the morning and find Diane sitting on my porch. I invite her in and make us some coffee.

Does Diane know? Are Drew and I the only ones?

"So what are we going to do?" I ask Diane. She tells me we do nothing. "Do you not remember last year? If you and Bobbie had just done nothing, I'd still be in South Winds, Rio would be raising my kids and my house would be mortgaged so that he could lose it all on some closeout center business."

"Not the same." Diane insists that we drink the coffee in

my living room where she can watch out the front window. "I'm up for a promotion," she says.

I tell her that's great, but it clearly isn't praise she wants. "What?"

"If I interfere with this investigation, I'm toast. The Department is watching me, waiting for me to screw up. I mean, who wants a lesbian cop on the force?"

"They know?" I ask.

She tells me that, of course, they know. It's not illegal and it's not something she's ashamed of. But that doesn't mean that all the good old boys are comfortable with the idea.

"I have to watch my back." She pulls the draperies back and sets down her cup. "I gotta go. Listen, Teddi. I'll do what it takes to clear Bobbie, but you have to stay out of it. Let the Department handle it. For my sake. You know I wouldn't let anything bad happen to Bobbie, right?"

"Where's the Diane I used to know?" I ask. "Now it's all about the Department. This is your sister, for Christ's sake."

Diane heads for the hallway. "She doesn't want you interfering, Teddi."

"Yeah, well you can't always get what you want," I tell her.

"Rolling Stones," Diane says and gives me a wave as she walks out my door.

I should post a tip on my Web site. I should figure out what Alyssa is going to wear for Halloween. I should invite the Lyons to have dinner with us and I should solve Elise's murder. Not necessarily in that order.

I open the freezer to see if the food fairy magically left anything, when the phone rings. I check the caller ID because I do not want to talk to Drew Scoones. Which doesn't mean that I don't want him to try to call and talk to me.

I'm relieved that it's my mother and not Drew. I should make note of this day somehow—the first time I'd choose talking to my mother over talking to anyone else in the world.

"Hello, Mother," I say, and my resignation rings through the line.

"I don't know why you insist on being mad at me," she says.

"Maybe because you asked a very nice man to measure his penis?" I respond.

"I was trying to be you," she says in her own defense, as if that makes it better.

If I had some other mother I might ask what would make her think *I'd* ask such a question. With my mother I'm afraid the answer would put me back on Ronnie Benjamin's couch for another year.

"Read Howie's column," she says. I suppose when you've been as intimate with the man as my mother has, you can call him "Howie."

I promise her I'll do it later. She asks what's wrong with now. "I'm kinda busy," I tell her.

"Oh." You can actually hear my mother's nose get out of joint. "Was I too busy for you when, on my way to the hospital, I made the driver stop to buy you nail polish? Was I too busy for you when I had pneumonia and I had to read your college application essays? Was I too busy—"

"Mom, the nail polish was for you. You wanted me to do your nails because your tech wouldn't come to the hospital. And you've never had pneumonia."

"I haven't?" She sounds disappointed, as though she's been cheated out of a life experience everyone ought to be able to fall back on. "You're sure?"

I am as sure of that as I am that I would never have asked her to read my college application essays since I really wasn't interested in having her star in them.

"I'll read Howie's review to you," she says. "Hold on while I get my glasses."

I open *Newsday* and turn to "Howie's" column because it may shorten this conversation by a nanosecond, and every nanosecond with my mother feels like a lifetime.

The title of the review is "Second Chances," so I really don't have to read more than that. Ostensibly, the article is about giving disappointing restaurants another chance, but with the first line, I know I'm being sent a message.

> There are places we have been that have such potential, such possibility, such promise, that they are worth revisiting. To risk missing out on such an experience is far worse than risking a second disappointment.

I hear my mother shout toward the phone that she's coming, but all I can think is "so's Christmas." I finish Howard's article and think he may be right. I berate myself for making stupid choices and I keep reading. There's a book review beneath Howard's column about an exposé that details the thefts of valuables from the Iraq National Museum at the beginning of the war. It deals with a sacred vase and a mask and an ivory of a lioness attacking a Nubian, and cylinder seals and coins.

Iraqi coins.

And as I wait for my mother to make her way back to the phone my call-waiting clicks. Without thinking, I answer it. Drew says hello.

"What do you want?" I bark into the phone so that he knows I am just as angry as last night. Maybe angrier.

He says he gets it, knows I'm still mad. "But I want to remind you that you are to drop it. You got that?" The police, he says, are doing their job, looking into it, following all leads, blah, blah, blah.

"And they've arrested the wrong person," I tell him. "So I'm supposed to just wait for them to get smarter?"

"You can trust me," he says. I snort. "Did I not tell you about the hit man? Did I not tell you about Jack Meyers's alibi? Did I not tell you all kinds of things the press doesn't know and neither should you?"

I have to admit this is true. Neither of us refers to what else he told me.

"But you're mad just the same," he says. It's not a question and I don't answer it. "Fine. I made arrangements for you to visit Bobbie in the Nassau County Jail. That is, if you want to. There'll be an officer present, but at least you'll be able to see she is all right."

I thank him because that's what polite people do, but I do it reluctantly. He warns me that I should not repeat anything he told me because it could endanger the investigation. When I don't seem impressed at that consequence he tells me the real reason—it could cost him his job.

At this point I have to ask myself, do I care?

CHAPTER 20

Design Tip of the Day

Vertical stripes make a room look taller. Spaced incorrectly, they can be very forbidding.
—From TipsfromTeddi.com

It should be a simple matter of posting bail. But because the money found in Bobbie's basement was foreign, the FBI is in on the case and they are refusing to release Bobbie. Frankly, I seem more concerned than she does.

"There's a handbag on eBay..." she tells me, as a matron eavesdrops on our conversation "...that I want. Just put in 'red and gold handbag' and it'll come up. The auction ends tomorrow and I have to get that bag. If you can't find it, just use my computer and my password. I bookmarked it before I left the house."

"Is this going to be your going-to-court-accused-of-murder-and-getting-acquitted purse?" I ask her. "Because otherwise I don't see how this could be of any particular importance." I am very cool to her, but she doesn't seem to notice.

"It's important," she tells me. "Just trust me." What is it with the rest of my world, that everyone just wants me to trust them on faith?

Then she wants to know how Bailey Manor is going. I tell her we have more important things to deal with, but she glances again at the matron and tells me she wants to talk about the showcase.

I tell her that I still haven't been able to get in touch with Helene.

"Her mother must be really sick for her to leave Gina in charge for more than a day and a half," Bobbie says. "Maybe she's dead."

"She *is* dead," I say, suddenly remembering how when I told Howard it was my mother he'd been e-screwing, he said his mother, *may she rest in peace*, would never have done something like that. "Would someone whose mother is dead use her as an excuse not to talk to someone? Is that allowed in the *Rules?*"

Bobbie says it's not, and she's the authority.

"So, then, where's Helene?" I ask.

Bobbie says she doesn't know, but that she's sure she'll turn up, and in the meantime she suggests I get busy on Bailey Manor. I ask if she's on drugs.

"I mean, Helene is missing, you're in jail, I slept with—" I look over my shoulder and the matron is definitely waiting for me to finish my sentence "—a *hunka-hunka*, and—"

"Oh, my God!" Bobbie shrieks. "You did? Was it rockets

and fireworks? Was it over the moon? Are you going to do it again?"

"Are you insane?" I ask her. "Are they feeding you crack in here, or what? It's over with *hunka*, and my primary concern at the moment is you, you idiot."

She looks at me like I'm the one who's on crack. "My lawyer's got it all under control. Truly. It is all under control. I'll be out of here in hours, and my life will go back to normal. Better than normal."

I ask what that is supposed to mean and she promises to explain after she is out.

"I promise to tell you all my deep dark secrets after I'm home, but only if you promise to stay out of the investigation."

I tell her the last thing I want to know are her deep dark secrets. She stares at me for a full minute, and then her mouth says, "Oh," but no sound comes out. I nod and she recovers herself.

"It could be dangerous and the police do not need your help, Teddi. My kids need your help. My husband needs your help. The police won't take care of them. Will you?"

I tell her that if the police think she's the one who killed Elise, they need my help more than her family and that I'm helping her family by trying to get her out of jail, but she is adamant.

"Look," she says. "You concentrate on Bailey Manor, and let the police do their job."

I tell her I don't think she's got a grasp on reality if she thinks that they are just going to let her walk.

"That's for me to worry about, not you," she says. "It was bad enough I let you go back into Elise's to get those stupid journals."

"They weren't so stupid, were they?" I ask.

She glances at the matron and tells me it's not something I have to worry about anymore.

Great. So now we all know she had a motive.

The matron apologetically tells me time is up. Personally, I think she's only sorry because she's been enjoying our conversation.

As I walk down the hall, Bobbie yells after me to feed her kids and not to forget about the handbag on eBay. Maybe it's her get-out-of-jail-before-dinner handbag. Or maybe there's something hidden in it, like a file.

Rio's car is in the driveway when I get home. There's no sign of him on the porch, so I go in and he's sitting in my living room, waiting.

"I knew you had another copy of Dana's key," I say, kicking myself because I didn't bother getting the locks changed with all that's been going on.

He says he knew I knew, so he figured that meant it was all right with me. Rio always reads what he wants into what people do. The truth is, I should have known better.

"So what are you doing here, anyway?" I ask him. He

can't claim he came to see the kids in the middle of a school day.

He tells me he can't find the old letters. I tell him to just let it go. "What about the old pictures?" he asks. "The ones we took with the Polaroid?"

Jeez. The things you do when you're young and in love and feeling safe. The things you write that you are sure no one else will read. The photos you take that no one else has to develop. You get the picture.

"I can't find them anywhere."

"Good." Maybe I destroyed them. My mind was mush back when I kicked Rio out—he'd seen to that. "They're gone. Now you go."

"Do you have any idea what they'd be worth?" he asks me. "Now that you're, you know, the 'Killer Decorator?'"

I tell him I have no idea what he means.

"*Playhouse Magazine* runs features like that all the time. Pictures of women in the news. In the nude in the news, if you get what I mean. They call it 'Women in the Newds,' I think. Like whistle stoppers—"

"Whistle *blowers*," I say.

"Even better," he says. With Rio it's full steam ahead. "So our angle is you're the 'Killer Decorator.' Get it? You decorate great and some of your clients get killed." He is actually smiling at me.

"You are out of your mind," I say.

"No," he says. "I pitched it to 'em. They're willing to pay twenty grand. That'd be ten for you and ten for me."

"Out!" I say, pointing to the door. I tell him not to say another word, just get out.

He shrugs. "Your loss," he says, but he goes too easily.

I order him to stop where he is and empty his pockets. Among gum wrappers and a few small bills is a Trojan foil. He smiles shyly. "You never know, Ted," he says. "I mighta got lucky."

I gesture for him to leave without saying a word, because when it comes to Rio Gallo, I'm at a loss for words.

After he's gone I drag myself into my office to turn on my computer. Apparently Rio's even looked in there because it's already on.

I type eBay into Mozilla and it comes up, but not without a pop-up ad. Who goes into someone else's computer without permission and changes the settings? They should take the *o* back from Rio Gallo's name and just leave it Gall.

Two more pop-ups appear before I can check the handbag, which, as Bobbie promised, comes up when I put in "red and gold handbag." It is definitely not Bobbie's usual style. Very Moroccan, very carpetbag-ish. Red and gold with jingly coins. Not at all what I expected. In fact, the handbags look a lot like Elise's bar stools. It's nearly three hundred dollars already, and I place her bid. I don't know how that woman knows what's hot and what's not. I wouldn't have thought it would bring more than twenty bucks. But then, I wouldn't think old nude pictures of me would be worth anything, either.

I decide I have to change the locks because I know Rio isn't going to give up the chance to get his hands on twenty thousand dollars. For just the smallest second I think what I could do with half of that. And then I smack myself because not only has that man got me thinking ridiculous thoughts, but he's got me splitting the take with him. Must be crossed wires because I don't know how the heck I'm going to pay the locksmith.

Which brings me to Bailey Manor and how I'm going to furnish that nook so that I can get some new clients and get rich. Or at least feed my kids and get the downstairs toilet repaired.

I've got to use a breakfast bar because the nook is too small for a table and chairs. I can fake the bar with a shelf and paper mache or plaster supports. I might even find something perfect at T.J.Maxx for that. And I can fancy up the shelf with *pique assiette*—those neat mosaics done with broken china and grout. That'll look great, and if anyone wants that, I can do it myself and charge a fortune with none of the money going to a middleman.

But the bar stools have to be strong enough for a prospective client to sit on. And there are no bar stools in my kitchen. And there are no bar stools in Bobbie's kitchen. And the only freakin' bar stools I can think of are in Jack

Meyers's kitchen, and he hates my guts and I'm not really looking forward to seeing him ever again.

Nonetheless, I call and tell him I can pick up the bar stools this afternoon.

He wants me to take back more than the bar stools and he wants a refund check. "Actually, make that cash."

I give him a song and dance about how custom work is not returnable but how under the circumstances I am making an exception. I tell him he'll have his money in thirty days. He tells me I can have the stools in thirty days, then. I tell him I don't want the stools in thirty days. I don't know where I get the nerve—when you don't have cash, it's handy to have guts—but I tell him to take it or leave it.

He tells me to be there in twenty minutes or the deal is off. I know I'm supposed to see him and raise him—tell him I'll be there in two hours—because this is about power and not about convenience, but I agree because I can't think of another place to get two bar stools before next week.

Jack takes his time answering the door. He's got on boxer shorts and a silk robe, open. The point he's making (pardon the pun) is that he isn't going anywhere and he's made me rush for nothing. He motions me in and closes the door behind me.

"Pretty brave of you, coming alone," he says. "Considering that you think I'm a murderer."

He has a good point and I do feel like I'm one of those too-stupid-to-live heroines. I tell him that the police know where I am. It occurs to me that too-stupid-to-live heroines always say that. It must occur to Jack, too, because he laughs.

"You think I'm kidding?" I say, gesturing toward the sidelights while bile rises in my throat.

We both look out the window and stare as a blue sedan with tinted windows pulls up to the curb and cuts the engine. Now, truthfully, it could be the Mafia. It could be two Jehovah's Witnesses getting ready to canvas the neighborhood. It could be the Orange Juice Queen herself, but from the look on Jack's face, he believes it's the police, and that's good enough for me. At least I can swallow again.

I tell him I can fit only the bar stools in my van and I march off toward the kitchen, hoping to get him away from the window before the occupants of the car turn out to be two old ladies in jogging suits.

Luckily, he follows me, and I suggest he close his robe as he does. He swaggers, ignoring me, and I'm sure that he was the kind of kid who said "make me" at every opportunity. I go straight for the stools, and Jack goes straight for me, coming up behind me and pushing me against the counter. There's nothing sexual about it. It's all about power as he hisses against my ear that whatever I know I'd better keep to myself.

"There's a cop in your backyard," I say, and I sound remarkably calm for someone who can't breathe and is convinced the end is near.

"Right," he says. But he bothers to look up, easing his

hold just enough for me to turn in his arms and raise my knee to his groin at the same moment we hear a knock at the French doors.

Jack moans as he crouches on the floor and a familiar voice shouts, "Police." I forget for a second that I hate the voice and its owner. A face I don't know appears in the window above the sink. Drew yells, "Open up."

I tell Jack, "I'll get it" and leap to let in Drew and the other plainclothes detective. Drew looks at Jack, appears amused, and asks his partner if he wasn't right about me. Then he asks if everything is all right.

I tell him it's dandy. That I am just picking up some bar stools Jack wishes to return, and though it isn't my policy to take returns on custom furniture, I am accommodating him.

Drew and his partner exchange a look that speaks volumes. It says, and not in any particular order:

I told her not to come near Jack Meyers, so what is the first thing she does?

Jack Meyers has something on her and that's why she's taking the stools back.

If, as she says, she's doing him a favor, why is Jack Meyers on the floor holding his privates?

"You all right, sir?" the partner asks Jack while Drew slips out the French doors, apparently to make a phone call. Jack kvetches about how I've assaulted him, but the detective merely sympathizes and doesn't bother responding to Jack's latest demand that I be arrested.

When Drew comes back in, he is visibly annoyed. Begrudgingly, he offers me a hand getting the stools out to my van.

My look says Costco will go out of business before I accept his help. He reads the look, shrugs, and leans against the wall while I try to carry both stools out of the kitchen and down the front hall. I picture the three men shaking their heads and saying, "Women!" but the kitchen is quiet except for the occasional moan from Jack.

I am still trying to get the bar stools in the van when Drew and his partner leave Jack's house. His partner veers toward my van, but Drew reminds him that I don't want help. "Knock yourself out," he shouts my way.

They wait by their car watching while I try to get the stools into my van like shoes in a box, and once I slide the side door closed and climb into the driver's seat, they take off.

As I turn to back up, I notice the shoddy job of stitching that was done on the seat nearest me, especially considering the price of the chairs. The thread doesn't even match. I get out of the car, go around and open the trunk to get a better look at the other seat. It's like two different workers did the jobs, which I suppose is possible.

Still, I don't remember noticing a difference when I delivered the stools, and those sorts of things are what I get paid for. And so, instead of heading straight for Bailey Manor, I run home, hoping that Rio Gallo's car won't be in my driveway when I get there.

Rio's not there, my computer's not on, nothing appears

amiss. Unless you count the fact that my hands are visibly shaking as I approach my keyboard. I tell myself I'm fine, that Jack Meyers didn't actually hurt me. In fact, I did more harm to him than the other way around. But I can't stop shaking and feeling that sleazy man in his silky robe pressing against my back.

Did he have an erection?

"Yech!" I say, brushing myself like I have cooties—Meyers cooties, I think, and my scalp begins to itch. I can feel bugs on my arms, bugs on my back where I can't reach and I'm doing that St. Vitus' dance thing in my office and all the way down my hall and up the stairs and into my bedroom, where I am already taking off all my clothes and heading for the shower.

I think about Rio walking in, promise myself that I will have the locks changed this very afternoon and jump into the shower. I could kill Rio for making even my own shower feel unsafe. I rub the steam from the glass doors and peer at my bathroom looking for signs that Rio has been here. Did I leave that extra bottle of Lavoris on the counter, or on top of the medicine chest where it is now? Did I stack the extra toilet paper two high, or one next to the other. Have I completely lost my mind or am I still in the process of losing it?

Having washed Jack Meyers's cooties from my hair, steamed them off my back and dislodged them from my psyche, I put on a robe and head for my computer, which comes to life with yet another pop-up ad, this one not for penis enhancement but for those little mini–nanny cams. I'd kill Rio for changing my settings if it didn't mean I'd have to see him again to do it. I wonder if Elise's hit man might be interested in another job.

And then I remember that the so-called hit man was really a cop, which brings Drew to mind and complete humiliation washes over me.

Self-pity, like the broken downstairs toilet, is a luxury I can't afford right now. I am on a mission, and I refuse to be distracted by my own problems when Bobbie's are greater than mine. I call up the pictures Elise took of her kitchen the night before she was killed and I enlarge them as much as I can. I pan the seat of one stool and then the other. They are identical, down to the matching threads.

CHAPTER 21

Design Tip of the Day

Sometimes life is crazy. This is one of those days. I promise to get a new tip up very soon. Please keep checking back.

—From TipsfromTeddi.com

In the morning, as soon as the kids are off to school and I think it'll be open, I call Precious Things, because I have a terrible suspicion that Helene isn't avoiding me at all. The Helene I know and love would have called and given me an earful. She'd have called my mother and given her an earful, too.

Gina answers the phone. She tells me she was just about to call me because she's just got off with Helene, who says it's fine to lend me a couple of pieces. I ask if there's a number I can reach Helene at and Gina says I should just try her on her cell phone, but that since she's at the hospital a lot, it's usually turned off.

And then she says she's got a customer and has to run and I'm left holding the phone and listening to a dial tone.

I don't know Howard's phone number, and I don't really want to actually talk to him, so I give in and call my mother for my JDate log-in and password.

"I knew you'd come around," she says. I tell her I just need to reach her e-lover. "Have you been reading his columns?"

I have to admit that it never occurred to me to read them, especially now that I was not going to get to go to any of the restaurants he'd be reviewing. But I probably could have got his e-mail address at *Newsday* and avoided having this conversation altogether.

"He sounds depressed," my mother says.

I tell her I'm sorry to hear that and could she just tell me my log-in and password as long as I've got her on the phone.

"Listen to this morning's column," she says, and I can hear her rustling the newspaper. She ignores the fact that I'm in a rush. "All is not what it seems at this pretentious little hideaway. Promises are broken, from the lack of certain items listed on the menu to switches and substitutions made without—"

"I get it, Mom," I say.

"He doesn't answer my e-mails," she tells me. "Your father says it's for the best, like he knows anything about these situations. You don't think your father is doing porn over the Net, do you?"

I admit it's not the sort of thing I think about. I tell her that since Howard isn't answering her e-mails at home, I'd be better off writing to him at *Newsday*. She says he doesn't answer the ones she sends there, either.

"They have *your* name attached to them as the sender," I tell her. "No matter how you sign them." She pretends she doesn't know what I mean.

"Well, tell him for me that I miss corresponding with him, and if he wants to get in touch with me he can reach me at my optimum online address."

"Mother, I am not telling him any such thing." Amazingly she replies that I didn't want him, anyway. "So who's it hurting?"

I tell her it hurt Howard. I hear her blow her cigarette smoke. "I thought you were giving up smoking because it would ruin your face lift."

"Face lifts arc easier on me than tummy tucks," she says, meaning that if she gives up smoking she'll replace it with eating.

"A few extra pounds are easier than cancer," I tell her.

She's silent for a moment while she takes another drag on her cigarette. "I wonder how much a lung weighs," she says before I hang up.

On the *Newsday* site I find Howard's e-mail address and send him a quick note asking if he's been in touch with Helene and telling him I'm concerned about her. Then I call the precinct and leave a message for Drew about how something is up with the bar stools that I think he ought to know about.

I tweak my site, throw in two loads of laundry, clean Alyssa's room, close Dana and Jesse's doors and finally post that Tip From Teddi I've been promising. I find half a roll of refrigerator cookies that we haven't yet consumed raw and slice them up and throw them in the oven.

When the kids walk in the door they are greeted with the aroma of freshly baked cookies and I hate myself for not doing this more often. Ronnie Benjamin would wonder aloud why I couldn't simply take pride in the fact that today I baked the children cookies.

Not that I consider slicing and throwing a few morsels on a sheet *baking*.

Since there is, in fact, no food fairy, I offer waffles to the kids for dinner and they balk at the idea of having breakfast for dinner. I tell them they need to be more flexible, throw in ice cream and whipped cream and they pretend they are doing me a favor.

As always, life is full of compromise.

After dinner I'm too fidgety to sit around at home, so I walk Maggie May, read Alyssa two stories and finally head for Bailey Manor. This close to the show, decorators must be working overtime to get ready and I'm sure I'll be able to get in.

Halfway there I get this creepy feeling that someone is following me, and I spend as much time looking in my rearview mirror as looking in front of me. At a light I punch Drew's number into my phone, figuring that way in an emergency I can just hit Send.

I make the left off the Turnpike and a Jeep two cars behind me does, as well. I make a right into a neighborhood, my eyes on the rearview mirror. The Jeep turns right behind me. By now, my heart is beating so hard it's interfering with my breathing. I turn up the AC and make a left. The Jeep makes that turn, too. Then it swerves around me and pulls into a driveway and a bunch of teenagers pile out of the car, laughing, singing, one of them shushing the others as they make their way up the walk.

I pull to the curb, put the car in Park, lay my head against the steering wheel and wait for my breathing to slow.

Now that was an overreaction, I tell myself.

When I'm calm enough to put the car into Drive again, I find my way out of the neighborhood and head for Bailey Manor. Only this time I refuse to let my eyes stray to the rearview mirror or my mind to murder and mayhem.

It seems as if all the decorators are gone for the night, but a few lights are still on. I drag one of the bar stools out of my van and carry it to the front entrance. A sign there says to go to the back doors after hours.

"Great," I mumble as I try to make my way around the Manor carrying a heavy Moroccan chair while my heels sink into soft ground I can't see. Bushes look like crouching stalkers. Shadows fall ominously from the lights on inside. I feel as if I am trapped in that Edward Gorey graphic that introduces public television's *Masterpiece Theater*.

I am reminded that my father didn't want me to become

an interior decorator, at least not a private one. "Going into stranger's houses," he'd said and shuddered. "Come work for me."

At this very moment it doesn't seem like that was such a bad idea. I'd have had a steady paycheck, could have made my own hours and I wouldn't be limping around a dark manor trying to find an open door.

Of course, I wouldn't be. I'd be in South Winds, regretting any more ties to my parents than are already strangling me.

The door is propped open with a two-by-four and I push my way in, happy to be able to put the stool down for a moment. "Hello?" I call out weakly, but no one answers.

I try to convince myself that I am just imagining things—ironic since only a year ago everyone else was convinced I was imagining things and I was fighting to prove I was not—but as a light goes off behind me, it's not easy.

I call out again, but still no one replies. Standing still I hear complete silence. I decide that this a very bad idea. Of course, if I leave now I've got to carry the stool back to the car with a bladder overflowing with fear.

The breakfast nook is just down the hall, the bathroom just a few steps beyond it. Throwing my shoulders back I stalk off, my heels clicking loudly on the stone floor, echoing as I go.

My breakfast nook looks good. The window painting was a great idea. Even at night it has the power to put the viewer on the beach. I will get some dishes that complement the bar stools at the Marshall's Megastore tomorrow and work on the *pique assiette* in the afternoon. That way I can be home when Bobbie gets back. *If* Bobbie gets back.

"Looks wonderful," a woman's voice says, and I jump only about five feet off the ground. She apologizes for scaring me. "Spooky here at night," she says. She's been putting finishing touches on one of the upstairs bedrooms. I'm afraid to ask her which one.

She asks if I want her to wait for me. I tell her I have one more chair to bring in and she looks at her watch. "I'll be fine," I say and she seems relieved.

"I've got to get home and sew sequins on some pillow slips," she says as she waves goodbye and saunters down the hall.

"You could have brought the other chair in tomorrow," I tell myself aloud. "You didn't have to play the big brave Bozo." With that, a door slams somewhere and I hurry to the bathroom with the idea that I'll just go and then head for home.

I'm fumbling with my jeans when I hear a little click and the doorknob rattles. "Out in a minute," I yell. No *okay*. No *take your time*. "Anyone out there?" No nothing.

As I reach for the door handle, the light goes out.

"Hey!" I yell. The door handle refuses to give. "I'm in here!"

I notice there is no light seeping in from under the door, either. I tell myself not to panic. I've got a spanking new cell phone with me and the door must simply be stuck. I feel around the floor for my handbag, praying the Manor isn't home to any small, furry creatures. I find it, dig around in it and find my father's phone. The screen reads 9:01. I figure the lights automatically go off at nine, which is a small comfort because it means I am alone here. Which wouldn't be particularly reassuring, except that the alternative—that someone turned off the lights, locked me in and is planning how to do away with me now that they have me, is worse.

I shine the phone light toward the door and try the handle again. It has no intention of giving. There are a limited number of people I could call in a situation like this. Rio, of course, could break in and get me out, but then he'd figure I "owe him," and I know what he wants. Mike has his hands full trying to get Bobbie out of jail and keep their kids and her mother calm. There's Bobbie's sister, Diane, but she's on duty tonight and if I call her, there's no way that Drew won't find out. And there's Drew, who I will not put in the position of knight in shining armor coming to rescue the damsel in distress.

There's my father, who could never leave the house without telling my mother, who would somehow, believe me, make things worse.

I dig in my purse and find the stylus to my BlackBerry. Using the phone light to find the key hole I try pushing the stylus in and wiggling it around. I learn I have no future as a burglar. I dig farther. There is the metal nail file Jesse gave me as a birthday present last year along with a CD he wanted for himself and asked if he could copy as soon as I opened it. Can it file through a bolt?

Ten minutes later I'd have to say *no* to that.

I resort to kicking the door until my foot hurts. It's dark. The bathroom is small. I'm quickly using up all the bravery I've got.

I clutch the phone for a few minutes—maybe less—okay, much less, and see that I only have one line left on my battery. I give in and punch Send. Drew picks up after only one ring.

"I am locked in a bathroom at Bailey Manor. All the lights are out. Everyone is gone." I am holding on to my self-control by a hair. And then I hear a shuffling on the other side of the door. My first instinct is to call out, but, whoever it is, they are moving something in the dark. I whisper into the phone that I may not be alone.

"Listen to me," Drew says. I hear him moving about. "Do not make a sound. Not a peep. Can you turn the ringer off your phone without turning it off?"

I nod, but of course he can't see me. "Yes," I whisper.

"I am coming," he says. I am praying I live to hear those words from him in a more exciting place, like maybe his bed. In my fantasy I get up and leave just before he does. Come, that is. I might change that if he gets me out of here alive. "Don't panic, and for God's sake, Teddi, don't do anything stupid."

Then again, maybe I won't change the fantasy.

He hangs up and I sit crouched, my ear pressed against the door. There isn't a single sound and I have to guess that the rustling I heard was just a raccoon on the roof. Of course, I'm on the ground floor and there are a couple of floors above me…I almost jump out of my skin when the phone vibrates in my hand. The caller ID says it's *Newsday* calling.

"This better not be about getting a subscription," I hiss into the phone.

A masculine laugh tickles my ear. "Catch you at a bad time?" Howard asks.

"Not if you want to take down my last words," I whisper.

"Depends what they are," he answers, and I tell him I'm not kidding, that I'm at Bailey Manor and someone might be trying to kill me. I tell him the police are coming but that hearing a voice in the dark is helping.

"Just please talk to me," I whisper.

His voice shakes while he talks. He tells me that he'll call me from his cell phone and talk to me as he drives over. I tell him not to hang up. He says he can't just sit in his office and wait for the police to go save me. I beg him not to hang up. He says if anything happens to me he'll never forgive himself. I ask about Helene.

He tells me he got my message about her, but he hasn't talked to her in several days. He also says that isn't unusual.

"Have you spoken to her since our last date?" I ask. At least Howard doesn't keep saying every dinner we have together isn't a date. He says he hasn't. "Don't you think it's odd that she didn't follow up with either of us?"

He doesn't answer.

"Howard?" The light on my phone goes dead.

It is really, really dark, and I am really, really frightened.

I keep thinking about my children and how I wouldn't want Rio or my parents to raise them. I have a brother in the Caribbean I've seen once in twenty years, and I know that Dana could be a beach bum in an hour. And all that incredible potential I see in her would be lost.

In the dark, huddled against the bathroom door, I don't bite my nails, don't clasp my hands in prayer. I am, quite honestly, paralyzed with fear.

I should have listened to Drew, to Mike, to Diane and Bobbie and just stayed out of it. I should not have risked my children's mother…

Just as I am about to make promises to the gods, I hear footsteps in the hall and the lights come back on.

I bang on the door and Drew opens it. "Did I not tell you not to make a sound?"

I point out that his sentence contains a double negative. He points out that they can put Good Grammarian on my tombstone.

Drew harps on how he hopes I've now learned my lesson and will stay out of the investigation. Safe in the light with my handsome-but-irritable detective I am bold enough to ask how bringing my stuff over to Bailey Manor has anything to do with his investigation and he merely humphs angrily at me. Humphs, but walks really close to me, hand on my elbow sort of thing and mumbles about how dark it is and how I have to be careful because he wouldn't want to have to carry me if I were to fall.

Doesn't, on the face of it, sound that bad to me.

His low, sexy sports car is parked behind my requisite suburban-mother van, and at a click of his key chain one of his headlights comes on and illuminates our way. I don't ask about why the other one doesn't pop up. I know why. He walks me to my van, waits while I get in, get buckled up, plug in my dead phone, get the motor started and turn my headlights on.

"I'll follow you," he says, and because I'm smart enough to be frightened, I say thank you.

I navigate the narrow, winding streets of Lattingtown, which were so pretty in the daytime but that now at night are very spooky, especially this close to Halloween, when bare tree branches cast long shadows beneath an overbright moon. And I try to figure out who could have hacked my BlackBerry. According to the synch log, I'm looking for Peanuts. I come up with two possibilities. Jack Meyers, with his "Take Me Out to the Ball Game," buy-me-some-peanuts ringer, or Gina, who has the Peanuts collection on her desk.

At my house Drew walks me to my door and waits for me to hand him my key. Before he can insert it in the lock, Jesse opens the door.

"Your boyfriend called," he tells me, and he gives Drew a *so there* smile.

I assume that he means Howard, and I realize I left him hanging half an hour ago.

"He said if he didn't hear from you in twenty minutes he was going to drive to Bailey Manor and rescue you."

"Backup plan?" Drew asks.

"Whatever," Jesse says with a shrug as Howard's repaired Mercedes pulls up at the curb. "You're gonna have to start giving out numbers, Mom, like at the bakery."

I tell Jesse to go to bed, and Drew and I watch Howard approach. The men acknowledge each other with a nod. Howard says something to the effect of "You again." I tell both of them my suspicions about who hacked my BlackBerry to no avail, and then Howard reports that he called his sister and got a timely message.

"You mean like, 'Hello, this is Helene and I am out of the office today, Tuesday, October 25th. Please leave me a message'?"

He beams at me, until I tell him it's an automated system. She could be anywhere, in any condition and that message would still be playing, *will* still be playing, until she turns it off.

"If we just put our heads together," I start to say, but Drew cuts me off.

"Sure, and while we're at it, let's trade cards to see if it's Colonel Mustard in the drawing room," he says. He glares at me. "I really thought that finding yourself locked in the dark bathroom at Bailey Manor would scare some sense into you, but I should have known better. I should have handcuffed you to the bedpost."

I turn three shades of red, Howard looks shocked, and Drew just looks smug.

"One woman is dead and another one is missing," I tell them, "and you two are—I don't know what you're doing."

Drew asks for the particulars regarding Helene, which unnerves Howard. I suppose learning your mother is near death after she's already died can do that. At any rate, Drew agrees to check out Helene's apartment and, at my suggestion, the phone records at Precious Things to see if Gina is really getting any calls from Helene, as she says.

And after Howard takes off, Drew tells me yet again that the police will look into it and that I should stay out of it. I ask him just when they are going to release Bobbie, trying to make it a quid pro quo, but he tells me it's out of his hands. I give him a look that says staying out of it is out of mine.

"Look, if your friend isn't involved, then the Department will clear her. We haven't closed the investigation, and we won't until every piece of the puzzle fits."

I tell him I'm handing him pieces of the puzzle and he's flushing them down the toilet.

He looks at his watch. "It's late and I'm tired and one of us is going to say something we'll regret. So I want your promise that you will just stay the hell out of it. Or I swear I'll have you arrested for your own safety. I've got better things to do than go rescuing you from locked latrines in the middle of the night."

I ask him whether or not he intends to investigate

Helene's disappearance. He has the nerve to tell me she is not officially missing.

"You are the only one who seems to think she's gone," he says. "But yes, I will, on one condition."

"That I stay out of it," I say.

He has the nerve to tweak my nose and say "Good girl," and if I didn't want to just get rid of him, I think I'd answer "*Arf.*" Or maybe I'd bite him. That has even more appeal.

I go up to check on the kids and find Jesse and Dana in Alyssa's room, surrounded by a pile of clothes.

"You should be asleep," I tell Alyssa before glaring at my two big ones. "What's going on?" Alyssa turns a tearful face my way.

"You promised I could go as Barbie," Alyssa says. I have no memory of this, but it sounds plausible. And Alyssa has a long memory. I could have made that promise last Halloween when she hated her pussycat costume. In fact, I do have a vague memory of saying that next year she could be a princess, or Barbie, or whatever she wanted.

"They're out of Barbie costumes at CVS," Dana tells me. "I went this afternoon."

I guess I don't hide my surprise because she sarcastically assures me that she can be nice when she wants to be. "And *someone* has to take care of Lys."

"It was nice of you to do that," I say. Not so nice to throw it in my face, but hey, from a twelve-year-old I'll take any niceness I can get.

"Barbie has a long blond ponytail," Alyssa tells me. My

three children and the dog all look at me like I've failed them by not having blond hair and passing it on to them.

I tell her that I have a long dark ponytail she can wear and get a grudging "Okay."

I head for my bathroom, trying to remember where the heck I put that clip-on pony I bought last year when my hair was going through that awkward stage between chin-length and long. Or maybe it was after the perm when I was pulling it back tightly and trying to hide it. My hair has had so many awkward stages.

The hairpiece is in a yellow and white striped box, waiting on top of the mirrored cabinet. I open the box and pull out the hairpiece, which is tangled on something. I untangle it and look at the small plastic box in my hand, trying to figure out what it is and what it is doing in with my ponytail.

It looks familiar. I've seen something like it recently. On the computer?

I realize what it is. I examine the yellow and white box and find a hole in the corner, but refuse to believe what is right before my eyes. *How much good did denial do you last year, Teddi?* I ask myself as I stare at the nanny cam/hidden camera thingy in my hand.

Alyssa comes into the bathroom and I find myself hiding my hands behind my back so she doesn't see what her father's done now. "Mommy?" she says, staring up at me with her big dark eyes. "Could I go as a princess instead of Barbie? A princess can have brown hair."

I assure her she will be the most beautiful princess on all of Long Island. Maybe in the whole world. With Halloween three days away, I promise she will have a gorgeous gown and a fake fur cape to wear over it in case it's cold, which it always is on Halloween.

Then I pull the "It's late" routine and send her to bed to dream about her beautiful gown, and I reach for the phone.

CHAPTER 22

Tip of the Day

Every house should reflect its owners' personality. Keep a sense of humor and lightheartedness about your decorating and watch people smile when then enter your home.

—From TipsfromTeddi.com

"**Is** this some kind of torture?" Drew asks me when I let him in and we stand in the hall. "Sleep deprivation? It seems to me every time I kick off my shoes and lie down—"

I see his blue and cranberry comforter and I don't want to go there. His tirade winds down when I don't bite.

"So what's the emergency this time?"

I put out my hand and open it, revealing the hidden camera. "I found it on the shelf in my bathroom."

He makes a face that shouts *kinky*. "Any idea how it got there?"

"I know how, I know who, I know why," I say. I just don't know what to do about it. He waits for me to elaborate and

I tell him how Rio wants to sell pictures of me to some nudie magazine and how he had duplicates of Dana's key and was in my house alone.

"Is this the only one?" he asks, taking the device from me. I realize they could be everywhere—in my bedroom, my office. He reads my face and gestures toward the stairs. At my nod, he takes them two at a time and heads for my bedroom.

"Mom, I need—" Dana starts, poking her head out her door and stopping midsentence when she sees a man preceding me into my bedroom. When she recognizes who it is, her eyes widen and she emits a little gasp.

"I think we had an intruder," I tell her and her look changes to contempt.

"Yeah," she says, eyeing the doorway where Drew has disappeared. "I saw."

I want her to know that nothing is going on between Drew and me, but I'm not going to invite her to join us in my bedroom while a policeman searches for another mini camera and theorizes about who put it there. I tell her that we'll talk about it in the morning and make it clear that the door to my bedroom is open and if she needs me, she can come in. "Without knocking," I add.

"There was really a burglar?" she asks, her arms wrapped around her middle.

I repeat that it was an intruder, not a robber, and that I might be mistaken. I add that it might have just been her dad looking for something. I don't say that "something" was trouble.

Reluctantly, she withdraws to her room, no doubt to call Kimmie and report on the latest drama in the never-ending soap opera we call life on Gregory Lane. And I stand in the doorway to my bedroom watching Drew Scoones search for hidden cameras while attempting to respect my privacy.

"Anything in here look new?" he asks as he looks around my room. "New clock radio? New clock? New VCR?"

He sits on the edge of my bed as he inspects my bedside lamp.

"New air freshener? New purifier? New bottles of perfume?" He goes over to my dresser and removes the top to my Kenzo Flowers, sprays it into the air, takes a whiff and smiles.

I examine all the items he's mentioned and admit that I can't swear the VCR is the same one we've always had. "This one could have been Dana's and we switched, or when we got a new one for the den I might have moved this one up from there or...I don't know." Now I take a seat on the edge of my bed.

"Where do you usually get undressed?" he asks, and I feel my cheeks redden. "He'd aim a camera where he expects you to disrobe," he explains.

I don't know where I get naked. In the bathroom if I'm going into the shower, by the dresser if I'm getting into my pajamas, by the closet if I'm getting dressed.

Drew stands by the closet and imitates a woman deciding what to wear and looks up.

"Bingo," he says, looking first at one corner of the room and then another. "Two motion detectors."

I look where he is pointing. To the best of my memory, which isn't all that great, I think the one across from the closet is new.

"Can I use your phone?" he asks as he lifts the receiver. I ask who he is calling. "The precinct. We'll need to issue a warrant for his arrest and—"

I break the connection with my finger on the phone's plunger.

"What?" he asks, looking blankly at me.

I tell him I don't want to have my ex-husband arrested. I just want to stop him from selling any of the pictures.

Drew folds his arms over his chest, leans against the wall and runs his tongue against the inside of his cheek. He stares at me and doesn't say a word.

"He's my children's father," I explain.

He still doesn't speak.

"I can't send their father to prison."

He pushes himself off the wall. "Good night, then," he says, and starts to head down the hall.

I hurry after him. "Aren't you going to do anything?"

He turns and glares at me. "What exactly would you like me to do?"

I blow out a deep, heartsick breath. "Scare him? Threaten him? Make sure you get the negatives?"

"I'm not a thug," he says, and his anger is so close to the surface I can feel it from ten feet away. "I'm a cop. I investigate crimes, and when they've been committed I seek warrants and make arrests. It's what I do. Take it or leave it."

"Look," I say, trying to be reasonable. "I'm a decorator. I go into a horrible room and I say we should gut it and start fresh. My client says she can't afford to do that, can't I just rearrange the furniture? I say that won't quite do it—how about we paint the walls and get new carpeting? She says she can afford to paint one wall and get an area rug. I say it won't be terrific, but it'll be better.

"See? Compromise."

"Okay," he says. "I say we execute him. You say we slap his wrist. I say that won't stop him from doing this again. Or from doing something worse—he needs to be arrested. You say no, he's really not a bad man. I stalk out of here. Guess compromise doesn't work in this case."

"He *isn't* a bad man," I say. "He's a conniver. He always thinks he can beat the system. But he isn't clever enough to do that."

He shakes his head at me. "Oh, isn't he? He seems to be smart enough to con you. But maybe you want to be conned. Is that it?"

Dana's head comes out her door again. "Are you talking about Daddy? Is that who you think was here?"

I stare at Drew, daring him to tell this child in her pink *Polar Bear Express* nightshirt that he wants to arrest her father. He opens his mouth but I jump in.

"He may have been, and you know he isn't supposed to be here when no one is home. I think he might need to be reminded, that's all."

"By the police?" she asks and her lip is trembling just a little.

"Apparently not," Drew says, and I say I'll be back to talk to her in a minute, that I just want to see "the officer" out.

At the front door we both turn and look at Dana, who is watching us. Drew gestures with his head that I should follow him outside. I step out onto the porch and the air is cold enough to turn our breath to clouds.

"What?" I ask him.

"You called me, lady. Again. It's getting a little tiresome, don't you think?"

I rub my arms against the cold, but Drew doesn't seem to notice. He's got his mad to keep him warm.

He waits to have my full attention, until my eyes are meeting his. Then, quite simply, he says, "The man you married is scum, Ms. Bayer, and you just don't want to admit that you made a big mistake, so you keep compounding it by making more mistakes." His voice is even and calm, but his look challenges me.

"Rio is not the issue," I say, trying to match my voice to his, to be full of resolute certainty instead of admitting fear and doubt. "The kids are what's important. Always have been, always will be. I have to do what's right for them, and having a convicted felon for a father is only going to pour salt into their gaping wounds."

"So it's all about the kids," he says, like he doesn't believe it. "Then I suggest you check that one's room for cameras, too." He gestures with his head toward the house, where Dana waits for me.

My hand goes up to slap him. It's a reflex action. He catches my wrist.

His reflexes are as good as mine.

"Next time you want to spin someone's wheels," he says, "don't call me."

In the morning I get the kids off with more hugs and kisses than usual because I feel like I've been rotten and neglectful even if it isn't my fault. And because I need the hugs myself.

Then I head for the computer to see why Drew would ask about Jack Meyers collecting coins. I'm the kind of person who can't resist a puzzle, and I try to see what pieces I have left. I know someone with the alias Peanuts hacked into my BlackBerry. But I don't know where that piece fits.

And then it hits me. I open up eBay and click on Advanced Search. Then I run a Search By Seller and enter Peanuts as the seller's user ID. A dozen variations come up and I check each one. The next-to-last one yields pay dirt. Antique coins, and from Iraq, no less.

But I still don't know how the bar stools fit in. Unless...and suddenly the hasty stitching on the bar stool makes sense. The coins came into the country in the seat pads. Coins and tapestry—I'm reminded of Bobbie's eBay handbag and feel like an idiot for not putting it together sooner. She could have been a little less cryptic, actually.

Anyway, Helene must have been supposed to take the coins out of the bar stools before delivering them. But then why give them to me before she'd removed them? Unless...

And then it all becomes clear.

My first inclination is to call Drew, but I know what he'll say. *Someone is selling coins on eBay and you think that has anything to do with this case?* And that's a best-case scenario. He could say a lot worse. I know what he thinks of my judgment.

So I'm going it alone, because someone has to exonerate Bobbie, and it looks like it's going to be me.

I consider bringing a weapon, but I'm so terrified that it could be used against me that the best I can come up with is a spoon. As I stand at my silverware drawer, I picture Drew Scoones kneeling over my dead body (shot full of holes) and finding the spoon clutched in my hand. Grieved as he is, sorry that he didn't take me seriously, ashamed of not being able to protect me, he'd still smirk at the sight of this spoon.

I put it back in the drawer, scrawl a note to my kids that says I love them, that they should do their homework and that it isn't only at Halloween that they are royalty to me.

I figure, on the off-chance that I don't get killed, they'll just chalk it up to their sentimental mother and toss it in the garbage. Which, if I'm not dead, is fine with me.

I grab my purse and head for Precious Things. When I get there, the Back In Ten Minutes sign is on the door. But I can see Gina and I tap on the glass. She looks up, sees me and tips over the candelabra on the counter. She sets it right before coming to open the door a crack.

"It's not a good time," she says, but lets me in anyway. She locks the door behind me, which I take to be a bad, bad sign. But not as bad as when the office door opens and a very big, very nasty looking man comes out and tells Gina she'd better look again.

"While you're looking for whatever it is he wants—" I say, gesturing toward the mountain behind her as though this is the most normal situation in the world "—could you check on the Pinsky order for me? I think it was supposed to be in a few days ago."

"It's not here, Teddi," Gina says, and I see the flash of recognition in the man's eyes at my name.

"I'm sure it was due in earlier this week," I say. "I have the order in here." I rummage in my bag until I find my father's video phone, hit and hold in the nine button, which goes directly to Drew's work phone, and then take it out with a sheaf of papers so that this guy won't notice it. I put some of the papers on the shelf behind me, drop a few on the floor, take out my wallet and pretend to look for the nonexistent receipt. And I start talking loudly so that if Drew says "Hello," Big Foot over there won't hear him.

"I'm sure I have the receipt here somewhere," I say.

"You're the broad who took my stools, aren't you?" he says.

I play dumb, loudly, because, let's face it, I am dumb. Maybe too dumb to live, I'm thinking. But I'm thinking about Alyssa and how she wants to be a princess and how I don't want to let her down. "This order isn't for stools," I say. "It's a gorgeous tablecloth. The kind you can only get at Precious Things on Jericho Turnpike. We did it in the same fabric as the pillows for the couch, but not the same as the couch fabric…"

I blather on, backing up toward the door. The man shakes his head at me and gives me an evil smile. "Screw me once, shame on you. Screw me twice, and I'll screw you."

I smile back, blankly.

Gina says the mixup wasn't my fault, but Helene's.

I say that if the Pinsky stuff isn't in, I'll just come back tomorrow. In two steps the man is between me and the door.

"I'm telling you, Helene is the one who screwed up," Gina says again.

"Well, she's about to pay for that, isn't she?" the man says.

"Clearly I have walked in on something that is none of my business," I say, stuffing things back into my purse, things that don't even belong to me. "I'll just take this up with Helene some other time…"

"You talk too much," the man says. I tell him that there

are many people who would agree with him. "There was a detective in my house last night," I say, and Gina and the man exchange a look that makes me think bringing up Drew was not such a good idea. "My ex-husband had these nanny cams…"

Another bad idea. The big man grabs my oversized purse and suddenly it looks puny. He dumps it on the counter.

"He wanted to get nude pictures of me," I explain. "Like people would pay to see me nude…"

The big man looks at me as though he can imagine that. As though he is imagining that. He licks the side of his mouth.

"I called the police about the nanny-cams." I babble some more about my children and not wanting to press charges because sometimes people make mistakes and they ought to be forgiven. "And I'm a very forgiving person. And forgetful, too. I forget a lot. Remember last summer, Gina?"

I am hoping she will tell the guy I'm nuts and just to let me go.

"I actually don't really remember it all that well," I say.

The big guy is going through the things in my purse. "Where's your phone?" he asks.

"See?" I say. "Forgot it. I forget everything. I have three children—darling, sweet kids—and I forget their names all the time." I repeat that I can just come back when Helene's around.

"Helene's not gonna be around," the man says. "Not much longer, anyway."

"You mean 'not for a while,'" I say. "Well, no rush on this. I can come back next week, or next month, or—"

"She's not coming back," he says. "So shut up."

I can't. It's like if I keep talking I'll talk my way out of this. If I keep talking I can't be, you know, the *D* word. "Has she sold the shop? That would be a shame. This shop, here on Jericho Turnpike has such unusual merchandise. I'll miss her—"

"You're gonna see her very soon," the man says. This does not sound like a good thing. He points a big, fat, scary finger at my face and adds, "Three women, and it's all on your head."

"I'm sorry?" I say. "I'm not really following." Spell it out, I think. Spell it all out for the videotape.

He pulls a gun out from behind his back and I figure he had it tucked into his waistband the way waiters put those check folders back there. If I live, I think my heart will race like crazy the next time a waiter reaches behind him to give me my check.

"I told Danny he never shoulda trusted a broad to pull this off." Bigfoot sneers at Gina and I think that this guy could have a career in Steven Seagal movies. Too bad I won't be around to see them.

"It wasn't my fault," Gina says. "She's the one who picked the stools up before I could get the coins out of them."

"Shut up," the man says.

"Don't tell me to shut up," Gina tells him. "You're the

one that Danny shouldn't have trusted. We had it all under control. He got the job guarding the museum. He stole the coins and I gave him the name of the furniture maker who was sending us the stool order. Danny made the contact, paid the guy to sew in the coins and ship the stools.

"It was all perfect until Helene gave the stools to her before I could get the coins out."

I'm not saying anything because I'm still trying to figure out who the three women on my head are. And I'm praying that there is someone on the other end of the phone line sending help.

"If it was so perfect, why'd Danny get in touch with me?" Big Foot asks. It's a rhetorical question but I can't help myself.

"Not to mention what I'm doing here. I mean you and me, we have nothing to do with this, right? Deal gone wrong. We should cut our losses and just get outta here."

The big guy looks at me, looks at Gina and looks back at me. "Are you nuts or something?"

"Yes," I say, enthusiastically. "I am. Certifiable. Last Summer. South Winds Psychiatric Hospital. Did I mention my ex is connected to the Mafia?" Not good for the police tape, but I can deny it if I live. And if I don't, maybe Rio won't wind up with custody.

"Well, you're going to be in a padded box before you know it," the guy says. I'm having trouble breathing at the thought.

"If only you hadn't picked up that furniture early, there wouldn't be three dead women."

"I knew Elise's impatience would be the death of me," I say.

"If that bitch had just let Gina take back the damn stools, we coulda been home free," the guy says.

"So she was number one, huh?" I ask.

The guy puts up one stocky finger, then another. "Two was Gina's stupid boss."

"She wasn't supposed to be in on a Tuesday," Gina says. "I had it planned perfectly—"

The big guy humphs, and, since I'm in mortal danger now, it seems hard to disagree with his assessment of Gina's "perfect" plan.

"How was I supposed to know she'd walk in on me opening the new cushions?"

"Maybe because that's what the first bitch did? Found you resewing the damn chairs after she'd told you that you couldn't have them back? Maybe that shoulda been, like, a hint?"

Gina says that Elise started it, that she pulled her hair and tried to drag her out of the house when she found her in the kitchen.

"So you picked up the faucet and hit her with it?" I say. "So it was an accident. You didn't mean to kill her."

"Well, duh," Gina says. "If I planned to kill her, don't you think I'd have brought a better weapon than a faucet?"

"So then you can't be charged with murder," I say, ignoring the whole smuggling business. "Probably you can't be charged with anything more than assault. You could probably get probation if you turned yourself in."

"You're forgetting the bitch in the back," he says. I take that to mean Helene, and I ask if she's dead.

Just as he is about to answer me, I see Drew's sleek little sports car with the dead eyeball headlight pull up in front of the store. Behind him there are two patrol cars. My eyes betray him, and Gina's thug takes aim at the door.

Before he can pull the trigger I grab up the carafe of complimentary coffee and throw it in his face. He growls as the police rush in.

And then I hear a gun go off. I feel myself crash to the floor.

Everyone is right. The world goes dark and I see stars.

CHAPTER 23

Tip of the Day

> Beware of shades of green. No one looks good in them and they do remind people of bad experiences in hospitals…
>
> —From TipsfromTeddi.com

When I wake up I'm in a hospital room. My head pounds and there seem to be too many people and too much noise. I want to yell that I am sick, but I don't think I am. I must not be dying because no one is looking at me, though Bobbie is holding my hand. She, like everyone else, is staring at the television set.

My throat is very dry. "Hello?" I croak, but no one hears me.

Helene is at the foot of my bed. Howard's arm is around her. They seem to be mesmerized by the TV.

"Did somebody die?" I ask.

Maybe I did, because no one answers me.

Drew is by the window talking to someone on the phone.

He shoots a look my way. "You're awake," he says, and everyone turns to look at me.

"What happened?" I ask.

"Here it comes! Here it comes!" Bobbie shouts and someone turns the television louder. I recognize the newscaster who covered last summer's fiasco. She is standing in front of Precious Things.

"The FBI today arrested two people in connection with a smuggling ring involving goods looted from the Iraq National Museum."

A man's face appears with the words *FBI Bureau Chief* at the bottom of the screen.

"This has been a long-standing investigation and we are happy to be able to close the books on this one, thanks to the cooperation of the Nassau County Police Department. I think that the Chief of Police has something he'd like to say, now."

The picture changes to another man and Drew comes over to the bed and squeezes my shoulder.

"Citizen cooperation," the Chief says. "This case was solved by the sharp ears and eyes of citizens. The Department would like to thank Teddi Bayer and Barbara Lyons for their heroism and self-sacrifice."

The reporter asks about my condition. I learn that I am in North Shore Hospital, where I am recovering from a concussion sustained during a gun battle between the suspects and the police. I also learn that I have saved the life of Helene Rosen-Feldstein.

When the report is over, Drew tells me that I am a bonafide hero and that the Department owes me and Bobbie their thanks. He and Bobbie exchange a look that says there was some bargain struck behind my back. My bet is that the Kate Spade journals have mysteriously disappeared from the precinct.

"I tried to tell you," Bobbie says. "But they swore me to secrecy. They said they needed a decoy to make the smugglers feel safe. Jeesh, I thought I'd dropped enough hints—cooking ahead before I was arrested, telling Kimmie she was a great actress like her mother. I'd have told you in jail but they sicced that matron on me so I couldn't."

"And the handbag on eBay was a hint about the coins in the bar stools. But how did you know about those?" My voice cracks as I speak.

Bobbie looks confused. "Huh?" she says. "It wasn't supposed to be any kind of clue—I just liked the damn bag and didn't want to miss getting it just because I was in jail."

I look at Drew and try to say that he could have told me, but my mouth is too dry. He gives me a glass of water with a bent straw in it without my having to ask. "Couldn't. Everything is written all over your face," he says, and I feel myself blush. He leans down and whispers in my ear. "Yeah, that too."

"You could have trusted me," I say.

"I could trust everything but the ability of your face to hide anything," he says. "Besides *you* could have trusted *me*."

With my history he expects me to make that leap of faith?

"I tried to stop you. I threatened, I pleaded, I ordered. I did everything I could, including trying to put the fear of God in you when I locked you in the bathroom at Bailey Manor. You just wouldn't be stopped."

"*You* locked me in?"

"Who locked who in where," a voice asks from the hallway and in walks my mother, my father trailing behind her.

"I'm reopening the store," my father says. "You're coming to work for me. No more of this dead people, life on the line, *goyisha* stuff."

"My daughter almost got killed," my mother tells the nurse who stands in the doorway reminding us that it's a hospital and asking us to keep it down. "Can you get me a Valium?" she asks the nurse as she pushes me over a little and sits on the edge of my bed.

"You saved the day, Daddy," I tell my father. "It was your phone that I used to call the police from the store."

My father beams as Drew tells him the images came through fabulously and the D.A. is investigating whether the tape can be used in court.

"Cutting edge," my father says and looks at my mother. "Didn't I tell you I was on the cutting edge?"

"Speaking of cutting edge," Drew says, and he doesn't meet my eyes. "You don't have to worry about that other cutting-edge mini camera."

I start to ask him why not when I notice someone lurking

just beyond the doorway. I gesture with my head and Drew sees it's Rio.

"You don't have to worry about that little secret camera," he says loudly, "because the *idiot* who planted it didn't wire it to anything."

I hear choking in the hall. "What?"

"Guy he bought them from probably told him they were wireless."

I'm thinking it's just like Rio to get them on the black market and get scammed.

"But—" Drew says and his voice takes on an ominous tone as he saunters toward the doorway "—should any unauthorized photos ever pop up in the press, or anywhere else, the Police Department will be the least of his worries."

I can't see from where I am, but I think he's probably nose to nose with my ex-husband when he asks, "You got that?"

And then Bobbie is shouting "Look, look!" she says, pointing at the TV.

A reporter is standing in front of Elise Meyers's house. She points to the house as the front door opens and Jack Meyers emerges in handcuffs. The next shot is of Elise's kitchen, where Elise was found murdered over a month ago. The reporter says that in an unusual twist, Jack Meyers is being indicted for the attempted murder of his dead wife.

Better still, the kitchen I did looks amazing!

* * * * *

Look for more books from Stevi Mittman featuring Teddi Bayer, her family and friends on Long Island in December 2006 in the anthology HOLIDAY WISHES.
Then, in January 2007, greet the new year with WHY IS MURDER ON THE MENU, ANYWAY?
Turn the page for a quick peek from WHY IS MURDER ON THE MENU, ANYWAY?
From Harlequin NEXT.

Design Tip of the Day

> Ambience is everything. Imagine eating foie gras at a luncheonette counter, or a side of cole slaw at Le Cirque. It's not a matter of food but one of atmosphere. Remember that when planning your dining room design.
>
> —Tips from Teddi.com

"Now that's the kind of man you should be looking for," my mother, the self-appointed keeper of my shelf-life stamp, says. She points with her fork at a man in the corner of The Steak-Out Restaurant, a dive I've just been hired to redecorate. Making this restaurant look four-star will be hard, but not half as hard as getting through lunch without strangling the woman across the table from me. "*He* would make a good husband."

"Oh, you can tell that from across the room?" I ask, wondering how it is she can forget that when we had trouble getting rid of my last husband, she shot him. "Besides being ten minutes away from death if he actually eats all that steak, he's twenty years too old for me and—shallow woman that I am—twenty pounds too heavy. Besides, I am *so* not looking for another husband here. I'm looking to design a new image for this place, looking for some sense of ambience, some feeling, something I can build a proposal on for them."

My mother studies the man in the corner, tilting her head, the better to gauge his age, I suppose. I think she's grimacing, but with all the Botox and Restylane injected into that face, it's hard to tell. She takes another bite of her steak salad, chews slowly so that I don't miss the fact that the steak is a poor cut and tougher than it should be. "You're concentrating on the wrong kind of proposal," she says finally. "Just look at this place, Teddi. It's a dive. There are hardly any other diners. What does *that* tell you about the food?"

"That they cater to a dinner crowd and it's lunchtime," I tell her.

I don't know what I was thinking bringing her here with me. I suppose I thought it would be better than eating alone. There really are days when my common sense goes on vacation. Clearly, this is one of them. I mean really, did I not resolve less than three weeks ago that I would not let my mother get to me anymore?

What good are New Year's resolutions, anyway?

Mario approaches the man's table and my mother studies

him while they converse. Eventually Mario leaves the table with a huff, after which the diner glances up and meets my mother's gaze. I think she's smiling at him. That or she's got indigestion. They size each other up.

I concentrate on making sketches in my notebook and try to ignore the fact that my mother is flirting. At nearly seventy, she's developed an unhealthy interest in members of the opposite sex to whom she isn't married.

According to my father, who has broken the TMI rule and given me Too Much Information, she has no interest in sex with him. Better, I suppose, to be clued in on what they aren't doing in the bedroom than have to hear what they might be.

"He's not so old," my mother says, noticing that I have barely touched the Chinese chicken salad she warned me not to get. "He's got about as many years on you as you have on your little cop friend."

She does this to make me crazy. I know it, but it works all the same. "Drew Scoones is not my little 'friend.' He's a detective with whom I—"

"Screwed around," my mother says. I must look shocked, because my mother laughs at me and asks if I think she doesn't know the "lingo."

What I thought she didn't know was that Drew and I actually tangled the sheets. And, since it's possible she's just fishing, I sidestep the issue and tell her that Drew is just a couple of years younger than me and that I don't need reminding. I dig into my salad with renewed vigor, determined to show my mother that Chinese chicken salad in a steak place was not the stupid choice it's proving to be.

After a few more minutes of my picking at the wilted leaves on my plate, the man my mother has me nearly engaged to pays his bill and heads past us toward the back of the restaurant. I watch my mother take in his shoes, his suit and the diamond pinkie ring that seems to be cutting off the circulation in his little finger.

"Such nice hands," she says after the man is out of sight. "Manicured." She and I both stare at my hands. I have two popped acrylics that are being held on at weird angles by bandages. My cuticles are ragged and there's marker decorating my right hand from measuring carelessly when I did a drawing for a customer.

Twenty minutes later she's disappointed that he managed to leave the restaurant without our noticing. He will join the list of the ones I let get away. I will hear about him twenty years from now when—according to my mother—my children will be grown and I will still be single, living pathetically alone with several dogs and cats.

After my ex, that sounds good to me.

The waitress tells us that our meal has been taken care of by the management and, after thanking Mario, the owner, complimenting him on the wonderful meal and assuring him that once I have redecorated his place people will be flocking here in droves (I actually use those words and ignore my mother when she rolls her eyes), my mother and I head for the restroom.

My father—unfortunately not with us today—has the patience of a saint. He got it over the years of living with my mother. She, perhaps as a result, figures he has the patience for both of them, and feels justified having none. For her, no rules apply, and a little thing like a picture of a man on the door to a public restroom is certainly no barrier to using the john. In all fairness, it does seem silly to stand and wait for the ladies' room if no one is using the men's room.

Still, it's the idea that rules don't apply to her, signs don't apply to her, conventions don't apply to her. She knocks on the door to the men's room. When no one answers she gestures to me to go ahead in. I tell her that I can certainly wait for the ladies' room to be free and she shrugs and goes in herself.

Not a minute later there is a blood-curdling scream from behind the men's room door.

"Mom!" I yell. "Are you all right?"

Mario comes running over, the waitress on his heels. Two customers head our way while my mother continues to scream.

I try the door, but it is locked. I yell for her to open it and she fumbles with the knob. When she finally manages to unlock and open it, she is white behind her two streaks of blush, but she is on her feet and appears shaken but not stirred.

"What happened?" I ask her. So do Mario and the waitress and the few customers who have migrated to the back of the place.

She points toward the bathroom and I go in, thinking it serves her right for using the men's room. But I see nothing amiss.

She gestures toward the stall, and, like any self-respecting and suspicious woman, I poke the door open with one finger, expecting the worst.

What I find is worse than the worst.

The husband my mother picked out for me is sitting on the toilet. His pants are puddled down around his ankles. His hands are hanging at his sides. Pinned to his chest is some sort of Health Department certificate.

Oh, and there is a large, round, bloodless bullet hole between his eyes.

Four Nassau County police officers are securing the area, waiting for the detectives and crime scene personnel to show up. They are trying, though not very hard, to comfort my mother, who in another era would be considered to be suffering from the vapors. Less tactful in the twenty-first century, I'd say she was losing it. That is, if I didn't know her better, know she was milking it for everything it was worth.

My mother loves attention. As it begins to flag, she swoons and claims to feel faint. Despite four No Smoking signs, my mother insists it's all right for her to light up because, after all, she's in shock. Not to mention that signs, as we know, don't apply to her.

When asked not to smoke, she collapses mournfully in a chair and lets her head loll to the side, all without mussing her hair.

Eventually, the detectives show up to find the four patrolmen all circled around her, debating whether to administer CPR, smelling salts or simply call the paramedics. I, however, know just what will snap her to attention.

"Detective Scoones," I say loudly. My mother parts the sea of cops.

"We have to stop meeting like this," he says lightly to me, but I can feel him checking me over with his eyes, making sure I'm all right while pretending not to care.

"What have you got in those pants?" my mother asks him, coming to her feet and staring at his crotch accusingly. "*Baydar?* Everywhere we Bayers are, you turn up. You don't expect me to buy that this is a coincidence, I hope."

Drew tells my mother that it's nice to see her, too, and asks if it's his fault that her daughter seems to attract disasters.

Charming to be made to feel like the bearer of a plague.

He asks how I am.

"Just peachy," I tell him. "I seem to be making a habit of finding dead bodies, my mother is driving me crazy and the catering hall I booked two freakin' years ago for Dana's bat mitzvah has just been shut down by the Board of Health!"

"Glad to see your luck's finally changing," he says, giving me a quick squeeze around the shoulders before turning his attention to the patrolmen, asking what they've got, whether they've taken any statements, moved anything, all the sort of stuff you see on TV, without any of the drama. That is, if you don't count my mother's threats to faint every few minutes when she senses no one paying attention to her.

Mario tells his wait staff to bring everyone espresso, which I decline because I'm wired enough. Drew pulls him aside and a minute later I'm handed a cup of coffee that smells divinely of Kahlúa.

The man knows me well. Too well.

His partner, whom I've met once or twice, says he'll interview the kitchen staff. Drew asks Mario if he minds if he takes statements from the patrons first and gets to him and the wait staff afterward.

"No, no," Mario tells him. "Do the patrons first." Drew raises his eyebrow at me like he wants to know if I get the double entendre. I try to look bored.

"What it is with you and murder victims?" he asks me when we sit down at a table in the corner.

I search them out so that I can see you again, I almost say, but I'm afraid it will sound desperate instead of sarcastic.

My mother, lighting up and daring him with a look to tell her not to, reminds him that *she* was the one to find the body.

Drew asks what happened *this time*. My mother tells him how the man in the john was "taken" with me, couldn't take his eyes off me and blatantly flirted with both of us. To his credit, Drew doesn't laugh, but his smirk is undeniable to the trained eye. And I've had my eye trained on him for over a year now.

"While he was noticing you," he asks me, "did *you* notice anything about him? Was he waiting for anyone? Watching for anything?"

I tell him that he didn't appear to be waiting or watching. That he made no phone calls, was fairly intent on eating and did, indeed, flirt with my mother. This last bit Drew takes with a grain of salt, which was the way it was intended.

"And he had a short conversation with Mario," I tell him. "I think he might have been unhappy with the food, though he didn't send it back."

Drew asks what makes me think he was dissatisfied, and I tell him that the discussion seemed acrimonious and that Mario looked distressed when he left the table. Drew makes a note and says he'll look into it and asks about anyone else in the restaurant. Did I see anyone who didn't seem to belong, anyone who was watching the victim, anyone looking suspicious?

"Besides my mother?" I ask him, and Mom huffs and blows her cigarette smoke in my direction.

I tell him that there were several deliveries, the kitchen staff going in and out the back door to grab a smoke. He stops me and asks what I was doing checking out the back door of the restaurant.

Proudly—because, while he was off forgetting me,

dropping by only once in a while to say hi to Jesse, my son, or drop something off for one of my daughters that he thought they might like, I was getting on with my life—I tell him that I'm decorating the place.

He looks genuinely impressed. "Commercial customers? That's great," he says. Okay, that's what he *ought* to say. What he actually says is, "Whatever pays the bills."

"Howard Rosen, the famous restaurant critic, got her the job," my mother says. "You met him—the good-looking, distinguished gentleman with the *real* job, something to be proud of. I guess you've never read his reviews in *Newsday*."

Drew, without missing a beat, tells her that Howard's reviews are on the top of his list, as soon as he learns how to read.

"I only meant—" my mother starts, but both of us assure her that we know just what she meant.

"So," Drew says. "Deliveries?"

I tell him that Mario would know better than I, but that I saw vegetables come in, maybe fish and linens.

"This is the second restaurant job Howard's got her," my mother tells Drew.

"At least she's getting *something* out of the relationship," he says.

"If he were here," my mother says, ignoring the insinuation, "he'd be comforting her instead of interrogating her. He'd be making sure we're both all right after such an ordeal."

"I'm sure he would," Drew agrees, then looks me in the

eyes as if he's measuring my tolerance for shock. Quietly he adds, "But then maybe he doesn't know just what strong stuff your daughter's made of."

It's the closest thing to a tender moment I can expect from Drew Scoones. My mother breaks the spell. "She gets that from me," she says.

Both Drew and I take a minute, probably to pray that's all I inherited from her.

"I'm just trying to save you some time and effort," my mother tells him. "My money's on Howard."

Drew withers her with a look and mutters something that sounds suspiciously like "Fool's gold." Then he excuses himself to go back to work.

I catch his sleeve and ask if it's all right for us to leave. He says sure, he knows where we live. I say goodbye to Mario. I assure him that I will have some sketches for him in a few days, all the while hoping that this murder doesn't cancel his redecorating plans. I need the money desperately, the alternative being borrowing from my parents and getting strangled by the strings.

My mother is strangely quiet all the way to her house. She doesn't tell me what a loser Drew Scoones is—despite his good looks—and how I was obviously drooling over him. She doesn't ask me where Howard is taking me tonight or warn me not to tell my father about what happened because he will worry about us both and no doubt insist we see our respective psychiatrists.

She fidgets nervously, opening and closing her purse over and over again.

"You okay?" I ask her. After all, she's just found a dead man on the toilet, and tough as she is that's got to be upsetting.

When she doesn't answer me I pull over to the side of the road.

"Mom?" She refuses to meet my eyes. "You want me to take you to see Dr. Cohen?"

She looks out the window as if she's just realized we're on Broadway in Woodmere. "Aren't we near Marvin's Jewelers?" she asks, pulling something out of her purse.

"What have you got, Mother?" I ask, prying open her fingers to find the murdered man's ring.

"It was on the sink," she says in answer to my dropped jaw. "I was going to get his name and address and have you return it to him so that he could ask you out. I thought it was a sign that the two of you were meant to be together."

"He's dead, Mom. You understand that, right?" I ask. You never can tell when my mother is fine and when she's in la-la land.

"Well, I didn't know that," she shouts at me. "Not at the time."

I ask why she didn't give it to Drew, realize that she wouldn't give Drew the time in a clock shop and add, "...or one of the other policemen?"

"For heaven's sake," she tells me. "The man is dead, Teddi, and I took his ring. How would that look?"

Before I can tell her it looks just the way it is, she pulls out a cigarette and threatens to light it.

"I mean really," she says, shaking her head like it's my brains that are loose. "What does he need with it now?"

* * * * *

HARLEQUIN®
Next™